SIGHT UNSEEN

SIGHT UNSEEN

REDONDO AND ROSE NEIGHBORS IN CRIME
BOOK 3

BONNIE HARDY

ON THE OTHER HAND BOOKS

Ebook ISBN 978-1-954995-29-1

Paperback ISBN 978-1-954995-30-7

Hardback ISBN 978-1-954995-31-4

Cover Design by Ebook Launch

Editing by Proof Positive

 Created with Vellum

VIVIENNE ROSE

The cruise ship's horn blast made talking impossible. Viv turned to Rex. "Too loud," she mouthed. When the blast stopped assaulting her ears she yelled, "I hope that doesn't happen very often." She patted both hands over her ears as if to give them encouragement.

A slight smile came to his lips. "Not exactly the peaceful sail I promised," he admitted. Instantly his charm worked its magic, settling over her frayed nerves.

Rex kept speaking in his warm, soothing voice. "I know it wasn't your idea, but I hope you enjoy our cruise. Honolulu is low-key and exotic. The perfect destination port. Why don't we sign in?"

He pointed to a woman wearing a navy-blue blazer over a white shirt who sat behind the table, tapping her pen.

"I think she wants to have a look at your driver's license," Rex said.

Viv handed over her identification with a smile, her ears still ringing.

"Welcome to Aloha Cruise Lines. Is this your first

excursion with us?" the brown-haired woman asked. Her bright blue eyes focused on Rex and then turned away.

Viv noted the stylized cruise pin with the wave logo on her jacket's lapel. *Allison Thompson, Information Technology Senior Manager* was printed on the badge.

When neither Viv nor Rex answered, Allison piped up. "*The Legend of the Sea* is our newest ship. We've heard nothing but rave reviews. Let me get you checked in right away." She glanced at her laptop. "Unfortunately your luggage has been delayed, not yet transferred to your room."

Viv frowned at the news.

Undaunted, Allison stretched her smile over perfectly aligned white teeth. "Nothing to worry about though," she assured them. "It takes time to get all the luggage in the right hands when we have nearly two thousand passengers. Once we've brought the bags up to your stateroom, we'll send a text and provide a personal escort.

"In the meanwhile, you can sit on the well-appointed outdoor lido deck with a view of the sea and look over the Welcome Aboard packet from our captain. Familiarize yourself with all of our amenities. I see you've purchased the unlimited drinks option."

Finally Allison took a breath. Viv cast a glare in Rex's direction. "Unlimited drinks?" She leaned closer to whisper, "Planning on getting me tipsy and having your way with me?"

"The drinks were a part of the deal I got online. Kind of an all-inclusive thing." He kept his pleasant smile, but his eyes twinkled in Viv's direction.

For the first time, Allison paid attention. First to Viv, then to Rex. Her blue eyes widened and remained on Rex. Her cheeks flushed pink. "I wouldn't mind an all-drinks package with my boyfriend." Allison blinked seductively.

"I see," Viv said primly. *And I do see. Rex is irresistible. Women of all ages can't keep their eyes off of him. Must be such a burden*, she chuckled to herself.

As she slid her driver's license back into her purse, a man dressed in navy slacks and a crisp white shirt approached. His badge read *Customer Service Coordinator*. Underneath was his name: Robert Redford.

Viv pointed. "Any relation to the movie star?"

"No, ma'am," he said. "I'm asked that all the time. My parents thought the name would turn me into a Sundance Kid kind of guy. Didn't work of course. We lived in a high-rise apartment in West Manhattan." He smiled sheepishly. "I majored in hotel management at Cornell and I've never ridden a horse, let alone jumped off a mountain."

His lack of pretense made Viv feel better about her luggage.

Redford leaned closer to Allison. She didn't acknowledge his presence, staring at her computer.

"Allison, take the next guest, would you? I need to speak to Mr. Redondo." This time he poked her shoulder with his index finger, making sure she gave him eye contact.

Rex brushed his hand over his hair, looking slightly amused. "You know my name already? I guess I'm a celebrity far and wide." He sounded quite pleased with himself.

Skepticism came over Viv at first, followed by curiosity. She'd agreed to Rex's cruise invitation recently. It was all his idea. For both of them to get away and get to know each other better. But now she wondered if Rex hadn't told her everything about the spontaneous trip.

She knew this wasn't his first cruise. He'd traveled all over the world with his mentalist act, aboard some very exotic ships. Her mind whirled. *What does Robert Redford want with Rex...* She began to speculate.

Maybe he's in trouble. A parking ticket in a foreign port; some indiscretion that caused alarm with the police...

"It's a pleasure to meet you." Redford moved around the table to shake Rex's hand. Viv stepped back to give them room. But not so much that she couldn't overhear their conversation.

"How can I be of help?" Rex asked.

Redford gave Viv a quick glance and then gestured with a sweep of his hand. "Ms. Rose may stand over here. She's fully checked in. This shouldn't take a minute."

Viv moved aside as directed, giving Rex a slight wave of her fingers.

Once they left she stood at the edge of the pier glancing toward the cruise ship. *The Legend of the Sea* flag waved from a pole high above the top deck. She felt a shiver of excitement. *My first cruise. At my age. Will wonders never cease.*

Workers bustled onto the pier, loading bags on wheeled platforms. Passengers straggled toward the ramp as staff greeted them. To Viv's eyes the ship seemed enormous. *Like a floating apartment building, with all the windows and levels.*

One open-air deck caught her attention. *I bet that's the swimming pool and fancy spa and gym that Rex told me about.*

"Excuse me, Ms. Rose." Allison Thompson stood at her elbow. "I've been asked to escort you to the lido deck while you wait. Apparently Mr. Redondo is still talking to Mr. Redford. It will take a bit longer."

"Of course." Viv stepped back, following Allison to the ramp. The smell of salt air tinged with diesel fuel clung to her nose. A seagull squawked overhead. The hint of anticipation brought on a giddy excitement. *It's been a long time since I've felt this way.*

Allison left Viv sitting in a chair on the lido deck. "It won't be long," she assured her.

"I don't mind waiting," Viv said. "I love people watching." Once Allison left, Viv realized how lame that must have sounded. *No one's here to watch right now.*

The pool water shimmered aqua blue, smelling slightly of bromine. A filter in the pool gurgled. She was familiar with the stories of people catching illnesses on cruise ships. She felt relieved that everything looked and smelled so clean.

Sitting back to make herself more comfortable, Viv watched as the glass door slid open and a staff member stepped onto the deck. They began work behind an expansive bar. Polished glasses were set in rows, and napkins fanned out over the bar's surface.

Another employee arrived. He released a large cloth and began to wipe down the chairs and stools. Within moments the area was alive with more workers, leaving small vases of flowers and cutlery wrapped in cloth napkins.

Viv's gaze took in the steaming spa on the far end of the pool. Behind that there were more doors with signs that read *Massage, Nail Treatments,* and *Saunas.* Lifting her eyes toward the sky, she saw that the lido deck included three levels.

She blinked at the brightness of the sun. Her gaze drifted downward again to stifle a sneeze. She lifted her gaze back toward the long line of elliptical machines. On the upper level machines could be seen through expansive glass windows. *The gym reminds me of New York. People exercising, looking down on the streets of Manhattan.* Except in this case they faced the pool area.

Only one man exercised on the elliptical. His hands braced on both handles of the machine as he pushed and pulled, bending his head down. Legs pumping, arms moving, he raised his head to look through the window. She felt as if he caught her staring.

She averted her eyes, but then something made her look back again. The man's arms began to flail, as if he'd suddenly lost his balance. Tumbling forward, his head bounced on the arm of the elliptical, his left temple heading straight toward the handle of the machine right next to him. Viv winced.

"Oh no!" she cried, jumping to her feet. She waited, watching as his body slumped to the floor. When he didn't move, she felt the rise of panic. One glance told her that the staff had left. And there was no other passenger in view.

From behind she heard the glass doors swish open. One glance revealed two stewards. They pushed a cart filled with food.

"Help," Viv called. "A man has fallen."

The men didn't seem to understand what she was saying. One shook his head and said, "No English."

She pointed to the window and to the bank of ellipticals.

Then her arm dropped, embarrassment flushing her cheeks.

She explained about the man but abruptly stopped. In the brief moment it had taken to turn and ask for help, the body had vanished. Sight unseen.

2

____

VIVIENNE ROSE

"But I saw him fall off the machine," she explained to Allison Thompson for the third time. Allison coughed and spoke in her measured voice.

"Ms. Rose. No one is allowed in the gym until everyone has been checked and boarded, reunited with their luggage. This is a strict policy. You must have thought you saw a man, but the sun's glare distorts the view." Allison tugged on her sunglasses to make her point.

Viv could tell by the tone in her voice that Allison had already decided Viv was one of those women who wanted special attention. She flinched inwardly at the obvious condescension. Even though at her age, she'd even used it herself on occasion.

When Viv didn't back down but tried yet again to tell her story, Allison's voice became clipped, though syrupy sweet, as if she were speaking to a small child. "The glass on the window is hard to see through. You can see the glare from the sun right now." She pointed upward. Her refusal to accept Viv's point of view along with the overly pleasant voice only irritated her more.

Taking a moment to calm herself, she glanced toward the wall of windows. She had to admit she couldn't see through the glare. *But then*, Viv rationally concluded, *the sun wasn't in the same position earlier.*

"I saw what I saw," Viv calmly stated. "A man, well-built, late thirties, working out on the elliptical. Then he toppled off. He might have had a heart attack." She shuddered. And because she'd had a recent experience with the police, she added more detail. "He was wearing a tank top, well-muscled, black pants. I'd say around six foot tall with curly dark hair."

The information technology senior manager's jaw tightened.

Maybe I got her attention, Viv thought.

Allison Thompson pulled out her cell phone and began to text as Viv watched. She pocketed her phone. "Your luggage has been delivered to your suite. May I lead the way? We'd like to offer complimentary champagne as our thank you for your patience."

"But..." Viv objected.

Allison turned her back, walking toward the sliding glass doors.

"Come along," Allison directed.

She had no choice but to go along.

Once they exited the elevator, Viv followed her escort down the narrow corridor. Each evenly spaced door they passed had a number over the peephole. Other than that, the doors looked identical.

"Are we there yet?" she asked Allison.

"Just a bit farther," was the curt reply.

She treated me like a child, and now I'm acting like one,

Viv thought. *I remember the opposite, when some childhood expert told me to treat my son like a grown-up and then he'd stop being such a baby. Is this one of those things that comes back to haunt you as you age?*

Viv couldn't wait to peel off Allison. Once she reunited with Rex, she knew he'd listen.

The door to stateroom 563 opened. Allison stopped as Rex, dressed in a fluffy white bathrobe and holding a flute of champaign, grinned at Viv. "You're right next door," he explained with a nod to room 561.

"I saw a man fall off—" the words tumbled past her lips.

"We'll talk soon," he said hastily, disappearing into his room. The door closed with a thud.

"The veranda between your rooms is connecting," explained Allison. "You can speak to him once I get you settled in."

Tapping a key card on the pad, Allison opened the door, letting Viv go first. Once they were both inside, she handed Viv a paper and her own key card. "Daily notices will be left either outside the door or on the counter under the TV. The only other thing..." Allison gave the room a quick glance. "The only other thing is to show you how the toilet works."

"I've got this," Viv told her, and then a tap came at the door. She opened the door. Rex stood on the other side.

"Did I hear you say you saw a man fall? Where was that exactly?" He took her in his arms. Fortunately he'd shed the bathrobe and dressed in slacks with a polo shirt. He smelled of patchouli and pine. She hugged him back.

"You can go now," he told Allison over Viv's shoulder. "Send the steward with a few snacks. I think the lady could use some cheese and crackers at least, after her experience."

"Yes, sir," Allison said smartly.

Before Viv could say thank you, the ship lurched under

her feet. Grabbing the end of the counter for balance, her stomach dropped.

"*Legend of the Sea* has stabilizers," Rex explained. "But it may be rough for a bit. We're heading out of the harbor toward open seas." He pulled her by the hand to sit next to him on the bed. "I'm sorry you had to wait so long. Tell me what happened."

"I'm not sure if I believe it myself," she began.

"Try starting again from the beginning."

"I feel a little queasy," she admitted.

"Let's step outside on the veranda. The fresh air will help."

Out of doors he offered her a chair, giving her time to catch her breath. He sat next to her, looking over the rail toward the vast expanse of sea. "I love this part: pulling away from the shore and heading into the unknown."

Viv heard longing in his voice. Then she remembered he'd also traveled on Navy ships during his time in the Marines.

"Your light respite is ready, sir," a man's voice interrupted. He held a silver tray. Viv closed her eyes to feel less queasy.

"I'll take care of this," Rex assured her.

He returned with a silver bucket under one arm. Placing it on the table, he explained, "Another complimentary bottle of champagne. The real stuff. I'll get the glasses and and be right back. You just stay put until you get your sea legs."

Three rhythmic blasts preceded an announcement from the loudspeaker. "This is your captain speaking. Operation Rising Star has begun."

Viv had no idea what he meant, so she closed her eyes

again. She leaned back in her chair, the sound of water splashing against the hull coming as a welcome relief.

She heard the door open and turned to see Rex carrying another tray.

"I hope there's a bottle of water and a lemon there," she said.

"Your wish is my command." The ship let out three more long blasts.

3

―――――――――

REX REDONDO

Rex observed Viv from the corner of his eye. *She's looking more relaxed.* He took a sip from his champagne flute. "Let's do a cheers and then dig in to some crackers."

She raised her glass, tipping it against his.

"Welcome aboard." He smiled taking a sip. "I'm going to spread some Brie on crackers for us both. You just watch the ocean. And then you can start your story again without interruption."

Once Viv finished telling him about the man and the elliptical, Rex took a moment to push back a surge of guilt. *I should have been there.* Instead of expressing his regrets, he smiled to say, "I can't leave you alone for a minute." He pulled the small charcuterie platter closer, watching her pick up another cracker.

"But maybe it didn't happen," Viv said in a thoughtful voice. "I could have imagined the whole thing. The body. Falling over the elliptical. The man most likely unconscious..." Her voice trailed off. He knew what she was thinking. That the guy could have been dead.

Rex knew it was his turn; he needed to tell her about what he'd agreed to. He didn't want to start because he felt terrible. Even more so since he'd heard her story.

"By the way," he began.

She interrupted. "It's amazing how nothing falls off the table, yet we're in the middle of the Pacific Ocean with waves crashing against the ship," Viv said.

"Like I said, they have stabilizers." Rex knew he sounded impatient. Not because of her, but because he had something to get off his chest. "I do have something to share with you. The conversation with Robert Redford, no relation." He hoped that she'd smile when he said the no relation part. But she continued to stare at the ocean.

Then she took a deep breath as if preparing herself for bad news. "I had time to wonder about your conversation with Redford. My imagination took me on a journey. Don't tell me what he said. Let me guess.

"Did the CIA finally catch up with you? Maybe an old arrest popped up when you used your passport for identification..." She continued, "Or maybe my bodyguard was the problem. Did he cause trouble when he couldn't come along? Did your conversation have something to do with that?"

"None of the above," he said. "Plus I convinced the police chief that I could keep an eye on you during the cruise. Fernando won't be joining us."

Viv reached for a cracker. "I assume when we return I'll be old news to the Palm Desert mob family. They have bigger fish to fry than an out-of-work doula with some time on her hands."

"I think you may be right," Rex mused. "Are you done guessing? Can I tell you what I got myself into?"

"Why do I think I'm not going to like what you have to say," she said.

Rex knew that he'd better get it out before things got worse. So he started in a rush. "What I wanted to tell you is that Aloha Cruises offered me a job on the ship."

"What?" Her eyes widened. "As a mentalist, you mean?"

"That's right." He began to explain, "The regular mentalist didn't show up last night. They tried to find him using all of their contacts, but they declared him a no-show early this morning. Everyone panicked. No decent cruise line can keep people busy at sea without a solid entertainer.

"Redford said my name came up. Someone realized that I was already on the passenger list. That's why he made a point to speak to me as soon as I showed up."

"That would be Robert Redford, customer service coordinator," Viv mumbled sarcastically.

"The very one. We're besties now." Rex held up two fingers close together. "I felt sorry for the guy, so I told him I'd help out."

To his surprise she didn't glower or disagree. She merely took another bite of cracker. He felt pleased and yet let down. Most women would have objected immediately.

"How many shows are we talking about?" Viv asked.

"They want me to do four shows. I guess there's a folk singer for the last night. I did get a look at the performing theater. It's really swanky. Lots of lights and microphones. I think I can work up some good material with no problem."

"Without Sutton?" she asked.

"That's the other part of my news," he added. "I was thinking you could be my Sutton. You could saunter around the ship and listen in to people's conversations. Then text me like she does. You'd be good, what with your mind for detail."

"I could do that," Viv agreed. "If it doesn't interfere with my busy schedule of sitting by the pool and getting my nails done." She held up her hand to inspect her fingers.

He felt slightly offended. He was Rex Redondo. Ladies' man and a renowned performer. *The indignity...* Then he saw her smirk. "You're pulling my leg, aren't you?"

"Yes, I am." She reached for her Champagne flute. "Someone has to. Otherwise you'd get overly impressed with yourself."

"Does that mean you'll help? The ship offered vouchers for us to take another cruise, open-ended dates. That would be fun!"

"It might work," she said. "But don't forget I may not like cruising. Let's plan our trips one at a time."

Rex reached for the champagne. He filled her flute and then his, placing the bottle back in the ice. *I just dodged a bullet. She didn't complain that I failed to consider her opinion. Which I would do next time. If it comes up again. She's the best.*

"I'm sure you're going to love cruising by the time we reach Honolulu," he said confidently. "We can have late night dinners brought to my suite after the show. Wouldn't that be romantic. The moon will shine over the waters as we access our unlimited drink package. You'll love it."

"Oh no, we can't do that," she disagreed. "If I'm to listen in and take notes on my fellow passengers, I'll have to eat in places where the people are. Not sequestered away on our private veranda. Out and about. That will be my motto for the next five days."

Disappointment hit him hard. He'd had high hopes that he'd get the best of both worlds. A little work and lots of time with her. But once again she'd set him reeling.

His plan wasn't working out quite like he wanted. She

seemed fine with the shift, but he was the one who would need time to adjust.

He turned to her. "I need to alert Sutton of the change of plans. One more phone call, then I'm all yours." He left her outside as he stepped inside the room. Closing the door he inhaled his disappointment.

4

REX REDONDO

Back in his stateroom Rex stood in his stateroom and put the phone to his ear after he dialed Sutton. She answered on the first ring.

"How's Kevin?" he asked before she could say hello.

"Living his best life," she replied. "I've made him a grilled sirloin burger for dinner, and he gets a minimum of three walks every day. He's in no hurry for you to come home."

"And Miss Kitty?" he asked after Viv's cat.

"She bit me yesterday," Sutton admitted. "I flicked her nose and told her no. Don't tell Viv."

Rex chuckled. "So it's not just me. That cat is feisty. But wait, I have news." He explained how he got the job on the cruise.

"You took a gig on your romantic getaway with Viv?" Sutton didn't hide her tone of incredulity.

"With her permission, of course," he exaggerated slightly. *Permission after the fact would explain it better.*

"She really has your number," Sutton chuckled. "She can have some alone time now that you're employed. I'm liking her more and more. That has to be a first for the silver-fox mentalist."

Rex felt disgruntled. If he wasn't mistaken, Sutton was laughing at his incomprehensible stupidity. Instead of admitting Sutton was right, he decided to be annoying.

"Just so you know, Viv may push you out of a job. I'm using her as my information gatherer in your absence."

Unfortunately Sutton only laughed louder. "Stop. You did what? Now I get a break from you as well. This is getting better and better. Viv will be using her doula skills before long, consulting with all the pregnant women on the ship. Giving advice on nursing and babies. Forgetting to eavesdrop for your show. You'll be the one begging for some company. That should be a nice change, you getting alone time."

Rex did his best to ignore Sutton's scoffing. It was never his first choice to be alone, but he hadn't realized that Sutton also knew. *I'm getting no sympathy from my personal assistant. And no sympathy from my... What do I call Viv. My lady friend? That sounds so less than.* He decided to change the subject.

"You won't believe what happened to Viv as she waited for me on the lido deck. She saw a guy fall off an elliptical and collapse in the gym."

Sutton stopped laughing. "Look, boss. Keep her out of trouble, would you? I've got enough to do, pushing back the enemies she made last time. Who are you two, Nick and Nora?"

Rex paused to consider Sutton's comparison of him and Viv to Nick and Nora Charles. The unforgettable characters penned by Dashiell Hammett in Rex's favorite crime novels from the 1930s. Sutton's comparison felt right.

Sutton continued, "Speaking of the last caper, Frank

Salucci has been arrested by the FBI. By the time the feds get done with him, Viv will hopefully be yesterday's news."

"I am happy to hear that. You told the bodyguard that his services are no longer required, right?"

"I did," she curtly responded.

"Okay, then let's wrap this up. It's time for me to get ready for the early seating in the dining room. Viv is taking her new job of being you very seriously. She refused a private romantic dinner for two on the veranda." He sniffed his annoyance into the phone.

He could still hear the echo of Sutton's laughter long after he disconnected.

Rex knocked on Viv's door. She opened it, looking stunning in a black cocktail dress and black high heels. He whistled. "You look amazing." His knees grew slightly weak.

"This old thing?" She swept her hand over the skirt with a grin. "My pal Jason fixed me up with cruise-worthy attire. He also put together something he called a cruise-wear wardrobe. Apparently basic black works for most evenings."

"Is that so?" Rex murmured. His glance drifting to her ankles and then back up her body, finishing on her lips.

"So lead on, Mr. Redondo." She closed her stateroom door, slipping her key card into a sequined clutch bag.

The corridor emptied into a busy lobby, where people waited for the elevator. Rex avoided standing in the midst of the crowd, keeping Viv close by his side. The elevator filled quickly, and they were the last to enter. Everyone exited on the dining room level, some breaking into a fast walk to get in line.

Rex leaned over to whisper, "Like a bunch of folks in a retirement home, all wanting to be first to dinner. I'm feeling no need to rush." He took her hand, pulling her toward the bar. "Want to sit by the table near the window for a bit? Then we can head to the dining room after everyone else has been seated."

"Why not." Viv smiled.

She placed her purse on the table and removed her cell phone. After glancing over the room, she made a note in her phone.

"Taking down info for my show?" he finally asked.

"Actually I started earlier. Right now, I'm putting everything into writing about the man on the elliptical. I might start to forget, and I want every detail written down. A flailing body, banging his head on metal and dropping to the ground, is nothing to ignore. He could be unconscious or dead. Have you thought of that?"

A server came to their table, stopping his response upon her arrival. He might have tried to talk her out of that conclusion, but so far he'd had little else to think about other than his stupidity and her guy in the gym.

"What can I get you?" the server asked.

"Just sparkling water for me," Rex said. *Because I'm the fool who made this a work night.*

"I'll take the same," Viv said. "With a twist of lemon, if you have one."

"Anything for Mr. Redondo and his guest."

Rex raised his eyebrows at Viv, wondering if she caught the use of his name.

"Mr. Redford told us we're to serve you whatever you want whenever you want it," the waitress assured him in a sultry voice.

Once she left, Rex picked up their conversation. Before he could do so, he spotted Robert Redford making a beeline toward their table. Pulling an empty chair with him, he sat down and leaned forward. "Good to see you both. I hope you're having a relaxing evening. Did you order anything yet? It's all on the house."

"We ordered water; I have to keep clear-headed for the show," Rex explained. "We're avoiding the dinner crowd."

Redford cleared his throat. "I forgot to mention something earlier. I've arranged for your berth to be downstairs with the rest of the crew. You can take your meals in the staff dining room and drink at their bar. How about I give you a tour right after dinner?"

Rex's jaw tightened. If he'd been told he'd lose his cabin next door to Viv earlier, he might not have considered taking the job. But now it was late to be annoyed. He couldn't quit and admit he'd made a mistake.

Plus Viv was still making notes on her phone. Since she had not objected, he agreed. "I suppose. You're the boss."

When the lull in the conversation grew uncomfortable, Viv looked up and glared at Redford. "I've made notes on my phone about the incident I saw on the lido deck."

"I'll tell my assistant to get in touch." Redford stood and wasted no time walking away.

5

VIVIENNE ROSE

Once Redford had left their table, Viv could tell Rex was in a terrible mood. He didn't smile or speak, but moved his knife over the tablecloth with one finger.

"I like my room," she told him, hoping to sound encouraging.

"I liked mine too." He tapped his fingers on the side of the table. "Until I got ousted. Okay, so I admit I may have complicated our plans, and for what? My ego wanted to take the job." He glared at her. "I am a professional mentalist. I've done cruise gigs on numerous occasions. I can't help myself."

Viv patted his hand. "I think all of that is true," she said. "But I also think there's something you're missing. The fact that you truly wanted to help. You said yes where your particular skill set was needed. I mean, how many other mentalists are on board this ship?" She looked around the room, her affectionate gaze returning to him.

"I never gave myself that much credit," he admitted. "That's really nice of you to see me that way. I've got to say

I'm flattered. No, not flattered exactly. More touched. That you would know me that well."

Relief brought a smile to Viv's lips. She didn't want Rex to be in a bad mood. Over the past months she'd grown fond of him. Even though he'd made a decision that upended their plans, she wasn't going to hold a grudge. But she also wasn't going to take responsibility for the consequences he'd brought on himself.

Her feelings had changed since when they first met. She couldn't stand him at all then, butting into her house and her life. But now she could see beneath his surface, and she realized how sensitive he was and that he didn't reveal himself easily. She wasn't sure what to do about it, but at least he seemed worth the fuss.

"I say we get the lay of the land on each of the passenger decks," she said. "As you know, I've never been on a cruise before. You can be my tour guide."

"But first I need a real meal. Plus I have to prep for my act. This one will be a bit iffy, since I don't have any intel yet," he said.

"Not so fast, Rex Redondo." Viv smirked. "Just you wait. I'm heading to the ladies' restroom. Give me about ten minutes and I'll have a few nuggets for you to work with on your unexpected opening night." She rose, placing her napkin by her glass.

Feeling his eyes follow as she walked across the room, she felt good about herself. *Shoulders back. Chin tucked. Eyes straight ahead. I'm not going to sway my hips or anything. No one wants to see sultry Viv in her sixties doing what came naturally in her twenties.*

Regardless, Viv knew she looked good, so she carried herself with aplomb, all the way to the corridor toward the sign that read *Ladies.*

. . .

Standing in front of the sink, Viv rinsed each finger in warm water. In no hurry she linger as long as she could without appearing out of place. Glancing to the left, she noticed a wooden box sitting on the counter. There was an engraved plaque attached to the top by small brass screws. The name Farley Hughes, along with a birth and recent death date, caught her eye. Viv shuddered. *Why would someone leave a box, possibly filled with ashes, on the counter?*

The stall door behind her slammed. A woman with light brown hair came closer. Likely in her early thirties, she stood close to the counter to bump the wooden box with her elbow. After a quick pump of the soap dispenser she bent closer to the sink, her curls falling over her shoulders.

Dressed in a short black dress and black high heels she seemed ready for a night out. If not for the wooden box Viv might have assumed she was on a date. Turning from the sink, the young woman smiled before holding her hands under the dryer.

"I don't want Daddy to get wet," she nodded to the box.

Viv debated. She could leave right now to avoid an obvious ploy for conversation. That would have been her first choice until she remembered, *I told Rex I'd get him info. What better than a young woman carrying her father's ashes to the restroom on a cruise ship to Honolulu...*

She reached for a paper towel. "I'm sorry for your loss. I assume when you say Daddy, that means Mr. Hughes. I couldn't help but read the inscription."

"Daddy passed just recently. We'd always wanted to take a cruise to Honolulu together, but the cancer got him before we could set sail." Tears welled in her eyes.

Viv stepped away from the sink as the younger woman

dropped a wet towel in the bin, taking the wooden box in her hands. She followed Viv across the room toward the wall of mirrors, continuing the conversation. "Would you mind holding Daddy for a minute? I need to put on some lipstick."

Viv opened her hands to receive the box. Just in time for the other woman to make a quick pivot facing the mirror. She reached into her purse, bringing out a bright red lipstick case.

Viv watched with fascination, knowing this was the perfect opportunity. *Before she asks for Daddy back, maybe I could draw her into conversation.* Viv glanced at the box for inspiration.

"I lost someone dear to me recently," Viv said quietly. It was the truth. Well, at least a partial truth. Because she had lost her friend, but that didn't mean she was dead.

"It's so hard," the young woman agreed. "Would you keep holding Daddy while I get another tissue?"

Viv longed to send Rex a text right then. Instead she held Daddy's ashes to her chest. Once the young woman returned, Viv said, "I hope you'll be attending the mentalist show tonight. You never know if Daddy will have a word for you. I've seen this man perform. He's very talented."

The young woman's eyes widened. "Oh, that's a really good idea. Thank you so much. I planned on being there."

6

VIVIENNE ROSE

They exited the ladies' restroom, and Viv quickly handed back the box.

Receiving it with a repressed sob, the young woman explained, "Like I said, Daddy really wanted for us to go on this cruise together." She held the box tightly to her chest. "Grandpa was a Pearl Harbor survivor. He told the stories to Daddy and then Daddy shared them with me. Once he passed, I knew what to do: take him on the Aloha cruise and have him buried at sea."

Up until now, Viv thought cruises were just for people looking for a good time. Where passengers ate and drank all day and into the night as they made their way across the ocean to Honolulu. Party, party, party. "I didn't realize you could do a burial at sea on a cruise ship," she said.

"Oh yes. I'm a frequent passenger on all the lines. It happens nearly every voyage," she explained. "By the way, my name is Cassandra Hughes, but people call me Sandi."

Viv felt disconcerted. She'd already held Daddy's ashes in her arms, yet only now had Sandi shared her name.

Maybe the introductions should have come first. She took the young woman's cue.

"My name is Vivienne Rose, but people call me Viv," she explained, deliberately echoing Sandi's form of introduction.

Viv and Sandi stood in a private alcove as passengers streamed by. "I'm on my way to the show this evening. Would you like to join me—and Daddy?" Sandi lifted the box she held in her hands.

Viv froze. She'd promised Rex she'd return to the table. "I can't tonight. But what about tomorrow? We could meet in the morning and chat then."

"Okay. Want to meet on the lido deck and go for a walk?" Sandi asked. "I can leave Daddy in the room for a while. The exercise would do me some good."

Viv sighed with relief. "That would be fantastic. How about I text you when I get up?"

"I'll add you to my contacts," Sandi offered. "If you don't mind holding Daddy, that is." She shoved the box into Viv's hands again, lifting her phone from her bag.

Viv handed the box back once she'd finished. "I have to get back to my stateroom and finish unpacking," Viv added with a smile.

"Okay then, see you tomorrow," Sandi replied.

Viv waited for Sandi to walk away before heading in the opposite direction. Circling back to avoid running into her again, Viv found Rex waiting for the elevator.

He looked relieved. "Turns out I'm not that hungry. You took long enough." She ignored his disappointment, realizing something new.

She yanked on his arm, pulling him aside. "I just realized that if I'm going to be your new Sutton, I can't be seen with you," she explained.

His eyebrows rose.

"But I have information. It's a doozy. I'll circle around to the coffee shop and text you right away."

"Good timing because I have to get to my dressing room." He leaned forward as if to kiss her, but she pulled away.

"We can't be seen as a couple," she insisted. "I'll blow my cover and then you won't have anyone to help with the act."

He straightened, his mouth twitching at the corners. "Of course. I didn't think that through. I will wait for your text. Until then." Instead of a kiss he gave her a wink.

It wasn't until she'd walked halfway down the hall that she realized she was not only on the wrong floor but on the starboard side of the ship. All the room numbers were even instead of odd.

She hesitated, nearly trampled by an eager couple laughing, obviously enjoying themselves and ignoring everyone in their path. She pushed her back against the wall to let them pass.

Taking that moment, she texted Rex her information. *He'll have plenty to go on with Sandi and Daddy. I think my first foray into being Sutton has gone pretty well.*

"Are you lost, miss?" A steward dressed in all blue waited for her reply.

"I think I've gotten turned around and misplaced my room," she explained.

"There's fore and aft. One side has staterooms ending in odd numbers, the other even. Each level has an elevator lobby in the center."

"Quite complicated," Viv murmured. "I'm in room 561."

"May I help you to the elevator?" the man asked politely.

"I've got this," she said firmly. It wasn't until she reached the end of the corridor that she realized she'd passed her own stateroom.

Sitting in the back row of the crowded performance venue, Viv admired the lavish decor. A glass chandelier hung over the uppermost balcony, the lights reflecting off the brass railings. She leaned back, appreciating the feel of the soft faux red velvet seat cushions.

Like the lido deck, the theater occupied three different levels of the ship. The seats could be accessed from several doorways. And now lights flickered across a back wall, creating mesmerizing designs.

As Frank Sinatra crooned over the loudspeaker, "Luck Be a Lady Tonight," Viv realized that the theater reminded her of the Palm Desert performing arts center at home. The couple in front of her seemed to be enjoying their conversation.

Maybe they won't notice if I lean closer to listen in.

Viv began her report to Rex.

Man named Barney just finished chemo.

Barney's wife seems distracted. She keeps glancing around as if looking for someone else.

Peeking past the people seated, she spotted her new friend, Sandi, sitting several rows ahead, chatting with a man next to her.

Sandi Hughes sitting in the seventh row on the aisle. She brought Daddy's ashes on the voyage.

Viv turned her phone over on her lap just as the curtain rose and people began to applaud.

"Please give a warm welcome to world-renowned performer and mentalist, Rex Redondo!"

The applause increased as Rex walked onto the stage. He picked up the microphone, the spotlight hovering from above. Skipping his usual chitter-chatter and introductory warm-up, he faced the front rows and pointed his finger. "Someone in the audience has a secret and she's holding it in plain sight."

The spotlight searched the audience. When Sandi tried to stand and then fell back into her chair, the spotlight stopped on her.

Rex kept his gaze focused, waiting until the audience followed his stare.

"I do have a secret," Sandi finally called out. "It's Daddy. He's here. In this box." She held the box aloft as people gasped.

"Come forward to the stage," Rex insisted. "I have a message from your father."

She stumbled into the aisle, as two ushers magically appeared to give assistance.

She made her way up the steps to stand next to Rex. He looked at her, speaking in a low but firm voice. "Your father wants you to know that he's happy, and that he's been chatting to your grandfather and that it's okay for you to enjoy your cruise without him."

Sandi's face lit up. "Is it true? Daddy spoke to you?"

"He said your grandfather has found other veterans and is having a great time talking old war stories. There's nothing to be sad about."

The audience broke into applause as Sandi burst into tears. Rex assisted her back down the steps.

He'd started off with a bang, wasting no time in getting the audience's attention. She felt a certain amount of pride in Rex. *He knows what he's doing and my information helped. Plus there's no harm done. Sandi obviously wasn't hiding her bereavement, carrying around her father's ashes.*

And Rex only told Sandi what she wanted to hear. That her father was all right and that he wasn't alone.

7

REX REDONDO

After the show, Rex sat in front of his mirror, removing the makeup around his eyes. He stared at himself and sighed. *Okay, Rex, old boy. You've made a big mistake. Just admit you won't be seeing much of Viv. The time on the ship will pass quickly if you stop wanting what you can't have.*

The thrust of the matter was that he no longer welcomed the extra attention from adoring fans when he wasn't on stage. Plus he had yet to settle in to his staff berth.

A knock came to the door. Robert Redford poked his head inside the dressing room. "Great show, Mr. Redondo. People loved your entrance and how you took over."

Rex tossed a soiled tissue into the trash and then turned in his chair. "Good to know. First night feedback is important. Plus I'll be seeing most of the same audience for another three performances, so I have to keep on my toes. Totally different at a casino..." His voice trailed off.

Stop talking. He doesn't need to know how you do your job. Oversharing had become a bad habit of late. He used anecdotes for a purpose; if he kept talking, he controlled the conversation. And then he'd make a quick exit without being waylaid.

Even now all he wanted to do was settle in and put his feet up. Maybe watch a show on television and get some sleep.

"Good to know," Redford responded politely. "We've readied your quarters. I can show you the way."

Minutes later, Redford began the tour. "Over here we have the staff bar and dining room. That's where we hold our get-togethers and parties. And there is a private lounge and library. If you look through that door, you'll even find a small dining room."

A giggling couple walked past coming from the opposite direction. Arms draped around each other, their laughter made Rex feel self-conscious. A stab of regret pierced his heart. *How did I let this cruise with Viv get away from me so easily?*

Redford seemed to sense his discomfort because he said, "We'll be sure to comp you and Miss Rose another cruise. One of your choice. It's Aloha's way of saying thank you for stepping in at the last minute." He stopped and used his key card to open a door. Rex followed him inside.

One look and he sighed. His mind raced, comparing his first stateroom to this. No veranda that connected to Viv's, for one. And it was smaller. He could barely walk past the end of the bed to get to the bathroom without bumping into the top of the dresser.

A tiny shower and a toilet with a basin. No fancy products or fluffy towels. Three dispensers hung on the shower wall, each one carefully labeled: shampoo, conditioner, and soap.

Back to the closet, he slid the door open. Only a few inches of rod space to hang his clothing. Rex was a man who felt particular about his wardrobe, and this would not accommodate even half of what Sutton had packed for the cruise.

Giggling sounded from the neighbors next to him. "The walls are thin," he commented dryly.

Redford spoke matter-of-factly. "To be honest, Aloha encourages their employees to take it easy when they're not working a shift." He sheepishly grinned. "Happy couples make for better workers. And then when the cruise is over, they go their separate ways, none the worse for wear. We have lots of double rooms for that purpose."

Rex shrugged. He didn't plan on making anyone else's acquaintance on this trip. He'd promised Viv a vacation with lots of luxury and he couldn't wait to make up for his bad decision as soon as they got back to shore. Then he saw his worn travel bag shoved into the corner.

"I'm going to unpack and get to bed early. But before you go... I brought one tux for the fancy dress dinner, which I wore tonight. I usually have at least two at my disposal, especially when I do gigs back-to-back."

Redford assured him. "Just leave it out and I'll have your cabin steward pick it up. It will be hung in your closet freshly pressed before each performance."

"Okay then," Rex muttered. When Redford continued standing in his room, he asked, "This has been quite the day. Do I have to get up at any special time for breakfast?"

"Oh no, sir," Redford spoke emphatically. "You're the performer and you can pretty much make your own hours for meals. Just call anytime and we'll get you room service." He pointed to an old-fashioned phone on the desk. "I'll leave you now to unpack."

Once the door closed behind Redford, Rex flung himself down on the bed, his face buried in a pillow. His eyes began to tear. *Come on, be a man*, he ordered himself, rubbing his sleeve across his forehead.

When he sniffed, he realized it wasn't his emotions bringing up the tears. It was some kind of burning plastic smell making them sting. *Probably coming from the air ducts.* He coughed to clear a scratch at the back of his throat. Rubbing his eyes, he thumped the flat pillow. *Allergies. They followed me on board.*

Early the next morning that Rex found Viv's text from the night before.

> Great show. The way you just jumped right
> in. Impressive.

> Thanks.

He added a thumbs-up emoji and then looked down at himself. *I didn't even undress last night*, he realized.

Sitting on the side of the bed, his stomach growled. *I think this whole job and upsetting Viv is making me feel terrible*, he concluded. *Might as well get out of bed and get this day over with.*

On his feet, he reached for the desk phone. "*Legend of the Sea*," came a familiar voice.

"It's me, Redondo," Rex said.

"I can see that on my phone," Redford replied. "By the way, a woman just stopped by the activities counter to sing your praises. I guess you know your stuff. She'd scheduled a burial at sea for her father a month ago and you picked up her daddy issues on stage."

Rex made it a point not to respond to compliments. He was not easily flattered when it came to his show. "I called to make sure my tux will be picked up and laundered before my next performance."

"It will be returned to your room well ahead of the next show," Redford assured him. "Just like I told you last night. No need to be concerned."

Rex hung up the phone and edged his way around the sharp corner of his dresser. Leaving his clothes draped over a chair, he stepped inside the small bathroom and straight into the shower. As cold water sprinkled over his chest, he braced his hand on the wall.

No matter how he turned the dial, the temperature refused to get warm. *Reminds me of the shower on a naval ship.* The space was so narrow that he was only able to lift one hand at a time to scrub under his arm. *At least there's plenty of water.* As if to prove him wrong the stream of water sputtered and died.

As he rubbed the rough towel over his skin, he realized the burning plastic smell before he fell asleep had somehow lodged itself in his nostrils. Rex scrubbed the towel over his hair, trying to recall what that smell reminded him of.

Because of his time in the Marines, he knew how ships collected bilge water in the lowest part of the hull. And that the water could contain grease, oil, and other contaminants. Waste from the showers, sinks, and laundry would be processed and then dumped at sea.

But the particular burning smell wasn't about bilge. *More like diesel fuel*, he thought. *But I think diesel is regulated as an environmental hazard, especially for cruise ships.*

He sniffed, then coughed as his head began to throb. *I'll take an aspirin later.*

After a quick cup of coffee in the staff dining room, Rex decided a quick glance at Viv would lift his spirits. *I don't have to talk and be seen with her.* After searching the dining room areas, hustling past passengers with his baseball cap pulled over his face, he finally found her.

She and the woman from the night before were engaged in an animated conversation. He ducked behind the life boats to stay out of sight. *This is complicated. I don't want to hear any more about Daddy in the box, and I don't want her to realize I know Viv.*

You're such a fool, Rex Redondo, he told himself. If I hadn't opened my big yap and said yes to stepping in, I'd be walking with Viv myself. After enjoying a leisurely cup of coffee and return trips to the buffet for eggs and crispy toast.

But oh no, I had to say yes one time too many. And now I've probably lost this chance to woo her into the next step of our relationship. I'm an idiot. He took a quick breath because he'd nearly shouted his frustration aloud.

He watched as Viv and Sandi turned the corner, coming straight at him. "Oh look, it's that handsome mentalist," Sandi said. She ran toward him.

"Good morning, Mr. Redondo. It's so good to see you because I wanted to thank you for last night. Just knowing that Daddy is happy..."

As she continued to talk in that breathy nonstop way, Rex pretended to listen. He glanced out of the corner of his eye at Viv. She looked slightly bemused, taking no part in his rescue.

He raised his eyebrow, but Viv looked away.

Once Sandi began to wind down, Viv interrupted. "I really must get going. I want to set up a spa treatment for later today. It seems I have a lot of time to spare." She turned on her heel, leaving him to fend off Sandi's attention.

Rex watched longingly as Viv disappeared around the corner.

8

REX REDONDO

Rex sat down at a round table on the lido deck. He wasn't that hungry, which surprised him, considering he missed dinner the night before.

When the server came by to take his order, he told her, "Dry toast." The choice came as an afterthought since he wasn't even hungry.

"I'll bring water and orange juice, butter, and jam just in case you change your mind and want more." Once she'd left, he sat back in his chair.

Rex thought that he'd be able to access both staff and passenger decks and that he'd spend the daytime going back and forth. He'd spy on Viv and hopefully get her to laugh. Text her ribald comments, maybe play a little hide-and-seek.

But her attitude this morning made him realize she wasn't playing games. At least with him. Viv didn't intend on spending her cruise wondering about where he was or when he would turn up. She'd made that obvious, slipping away to get a spa treatment.

The server reappeared. "Here's your order, Mr. Redondo." She reached to flip over a cup for coffee, and he raised his hand.

"None for me this morning," he said.

His anxious stomach had made the turn to slightly nauseous. "Would you prefer juice or water?" she asked.

"I'm fine without," he assured her, his eyes on the distant horizon.

After nibbling the corner of the toast, he put it down and turned around to get a good view of the gym. Raising his eyes upward, he had a clear shot of the row of ellipticals. Every one was in use. Men and women pumped their arms and legs. Most were wearing Airbuds or headphones.

When Viv first told him what she'd seen, he'd wondered if she might have been mistaken. Given the gym was two levels up from the pool. And of course the sun bounced off the glass, creating a glare. And she might have been tired and a bit irritated at being left alone...

But now that he had the same view, he wasn't so certain. The gym wasn't as far away as he'd thought originally. Viv's eyesight was as good if not better than his, especially if she was wearing her tinted progressives.

She looks so sexy wearing those glasses when we walk every morning with Kevin, in her athletic skintight pants and t-shirt.

He shook his head. *Stop it. Not gonna help your mood any, thinking about Viv.*

He looked up at the wall of ellipticals one more time. *I need to tell her that I heard what she was saying. She probably thinks I'm an ass for not paying more attention to her feelings.*

He pulled out his phone. Viv's bright voice answered.

"Yes," she said.

"Good morning," he replied. "How are things?"

"Oh, I'm just out of the shower. I had a wonderful break-fast delivered to my room, and then you know what? I had a second breakfast after my walk on the promenade deck. Isn't the ocean amazing? So vast and so very blue."

He found her cheerful account slightly irritating. Two breakfasts. He lowered his voice. "Wish I could be sharing that second breakfast."

"I know you do, but then there's not a chance of that, is there?" A bit of the brightness left her voice. Suddenly he felt better.

"So I called because I'm sitting on the lido deck, pretty much where you were yesterday. And I can see right up into the gym to the lineup of ellipticals. I can see faces very clearly. You had that view, right?"

Her words came quickly. "Yes, I did. I saw that man with my own eyes. He fell over and hit his head on the handle of the elliptical just like I said."

"I'm thinking we'd better follow up," he said. "Maybe he's injured or maybe he's dead."

"When I turned back around, he'd just disappeared." Her voice sounded thoughtful. "I'm so relieved you believe me. I tried to put it out of my mind last night. As long as I was helping you with the intel gathering, I was fine. But when I got to bed, I couldn't get to sleep. I kept seeing him falling, his head slamming against the metal arm. Terrifying."

"So what are we going to do?" Rex asked.

"Well I'm a bit worried about all of that," she said right away. "When I left you with Sandi I did make an appoint-ment at the spa. Since it's right beside the gym I thought I could listen and gather info for you and also pay attention, just in case someone might have noticed the man. Surely someone besides me witnessed the fall." Her voice trailed away.

One of the qualities Rex appreciated about Viv was the way she took on a challenge without so much as a flinch.

"I think you're on to something," he said immediately. "I can listen to conversations among the staff. I know there's someone with loose lips who will know what happened to the guy. How about we check in again around lunchtime?"

"My massage is at noon," she answered in the irritating bright voice.

"You're getting a massage?" He felt his pulse quicken. "And you'll be naked and everything, with oil on your body."

"That's the way they usually do massages," Viv said tartly.

"I am such an idiot," he groaned. "I never should have taken this job."

"Yes, you are. An idiot. We can talk more about that later."

After Viv hung up, he put his phone in his pocket with a sigh.

9

VIVIENNE ROSE

"A little bubbly before your massage?" the spa attendant offered. Dressed in a white formfitting blazer and white pants, she looked very clean and efficient.

Viv reached for the flute and then pulled back. *It's barely eleven o'clock, for heaven's sake.* She'd arrived early for her appointment to give herself plenty of time to eavesdrop. Left in the waiting lounge, no one else had joined her.

"Do you have water instead?" she asked the attendant.

Disappointment showed on the woman's face. "Of course. We have clear distilled, fruit-infused, or sparkling bottled—"

"Fruit-infused," Viv said hastily.

"Follow the signs to the dressing room, and when you're finished undressing I'll meet you at the reservation desk with your beverage." The woman walked away, looking crisp and germ-free. Hair tucked back into a neat bun, she could have been mistaken for a hospital employee.

Strolling down the quiet corridor, Viv inhaled a pleasant flowery plumeria scent. In the dressing room, she took a towel from the top of the pile before looking around.

Everything looked and smelled welcoming. Cloth towels, pristine tile and fresh paint, light music in the background, and the scent—not too flowery, nor too spicy, nor familiar for that matter. *Plumeria,* she thought. *Plus something else I can't identify. Maybe a unique creation for this particular location.*

She looked at an advertisement that lay on the counter. *The spa has its own name,* she thought. *Embrace. Where your every need is met.* On the back of the card they'd listed every possible package treatment for nails, hair, body, and spirit. The spirit option included mantras and oil-infusion aroma therapy.

Her eyebrows lifted.

She put the card back, looking toward the sinks and counters. *Also very clean. But not fussy.* Stopping to listen, she realized even the New Age music wasn't over the top. *No pan flutes. They put my nerves on edge.*

At least my brain won't exhaust itself pushing away the sounds.

Further down the hall, she found an empty dressing room. A fluffy white robe with the spa's logo had been hung inside. When she slipped it off the hanger she found a note: This item can be purchased in our gift shop and put on your account.

"Sure it can," Viv murmured. *And wouldn't I like one just like this, with the Embrace logo on the front to remind me of my cruise. And once I bought the robe I'd end up needing the scent.*

So I'd inquire about the fragrance, and by the time I realized how easy it is to buy items and just put them on my room number, I'd remember someone at home who'd like a bottle. So it would be two. And then maybe I'd be convinced to add the lotion. Just to treat myself...

She slid her feet into the white oversized slippers that were placed in a basket labeled "for your use." Then she folded her clothes into a bundle. But before she could pull the curtain back, she heard voices rise and fall in conversation.

"They replaced Mulroy," came the light tone of a female voice. "This guy is better, actually. They found him on the passenger manifesto of all things, and now he's sleeping in staff quarters."

"Older guy. Silver fox, right?" Another woman's voice, this one deeper.

"That's him. Rex is his name. I tried to chat him up before the show, but he seemed distracted. Kind of abrupt. Too bad. He'd be good for a week—you know, older guy boyfriend material."

"You already have your hands full, if I'm not mistaken," the deeper voice said.

"Stop that. I have to keep it under wraps. At least until his divorce."

Viv pulled the dressing room curtain aside with a flourish. Stepping out she called, "Where are the lockers?"

A woman came from around the corner. She wore a different uniform, one with a matching blue top and slacks. "I can help you," the woman said. Viv recognized her voice as one of the women she'd heard talking earlier. The one with the deeper voice. "Right over here. Just take the key with you and keep it in your bathrobe pocket. It will be safe."

"Thank you so much," Viv said. "Are you a spa employee?"

"Oh no. I'm just walking through on my way to the Crow's Nest Beverage Bar. I'm the manager there."

"Where is that exactly?" Viv reached for a key on a locker door.

"It's right inside the gym, tucked behind an alcove. After people shower and work out they often stop to rehydrate and get a coffee. Enjoy your treatment. Try the Turkish Bath Gold Massage package. It's the most popular and well worth the cost."

Viv meandered her way toward the reception desk. A woman held out her fruit-infused water with a lemon. "Here you go. If you sit over there, Courtney will be with you shortly. She's just finishing with another client."

Drinks in hand she sat down, carefully arranging her robe to cover her legs.

A phone rang. "Embrace." She spoke in a low voice. "How can I help you?"

The staff person tapped her pen on the counter as she listened.

"Yes, I have you down for noon. Oh, that won't be a problem. We'll have someone walk the dog while you're getting your manicure. Would you like to add a foot massage to your package? Of course, I'll put you down for another half an hour. See you soon." The woman placed the phone back in the cradle.

Viv hid her smile behind her hand. *Another upsell. I wonder how much that cost...*

Minutes later Viv stood in the massage room. As the door closed behind her she inhaled deeply. On her belly, she relaxed her face into the horseshoe-shaped pillow. The now familiar flower scent permeating the air. Viv inhaled again. *I do love plumeria.* Eyes closed, she thought about the conversation she'd just had with her massage therapist.

The name tag told her the therapist's name was Courtney. "We have several packages for you to choose from." She handed her a sheet with a smile.

Even though the sheet listed a number of options—with no price listing—Viv pointed to Ayurveda massage. The one she'd booked originally.

She knew better than to ask about the cost. If she did, Courtney might conclude that she wasn't used to this kind of luxury. And Courtney might hurry the massage, hoping the next customer might be more lucrative.

Feeling of two minds, she vacillated while Courtney continued her sales pitch.

"I can also take you next door after I'm done for a lymphatic drainage. Women of your age benefit from the process."

"That will reduce my facial puffiness then?" She made every effort to sound interested and not annoyed.

Courtney warmed to her subject. "If you have special plans this evening, you'll be looking your best!"

Viv knew that special plans was code for having a date. And that she wouldn't be that person, since Rex was no longer available. She felt a tinge of disappointment. *Maybe I should treat myself...*

That's just what they want. To keep adding on the treatments, hoping I'm planning for a special night or that I'm just the opposite, sad I don't have a plan. Cruises are seductive. I might have been coerced if I were here with a partner, but I'm alone and not interested in anyone else.

She handed the sheet back to Courtney. "I won't be needing any other treatments."

Courtney's face grew stony with disappointment. "Okay then. Take off your robe. Lie back on the table face down. I'll be right back."

Still appreciating the scent and the music, Viv heard the door close.

Minutes later she felt smooth hands travel down her back.

"Worked here long?" Viv asked, hoping she'd been forgiven.

10

VIVIENNE ROSE

Five hundred dollars later, Viv departed from Embrace feeling quite pleased with herself. Her toenails and fingernails sparkled with Delicious Apple, a color she'd never wear at home but one she fully embraced for her cruise. She'd been assured that the lacquer would stay on for days, as long as she let it thoroughly dry.

It better, considering I paid two dollars extra per nail over and above what I initially booked.

She wafted her way down the hall smelling of exorbitant amounts of body oil. She sniffed. *Okay, so I smell a bit like Kevin when he comes back from the groomer. But at least I didn't buy into the upsell post-massage.*

"I don't think I want to bring any home with me," she assured the attendant at the checkout desk. "I want to experience the scent and enjoy its essence on the cruise." Keeping her face straight was the hardest part after that overblown and overly wordy explanation.

So now Viv felt ready to take on her day. Until she remembered...

No matter how many questions she asked of her

massage therapist or the nice girl who did her nails, they only smiled and kept working. Even when she brought up the elliptical incident, she'd received a polite, "Um-hum," from the massage therapist, and an, "Oh really?" from the nail technician.

Stepping into the ladies' locker room, it took her five minutes to retrieve her clothes and get dressed. It was a relief to return her feet to her flip-flops. The Delicious Apple toenail polish made them look expensive. Once she'd returned her key to the locker, she made her way toward the gym and the coffee bar.

The Crow's Nest manager she'd talked to at the spa, wearing a name tag with Tonya written on it, stood behind the counter. The woman handed a coffee to a man who smiled back at her. "Have a good workout?" she asked in a conversational tone.

"I did. My plan is to show up every morning of the cruise. Burn some calories. Add to my steps. That way I can consume more calories the rest of the day."

"This will be a good beginning," came her chipper reply.

He moved aside for Viv to give her order.

"Hello again," she said. "I'll have a large coffee, black."

"How was the massage?" Before Viv could answer, Tonya turned her back to grab a mug.

"Great. I feel wonderful. How's business?" Having failed to get any gossip from the spa people, Viv felt more determined than ever.

Tonya slid the full mug across the counter. "You get one free refill. Just write down your room number and that should do it."

Viv filled out the chit. "So I'm curious... How many people come and go during the day?"

"We're busy as soon as the gym opens at around six

o'clock. We shoo people out for dinner and the show, then reopen for those who want a late-night beverage."

"How long have you worked for Aloha Cruises?"

"This will be my third year. My ninth voyage. I'm hoping to get promoted, maybe into management."

Viv felt confident that she and Tonya were hitting it off. *I've got a talker. Now I just have to ask the right questions.*

One more sip of coffee, then I'll ease my way into the elliptical guy.

She took advantage of the pause while Tonya wiped the counter. Once she was finished, Viv glanced over her shoulder to make sure no one else was in line. Then she leaned closer and spoke in a conspiratorial tone. "I got early boarding. Sat right over there." She pointed toward the pool area. "I saw a man fall off the elliptical."

"That's unlikely," Tonya said curtly. "Maybe you imagined it, because no one's allowed in the gym until everyone's boarded and assigned their room." Tonya dropped her hand under the counter.

"Oh, I know the regular customers aren't allowed that soon. But what about the special ones... I heard there are all sorts of extra perks, depending on how often you cruise and what you pay. Maybe the guy was one of those people and got to use the gym before everyone else."

Viv felt especially pleased with herself now. If staff was encouraged to upsell at the spa, she was pretty certain that carried over into the rest of the cruise line business practice, and it looked like she was right.

"There are special perks." Tonya took another swipe of the counter with her cloth. "Actually, there's an entire section of high-cost suites with a members-only lounge."

"And how do I qualify for that?" Viv asked.

"Spend lots of money and book another cruise before

you leave. That will help. You can inquire at the concierge desk."

"So those special people board earlier and get to use the gym before other people get settled?" She felt sure that she was on to something. *If I can narrow down my guy as a special passenger, then my search will be less cumbersome.*

But to her disappointment Tonya shook her head.

"Nope. Not how it works. The private-hideaway people have their own exclusive gym. It's separate and located on their level. No one else can work out there. It's against the rules."

Viv put her empty mug down with a thump.

"Would you like a refill?" Tonya asked.

"I think I'll try signing up for an aerobic class before I head back to my stateroom. I can do that right over there?" She pointed to a counter close by.

"Yes, you can." Tonya turned to assist another customer.

Making her way out of the coffee bar, Viv stepped closer into an alcove. She paused to look in a display window and then made a right turn into into the gym. The familiar smell of hardwood floor polish and perspiration met her nose. All of the elliptical machines were in use, men and women with headphones, arms and legs pumping.

Viv drew closer. She stood against the wall and glanced at her phone. *People will think I'm waiting for a machine,* she told herself. *It's a good thing I wore clothes that could pass for exercise garb.* Each time she looked up she made a mental note.

If I'm not mistaken the fifth elliptical from the left is the one my guy fell off of. When he toppled over, he hit his head on the handle of elliptical number four.

A woman stepped off the machine, stopping to blot her forehead with a towel.

Viv hurried forward as the woman walked away. When no one else claimed the machine, she hoisted herself onto the elliptical.When no one told her to get off, she pedaled for a minute and then stopped, pretending to inspect her foot and shoe on the right side.

Hopping off, she ran her hands over the foot pedal. Her nose twitched with distaste. *So many people sweating on these machines every day. I hope they clean all the surfaces.*

She lifted the corner of the rubber mat underneath the flywheel, looking for a clue. Maybe a trace of blood. Coming up with nothing unusual, she lay on her back to see underneath the seat.

A loud voice interrupted her search.

"Excuse me. This is my machine. My time slot, according to the schedule." The voice sounded like Cary Grant. Or someone trying to imitate the famous actor.

On her feet she faced the complainer. Rex Redondo grinned back.

"Are you trying to sound like Cary Grant?"

"I'm a good mimic. I used to do impersonations in the early days."

Viv's heart skipped a beat. He did have that suave Cary Grant thing going for him. That was for sure. Her eyes drifted over Rex's comfy but obviously expensive tracksuit. If she didn't know better she'd think he was a handsome guy looking for company, the way his eyes widened as they continued to stare at her. She pointed to a bit of ecru-colored fabric hanging from his pants pocket.

"What's that?" Viv smirked. "A Cary Grant silk hand-kerchief?"

His face turned red. He shoved the fabric deeper into his pocket before explaining.

"If I'm not mistaken, those are a pair of panties," Viv said.

"I believe this is my elliptical time," announced a loud voice.

A stranger glared at Rex, and then his eyes rested on Viv before turning his gaze back to Rex. "Aren't you that mentalist guy? I saw you last night."

Viv chuckled. "See you," she muttered under her breath.

On the elevator ride down to poolside, she pondered the panties. Has he been keeping busy down in staff quarters. *I wonder what he's up to.*

11

REX REDONDO

Earlier that morning, Rex stretched his leg in bed, warding off a cramp in his calf. He felt awful, including a quickly burgeoning headache, but he didn't know exactly why. Thinking back over the evening, he still wasn't certain. The show went well. He'd done a great job with that woman and her father's ashes, for instance. At least she seemed satisfied, and so did the audience.

But then his thoughts flooded back. *What about Viv...*

His calf continued to cramp, so he got out of bed to hop on his foot. Finally he got relief. Hobbling toward the bathroom, he knew he couldn't leave things with Viv alone. *I'm going to track her down and apologize again.*

It didn't take but twenty minutes to shower and dress. *Viv will be heading to the spa and to check out the gym. Maybe I can just run into her by chance. Pretend we don't know each other. Have a cup of coffee like we just met.*

When Rex reached for the door handle, an uneasy feeling came over him. Not a cramp in his calf this time. An overall sense of something not right. He steadied himself against the door.

Used to the images that spun in his head, Rex closed his eyes, waiting for his brain to deliver. *Come on, then. Tell me what I need to know.* To his surprise the usual pictures behind his eyes did not arrive.

Rex blinked a few times and tried again. When nothing came up that time, he stared at the door.

I wonder what's going on...

Instead of opening the door, he turned to face the room. *Maybe it was the stuffy hot air and the stale smell. Like that time in Afghanistan.* In the infirmary tent. In an instant it all came back to him.

He'd gone to sick call, needing something for a cold. He'd found the makeshift infirmary filled with younger Marines coughing and hacking. In the past, Rex would have assumed that most were malingering, needing some attention and a few hours off the job.

The doc would evaluate and determine and do the proper report.

But that day Rex knew something was different. His intuition kicked in, informing him that eight of the men waiting to be seen were genuinely ill.

That place. Rex shuddered. He forced himself to release that memory and to stay present. A new suspicious came up. *Maybe I'm picking up the vibes of the previous occupant.* He felt an anticipatory tingling in his hands and feet.

At least I can still read a room.

He blinked and his mood changed instantly. From uneasy to insecure. Thoughts of another show that evening caused him to shake. His heart began to race.

I'd better pay attention. Because if I go on stage tonight without my full-on skills...I'll be stuck making things up to please the audience.

Rex walked away from the door to sit on the edge of the

bed. Holding his head in his hands, he willed the images to come. He opened his eyes, his heart still pounding.

I can't just sit here. I need to take action. I can do this by logic. So I think it's the room. It has to be. I need to search this place. Maybe the previous occupant left something behind that's blocking my energy.

Rex checked every drawer in the small dresser a foot away from the bed. Then he rifled through the bedside table. On his hands and knees he looked under the bed, which only revealed his suitcase.

Finally he pushed open the sliding door to the small closet. His clothes for the evening had been left hanging, pressed and smelling fresh. *So they delivered my laundry at least. Was I asleep?*

He pushed the clothing aside to reveal a metal safe. On the front was a lock with a red dial. He tried a few combinations and was not rewarded with the satisfying click of the door opening. Rex scratched his head.

Though his thinking still felt muddled, his logic told him that he needed access to the safe. With people coming and going to drop off his tux, he needed to store his wallet in a safe place.

I'll ask someone about how to reset the combination, he thought.

The staff dining room hummed with morning activity. There were several tables set for two and four, with one long communal table in the middle. The officers and heads of departments were easy to spot dressed in all white. The stewards and other personnel were dressed in all blue.

The smell of bacon drifted from the kitchen. Rex felt his stomach clench. Ignoring the food, he spotted Robert Redford sitting by himself. "Mind if I join you?" Rex pulled out a chair.

"Not at all." Redford smiled. He took off and cleaned his glasses before slipping them back over the bridge of his nose.

"I'll get my food and be right back," Rex told him.

Once he'd returned with two pieces of dry toast, he started the conversation. "I don't remember you wearing glasses when we first met."

"Contacts," Redford explained. "Now that we're underway, I spend most of my time at the computer, helping guests at the IT desk. The glasses work better. Anyway, I wanted to talk to you. Did you find your laundered tux?"

Rex got right to the point. "I did. Hung up in my closet. But I wanted to put something in my room safe, and I couldn't get it to open."

A surprised look came over Redford's face. "Usually the steward resets the safe on the final clean out." He wiped his lips with the cloth napkin. "Funny story. Stewards often find the oddest things left over in a safe. They occasionally forget to clean it out in the excitement of heading ashore. Last year we found a year's supply of condoms and a two-carat diamond ring."

Rex chuckled. "Well we know what was going on in that occupant's mind, don't we." He squirmed. *I may have been that guy a while back.*

"Yeah, we do. But like I was saying, it's not usual for staff to be forgetful. I can ask your steward to straighten that out for you right away." Redford pushed his plate aside. "Heading to the smoking deck, care to join me?"

"No, I gave it up. But before you go..." Rex placed his toast back on the plate, not feeling remotely hungry. "I'd prefer to keep the stewards out of my room. As much as I appreciate the help, I also value my privacy. So would it be possible to leave my tux hanging outside the door in the hallway, and also to give me the necessary information to reset the safe combination myself?"

Redford frowned. "I suppose I could do that." He pulled up his phone and tapped around." I just sent you the universal code for clearing any leftover combinations. Once you use this, you can put in your own code. And then when you leave, let the door to the safe remain open for the next person."

"Thanks, I appreciate that."

After saying goodbye to Redford, Rex walked down the corridor to his room.

He opened his stateroom door with a heavy sigh. *I don't know what to do now. Maybe take a nap.*

He'd completely forgotten about his plan to find Viv.

12

REX REDONDO

Rex laid his head on a pillow to rest. With conscious effort he inhaled and exhaled until his heart rate throttled down. They'd taught him to do that when he retired from the military.

Breathe in for five. Hold the breath for five. Then exhale to five. It always works. He fell asleep.

Opening his eyes with a start, he swung his legs to the ground. Lifting his phone, he looked at the text from Redford with the combination.

In three spins he cleared the previous numbers and then set his own. Now that the door was open he reached inside to the back of the safe. To his surprise he touched fabric airy and soft.

It didn't take an expert to know that what he held in his hand was a pair of silk panties. Rex was, in fact, kind of an expert about this particular pair. It would embarrass him to admit to Viv, but he'd purchased panties much like this for a young woman more than once. The last time was before he met his neighbor, not quite a year ago.

Though he couldn't remember the woman's name, he'd never forget the look of delight when she opened her gift. Plus she knew the brand.

"The La Perla Maison lace thong!" she'd exclaimed with delight.

She'd better be happy. Those panties set me back three hundred bucks.

Gently rubbing the fine fabric between his fingers, he waited for his intuition to kick in with an insight. Maybe who they belonged to and why they were left behind. Yet his mind offered no image or inclination. Just the blank fog he'd woken up with that morning.

He tried again. Closing his eyes, he waited. There was no roll of images. Only his fingers turning ice cold.

"I got nothin'," he announced to the empty room.

Shoving the panties in his pocket, he remembered his plan to reconnect with Viv. *I need to keep apologizing until she forgives me.*

Rex put the Do Not Disturb sign over the door handle, then made his way to the elevator.

Once inside the gym, he stood to the side to look for Viv. He finally spotted her by the elliptical, standing astride with one foot on each pedal bar.

As if she'd heard him, she popped off the machine. Bending over, she glanced under the foot pedals. He knew immediately what she was up to. *Looking for evidence. Good for her.*

He reached to straighten an imaginary bow tie. Shifting to his Cary Grant persona, he walked closer, hoping to catch her by surprise.

· · ·

Rex felt worried. *She saw those panties and I didn't have a chance to explain. She might think I'm...*

Okay, I have to set this straight. Maybe I can find her sitting poolside.

Sure enough Viv had selected a chaise lounge near the jacuzzi. The one next to her didn't have an occupant, but someone had left a towel to save their place. Rex reasoned to himself, *I'll give them five minutes. If no one claims the chaise, then I'll sit down. No decent cruise line lets people save places indefinitely.*

He kept his focus on Viv as he waited. She occupied herself by carefully shaking and then spreading out the Aloha-brand cruise line towel. Once she sat down, she pulled a paperback book out of her purse. No glance in his direction.

Okay, I'm done waiting. His shoes squished against the wet pavement as he made his way to the foot of her chaise. Lowering his sunglasses he said, "Mind if I sit there?"

Viv kept her eyes on her book. "Better not. Sandi Hughes is sitting with Daddy at that round table. One glance in this direction and she'll see us together." Viv kept reading.

Rex decided to walk around the pool. Maybe Sandi would go away and he could try again. After three laps, he looked over. When Viv didn't return his gaze, he felt miffed. *She's getting along all too well without me, but without Viv's company, this cruise is just a big bore for me.*

Continuing to stroll, he rounded the jacuzzi and then came to a halt.

A small gaggle of passengers stood close to an old woman. She was seated at a table, her cane propped against a chair. Rex came closer to listen.

"Oh yes, I've traveled the seas for decades," the woman said in a gravelly voice, her pronunciation precise. "In fact, I go from cruise to cruise, and I keep all of my worldly belongings in my stateroom. I sold my home years ago. This really is the best way to live. And now they call me the Old Lady of the Sea. I'm a legend." The pride in her tone could not be mistaken.

"How old were you when you made your first voyage?" one woman asked.

Rex sat at an empty table close by. He ducked his head to stare at a menu, finding the woman's story more than fascinating. After a short time, he realized it was hard to concentrate because her tone of voice grated on his nerves. On his feet again, he began to circle the pool.

Instead of coming around to Viv, he walked straight ahead, past the swooshing glass doors and into the lobby. *Maybe I need to forget about her and focus on me.* Then he remembered the staff had their own workout room.

You're not a passenger, he reminded himself. *Go to your place.* Rex felt his heart drop. Those were the words he'd used to train his puppy, Kevin, when he wanted him to sit in his kennel. A very pricy dog trainer instructed him on tone of voice. Of course Sutton was better than he was on the follow-through.

It wasn't until he opened the door of his stateroom that he realized he didn't have the energy to work out. Plus he felt dizzy and he still had a headache. *You sound like you're malingering, Redondo.*

He lifted his phone to text Viv.

> I found the panties left behind in the room
> safe. Might belong to the previous
> occupant or maybe a friend of theirs.
> Taking a zap.

He felt too tired to correct spell check. But he did manage to take a photo of the panties to send along with the text. Then he flopped down on his bed and fell back to sleep.

13

VIVIENNE ROSE

Viv watched from behind her sunglasses. Rex lingered behind the crowd speaking to the Old Lady of the Sea. Then he sat down but got right up again. Once he'd disappeared past the sliding glass doors to the lobby, she felt better. *I'm supposed to be listening to conversations, not keeping him company.*

Using her book as a decoy, Viv paid attention as random people stopped at the older woman's table to chat her up. She made a note in her mind of the juicier bits of conversation. Once she'd heard enough, she put her book down to compose a text.

That was when she saw the photo of the panties.

What's this about? she asked herself.

Rex's text seemed a bit garbled. *What's a zap? Probably autocorrect. Does he mean nap?* Since when did Rex Redondo snooze in the middle of the day? Then she heard Sandi's voice. Viv put her cell away.

"Yes, I'm here because of Daddy," came her now familiar words. "He passed away. He always wanted to take me on this cruise across the ocean to Honolulu. You see, his uncle

Dick was a Pearl Harbor survivor. They planned to make the trip, but Dick passed away. And now Daddy has passed too."

Viv felt a jolt. Uncle Dick. That didn't feel right. Hadn't she said...

Wait a minute. She said her grandfather was a Pearl Harbor survivor that time. Has she changed her story, or did her entire family wear a uniform and serve in WW II?

Viv watched as a couple who'd spent a good deal of time chatting with the Old Lady of the Sea made their way toward Sandi.

Maybe her story is more interesting, thought Viv. *People are begging for something to do on these cruises. It's as if the free time is too much for them.*

Sandi's voice continued as Viv picked up her book. She didn't know what to text Rex after receiving the photo of the panties. Obviously it was important to him. But it didn't seem that complicated or necessary. Not missing-body-in-the-gym complicated.

Lifting her phone, she texted.

> Nice panties.

That was the only thing she could think of saying. It wasn't as if they interested her. She wore all cotton briefs that came six in a package. Obviously not in the same league. She huffed and picked up her phone to text him again.

> Sandi says her uncle Dick was at Pearl Harbor. Yesterday she said it was her grandfather. Can you make something of that for the show?

Viv took her book and stood, exasperated. She was tired of eavesdropping; her mind consistently returned to the guy and the elliptical. *No one wants to admit I actually saw what I saw...*

Maybe that was the point. *Am I being gaslighted? He could be dead or seriously injured.* Her chest tightened. *That's it. He was whisked away because he was an inconvenience. Bad for the Aloha brand. They probably put him in some back room somewhere.*

Indignation filled Viv, now she felt even more determined. *I'm going to make someone pay attention to me,* she resolved. *Or at least tell me the man is being cared for.*

Rex paid good money for us to travel on this cruise. Up until he was employed, we were customers. I may not be able to demand his money back, but I can write a nasty review and make them squirm.

She pulled up her phone and composed a message. *There. I'm ready to press send if there's any more nonsense.*

Viv stood behind five other people at the IT desk. Listening to everyone's complaints, one by one, she noted more information to alert Rex for the next show. *I'm getting the hang of this,* she thought. *Snoopy, just like a regular Miss Marple. With my phone I don't even need to knit. Just look down and pretend to be scrolling.* Viv paused to think: *I'll get some more info before I send to him. I bet he'll be pleased.* Then she put her phone away without sending.

Which she was still doing twenty minutes later, when she was still fourth in line. Viv stared at her screen as the woman ahead of her continued to explain.

"I can't connect to the on-board website, so I don't know what I've scheduled for my day. Or what's on the menu. Or what time it is, since we're at sea. My husband is connected, but I'm not. He won't stop telling me what to do, and it's annoying."

Allison Thompson, dark hair amassed clipped on the top of her head, held an expression of displeasure. "That's so frustrating. I hate when that happens to me and my husband. We live in Maine, kind of a remote part, and have unreliable internet providers." The words were right, but the tone of condescension was off putting.Viv had to admit that her smile looked genuine enough.

All of the senior staff on the cruise ship have that interesting way of acting like they care. The nods. The slight smiles. The sincere modulated manner of speaking.

"Is Redford behind the desk?" came a rough loud voice.

The Old Lady of the Sea leaned on her cane. She'd walked right up to the desk, not bothering to stand in line. No one suggested that she should do otherwise.

"Just a minute, everyone," Allison said to those waiting. "I need to help Ms. Alcott next."

Viv smirked. *Well, we know who gets the special treatment here.*

She texted.

> Old Lady has the last name of Alcott. Will research her later for more details.

Robert Redford walked briskly from the back room. "Hello, Ms. Alcott, how can I help this morning? Please step over here." Unlike when he spoke to her, he now sounded genuinely concerned.

She took a small step to the side to see if she could hear their conversation. When the woman ahead of her left the line, she moved closer to the desk. "Allison Thompson,

Information Technology Senior Manager," Viv said firmly as a greeting. "I have a problem."

"Oh, I remember you." Allison pulled on the lapels of her blue blazer in a nervous gesture. "You remind me of my neighbor in Maine. Such a nice woman. An extraordinary baker. She's very smart too."

Viv felt her resolve soften. *It works, to bring up personal information to disarm people.* But then she pushed against that feeling as her eyes narrowed. Every time Allison mentioned Maine, she was trying to make a connection. Viv doubted Allison even lived in Maine. She'd heard her refer to her husband and children too many times to everyone ahead of her in line.

"I've never been to Maine. I don't bake. And I'm even smarter than you think," she stated firmly. "That's why I'm here to tell you, yet again, that I saw a man fall off an elliptical and hit his head and collapse to the floor. And I'm not going to be talked out of what I saw no matter how hard you try."

The color in Allison's face drained. She cleared her throat. "I see," she said in a tight voice. "I'll have you fill out this form so that I can take your complaint to the next level. May I have your cell phone?"

Viv extended her phone with misgivings.

Allison held it in one hand, relentlessly scrolling with her thumb. "Are you looking at my messages?" Viv demanded.

"I am so sorry. I have to add a phone number and email to your contacts and then save. Give me another minute."

Apology not accepted, Viv thought.

Allison finally handed her phone back. "We only offer to input things into the phones of our senior passengers.

They aren't technologically savvy, and it saves time that way," she said tartly.

There it is. The real Allison Thompson. Condescending and slightly pompous. The pompous part will only get worse as she ages, Viv thought. *Just wait until you get called a senior.*

"I sent an email and an attachment," Allison mumbled, then added, "You can fill out the form if you still want to make a complaint. May I help the next person in line?"

Considering her small success a minor victory, Viv squared her shoulders and she turned to walk away. It was all she could do not to high-five each of the ten people who stood in the line, waiting for their turn at the desk.

It wasn't until she was on the elevator that she turned to gaze out the glass side toward the ocean. Her shoulders slumped. *Maybe I won the battle, but the war goes on. Filling out a form isn't an answer. It's just one more obstacle until I get to the truth.*

14

VIVIENNE ROSE

Viv spent the rest of the day in her stateroom. After resting with a book and a long bath, she selected her outfit for dinner. Placing each item on her bed, she added a purse next to the ensemble. Then she picked up her room phone. She waited for the pleasant person to stop talking before asking, "May I have a pot of lavender herbal tea and a few shortbread cookies sent to my room?"

"Yes, ma'am," came the voice. "I'll tell your steward. It will only be a few minutes."

"Oh and would you also bring honey?" Viv turned on the television, clicking her remote to find a news station. Global or local, she didn't care. Anything to remind her that there was a real world out there, beyond the sea.

Sitting on the edge of her bed, she waited for the knock on the door. In the pause, she realized her experiences, connected like a daisy chain, felt connected.

Like Rex's voice at the gym. He'd done a really good impersonation of the actor Cary Grant. The movie *An Affair to Remember* came to mind.

And now the phrase "beyond the sea." She thought of

an old song of that same title. She hummed, thinking of a boy in junior high school. How everyone attended the monthly sports nights.

What was his name again... Anyway, he'd asked her to dance on the last song of the evening. This request, due to its significance in the lineup of tunes, would be groundwork for all the gossip the following school week.

He held me with both arms wrapped around my body. So close I could smell the peppermint gum he'd tucked into his cheek. He ducked his lips into my neck and dared to take a small bite. That Ricky. He became my badge of honor for the next month—until the next sports night when we'd become old news.

He'd asked her to go steady. Lifting a silver chain over his head to hand her his St. Christopher medal. That's what boys did then. Couples would go steady for a month. She ended their relationship in two weeks because she didn't see the point in it really—he never called or spoke to her after he'd handed over the medal.

A knock at the door snapped Viv out of her reminiscence. She rose and opened the door, standing aside as room service ushered past holding a tray. "Here you are, ma'am," he added a slight bow. "Would you like me to leave this outside on the veranda or inside, here at the desk?"

"Outside, please."

Once he'd left, Viv lifted the cozy off the teapot and poured a cup. Adding a bit of honey was her afternoon treat to herself. She took a sip and then looked to the veranda next door. The one Rex was supposed to occupy. Viv bit into a cookie as she wondered if Rex's stateroom had been given to another occupant, since he now stayed with staff on the third level.

After she'd finished a second cookie, she heard the

scraping of a chair from the other side. Curiosity made her stand and draw closer. She leaned out over the rail and looked over her left shoulder. A pair of bare feet poked over the end of a chaise lounge.

Afraid of being observed, she took a hasty step backward. The feet were large and the toes slender. *Man or woman?* Viv wondered. *I guess it doesn't matter.*

The ship unexpectedly lurched, and Viv's stomach clenched. Sitting back down at the table, she reached for the last cookie. *I need to keep a little bit of food coming at regular intervals,* she concluded. *That's the best way to avoid feeling queasy.*

If she were at home, she wouldn't allow herself the privilege of cookies with her afternoon tea. But now that she had her stomach to settle, she had the perfect excuse.

The tip of her tongue tingled with sweetness. *I think I'll take a short snooze before dinner.*

An hour later Viv awoke from a nap. It was seven o'clock. Her stomach growled. *I'm always hungry on this cruise,* she realized. *Instead of eating I'll call Rex.* She wanted to hear his voice. *Maybe I'll catch him before he has to get dressed for his show tonight.*

When the phone refused to ring, Viv frowned. *Did he turn it off? I bet he's found other friends in his new location.* Though he'd seemed eager at the gym, maybe he'd finally realized they couldn't be seen together and given up trying.

Or maybe someone belonged to those panties, and they weren't left behind after all...

Viv felt her disappointment keenly. This cruise was not going as planned. No matter how many spa treatments or cookies, she couldn't deny her true feelings about the circumstances.

I'm alone and a bit out of sorts. I'd better make the best of this before I get really angry and take it out on Rex.

Viv reached for her journal and began jotting a few notes. This time she wasn't keeping track of the other passengers on her phone. This time she wrote what she felt. Writing helped to clarify her feelings, especially when she'd pushed them aside for too long.

Finished with her journaling, she felt better. For a moment she thought about the bare feet she'd spotted on the person next door. *Being left by myself must have made me unnecessarily nosy*, she told herself. The residue of embarrassment still lingered making her feel uncomfortable.

She tried to call Rex one more time, with the same result. Then she texted, but it wouldn't send. *Maybe another trip to the IT desk*, she thought. *Ugh. I don't want to wait in line.*

Time to get dressed, she concluded. Black slacks slipped on easily. The loose-fitting blouse with the gold accents fell gracefully to her waist. The gold sandals made her outfit look intentional. *With my hair up, I'll blend with the other women of a certain age.*

She stood in the corridor, feeling self-conscious anyway. Eating alone didn't bother her at home. But on a cruise it felt very different. Pulling her shoulders back, she made her way to the elevator lobby.

The door slid open, revealing several other people dressed for dinner. Viv stepped inside. "Room for one more?" she said lightly, turning to face the closing door.

15

REX REDONDO

Rex leaned back in bed, his arms behind his head. *At least the mattress is comfortable,* he thought. *But I still have a headache.* He rubbed his temple where it hurt the most. Then he remembered. Digging into his pocket to pull out the panties, he quickly shoved them into his nightstand.

Reaching for his phone, he sat up with a start. *It's nearly five o'clock and I'm not dressed. Why hasn't Viv sent any intel?*

He scrolled on his phone, noting her last text. *Alcott, huh? Like the* Little Women *author.* Another sharp stab of pain in his temple made him blink. *I don't have time to worry about my aches and pains. Without more from Viv, I need to prep for my show.*

Standing by the closet, he reached for his tuxedo, considering his options. He couldn't remember ever being this flummoxed over information before a performance. At the casino he had any number of avenues he could explore. Of course his usual way—information from Sutton—was immensely helpful. But then he had those images that spun behind his eyes. They gave his act an unexpected flair. Activating his intuition, making him seem psychic.

But neither of those were available right now. Rex had to admit he felt a bit ashamed. Vulnerability had always made him wince, especially in himself.

On top of that, he hadn't realized until now how he'd come to rely on the information provided by the internet. *What did mentalists do in the old days when there was no texting or instant feedback?* he wondered.

Rex adjusted his bow tie. Standing in front of the mirror, he confirmed that he looked the part. *At least I have that going for me. Maybe I'll have to improvise.* He reached for his phone, noting there was no message from Viv. *I wonder why she stopped texting...*

Closing his stateroom door, he slipped the Do Not Disturb sign over the handle. As he approached the staff dining room, he could hear the familiar din of voices. Staffers, talking animatedly over plates of food, were dressed in their evening uniforms.

Standing in front of the seafood buffet, Rex pointed to the grilled salmon. "I'll take that," he told the server. She looked familiar. Her tag read *Cricket Hicks* and she was very thin. Too thin in his opinion. *She's in dire need of a sandwich.* Then he corrected his attitude. *Stop body-shaming. What would Viv say?*

"This piece?" Cricket asked him with a smile.

Rex nodded. "That's the one." He watched her slide the perfectly grilled piece of salmon onto a plate. It dawned on him where'd he'd seen her before.

"Weren't you in my room a day ago? You're my room steward, right?"

"You did." She gave him a friendly nod. "I do whatever needs doing. Lots of us are like that. The captain, for instance? He'll clear a table if he's in the upstairs dining room. No problem for him. It's kind of company policy."

"I'd like to talk with you when you have time," Rex said.

Cricket's eyes grew wide. "Your room needs an extra service?" Her voice dropped to a low register, sounding sultry.

Rex realized his mistake. But before he could correct her impression, he stopped himself. *Maybe she wants to get cozy. An on-board fling. Flattering of course, but not for me. But I want to know why she still comes into my room when I put the Do Not Disturb out. And maybe she could explain about the silk panties.*

Rex felt uncharacteristically self-conscious, leading Cricket on. He turned his head, glancing around behind his back to see if anyone was listening. "I'll be done at midnight. Why don't we meet in the staff bar. I'll buy you a drink."

Cricket smirked. "That's an offer I can't refuse."

Rex slid his tray on the counter toward the array of salads, choosing the first one he saw. Then he made his way to an empty seat in the dining room. After arranging the napkin on his lap, he poked at his salmon, moving bits and pieces around his plate with his fork. After the first bite, he made a face. It left an odd taste in his mouth. He tried squishing more lemon over the pink meat, but even that didn't help.

Maybe something sweet will settle my stomach. He left the plate to check out the dessert buffet and watched as the server slid pieces of chocolate cake with thick chocolate icing onto plates. His stomach turned over, changing his mind about dessert.

"May I offer you cake?" he asked politely.

"Actually, I need a piece of that waxed paper." He pointed to the box next to the server's hand.

"That's weird. Why do you want that?" The server shot him a quizzical look.

"I want to wrap my salmon up and take it back to my room," Rex explained.

The server shrugged. "Sure, man. Whatever." He handed Rex several pieces. "Be careful where you put that fish. They don't like food left in the rooms. Attracts all kinds of bugs."

"I'll be sure to remember that." Rex took the sheets of waxed paper and walked back to his table. Once seated, he used his fork to lift a piece of the fish onto the paper. He folded the edges securely before slipping the packet into a pocket of his tux pants. *That should do the trick.*

"Ladies and gentleman, Rex Redondo!" the announcer's voice blared over the loudspeaker. The sheer intensity made Rex's ears ring.

He walked on the stage to mild applause. Turning to face the audience, he glanced to the back row, where he hoped to catch sight of Viv. The spotlight glared, making it impossible to see beyond the first few rows.

His head began to spin, and he blinked to focus. Then he swallowed, pushing back a feeling of foreboding. *Focus, Rex,* he told himself sternly.

You'll have to make due with Viv's last texts. Something about Pearl Harbor...

16

REX REDONDO

After the show Rex stared at himself in the dressing room mirror. *Not my best performance*, he lamented.

He reached for the box of tissues. Unscrewing the container of cold cream, he dipped his fingers inside, then smeared the cream liberally over his face. He used the tissue to remove his stage makeup.

If it hadn't been for that dog... He'd spotted the eager mutt in the audience right away. Rex knew he could get a good ten minutes working with someone's beloved pet. He'd done that at the casino and many other venues over the years.

It surprised him that dogs were allowed on the cruise ship. He used his own curiosity to fuel the first salvo of the night. "There's someone in the audience who pees outdoors." The crowd predictably laughed as a woman with a French bulldog stood up. "That's my Alfred." She held up the dog for everyone to see.

Rex spent longer than usual interviewing the woman and Alfred on stage. "So he goes on the promenade deck?" Rex quirked his right eyebrow.

"They have this special place for dogs," the woman explained.

He posed an interested expression, grateful for her eagerness to talk about her pet. The crowd helped a lot, laughing right along.

As the audience laughter dimmed, Rex reached to pat the dog's head. He let Alfred smell his fingers. The dog struggled to get out of his owner's grasp, while Rex pretended to look shocked.

A loud whine and a lunge made the audience laugh harder. Struggling against the owner's bosom, Alfred let out a series of yips. No matter how hard she tried to hug him closer, Alfred wasn't going to be subdued. Finally she loosened her grasp and he twisted in her arms, lifting his front paws to scratch at her chest.

"Looks like Alfred is tired of the spotlight," Rex commented. He waited for the audience to stop laughing before adding, "I bet he could use a treat." Rex reached into his pants pocket, bringing out the packet of salmon. He held it closer, and Alfred went wild, breaking into a series of heartfelt barks.

Scratching vigorously at his owner, he finally got loose, jumping down to the stage floor. He looked up at Rex, pawing at his shin.

"Salmon." Rex bent down to give Alfred a sniff. He unwrapped the packet.

"I didn't know he ate seafood," his owner said.

"Well that's the thing. He hasn't mentioned it before. You see, Alfred spoke to me." Rex handed Alfred a bite, which was quickly lapped up. "Alfred wanted me to tell you that he's tired of kibble and beef."

Rex kept talking. "Alfred's been quite patient. You may not know that he's been longing for a change in diet for the past two days. Once he smelled the salmon, he just had to give it a try."

As if on cue, Alfred lunged at Rex's hand. He swallowed the rest of the salmon in one gulp. The audience cheered and clapped.

The owner lifted her dog with both hands, hugging him to her chest. She made her way back to her seat as people applauded.

This gave Rex a chance to glance at his wristwatch. *Only twenty-seven minutes to go.*

Instead of launching into his next bit, he stood in the middle of the stage and closed his eyes. The audience grew very quiet, anticipating his next reading.

There were times like this that Rex longed for another prop. Some mentalists used them. Like crystal balls, for example. They called it scrying. Using the shimmering reflections cast by the crystal due to the spotlights, mentalists would activate a trance, and then, with a shift of voice, access people who had already transitioned.

Though it had never been part of his act, Rex believed a skilled mentalist could make scrying work. He took another quick glance at his wristwatch. *Gosh I wish I had that crystal ball now.*

For the first time in his career, Rex was frightened. *What if I'm done? I've got nothing and I'm in a jam. This looks so unprofessional.*

His finger inched up to his temple. The throb had turned to a dull ache. As he rubbed vigorously right as a new idea popped into his head. *I could do that*, he thought. *I've never resorted to anything remotely like that before. But desperate times require...* He couldn't remember the rest of the quote. But he did have a plan for sure.

He opened his eyes and told the truth.

"I've got to say, ladies and gentlemen, I'm in a pickle. It seems I've got nothing for you this evening except this terrible headache." His fingers massaged his temple. "I've never been in this situation before." He looked toward the first row of faces. Some held skepticism.

As Rex scanned each face, his eyes stopped on one. It was Sandi, holding the box of ashes in her lap. She looked hopeful. He'd never been in this position before, willing to use the same person from the audience two nights in a row. But now he felt desperate, so he took the plunge.

"I think this woman knows what I'm feeling." He pointed to Sandi. "She's trying to make another connection with her father who recently passed over." He held his finger to his temple again, but this time his voice shifted into a lower register, a strong singsong cadence. "Speak to Sandi. She needs you."

Sandi, highly suggestible as he suspected, spoke in a bell-like voice. "Why won't you talk to me, Daddy?"

Rex spoke to her directly. "Why don't you come up here and we'll see if we can get in touch with him, find out why." The audience noted their approval with polite clapping.

As Sandi came forward, he glanced at his watch again. *Only a few more minutes. I think I can wing it from here. I've done so many cold readings, I know what she wants to hear. That Daddy doesn't hold any grudges, that he misses her more than he can say. Who in the world doesn't want to hear that universal truth?*

17

VIVIENNE ROSE

That evening Viv thought she'd get an after-dinner cup of tea at the Crow's Nest Beverage Bar. During the day, the view of the ocean drew people away from the fray of sitting poolside to sit and sip their hot beverages. After the last show, people also gathered in the evening to view the dark expanse of sea.

A female member of staff held a ceramic mug under a dispenser, her back to Viv. The woman turned. "May I help you?"

"We meet again," Viv replied in a friendly voice.

"What can I get you?" Tonya asked.

"Lavender tea, no sugar," Viv responded.

As Tonya reached for a fresh mug, Viv wondered about how many hours the staff worked before they got a break. *Hopefully they have an airtight contract and a union.* Her doula agency made her sensitive to such matters since doulas worked long hours.

Tonya put a napkin under the mug and placed it in front of Viv on the counter. "Anything else? A cookie maybe?"

"Oh no. I had dessert in the dining room. Thank you so much."

Viv took a sip and continued to make conversation. "You must be exhausted, working all these hours. Didn't I see you earlier this morning?"

Tonya looked away and then back at her. "You're right. I'm beat. I got a break in the middle of the day, but this shift is the hardest. My feet hurt." She offered a half-hearted smile.

"Not that it's any of my business," Viv said, sipping her tea again casually. "But if you want to put your feet up, is there a break room for employees?" Aware that she might sound too inquisitive, Viv smiled again, trying to make it seem like she was only interested in Tonya's well-being.

"Below on deck three. The fore side is for exclusive passenger berths. Celebrities and people who basically go from cruise to cruise live there. The middle is for staff. We have a little community. Lots of partying too. At least we did until..."

When Tonya's voice trailed off, Viv's skin prickled. *She's hiding something. And she nearly let it slip.*

"I used to have a small group of good friends," Viv said quietly. "We had each other's back for a long time. Until just this past year when..." She let her voice drop in the same way, deliberately using her own experience to commiserate with Tonya.

Tonya looked over Viv's head. "I'm not supposed to tell passengers my sob story," she explained. "But you seem really nice. And it's late. Want a refill?" She pointed to Viv's empty mug.

"One more and then I'll head back to my stateroom." Viv slid the mug closer.

After Tonya poured the hot water, she offered a fresh

tea bag. Leaning her arms on the counter she asked, "You cruising alone?"

"All by myself." Viv dunked her tea bag, biting her bottom lip at the sympathetic tone of Tonya's voice. *It's as if being alone is a bad thing. I thought women were more independent nowadays.*

"I like it that way," Viv added. "It's fun to wander by myself and be treated so well. I think I'll book another cruise before we disembark."

"You get a discount if you do it now," Tonya explained. "Someone from staff will come talk to you, if you like. I can tell them to give you a good deal."

Viv took her time before answering. "Sure, go ahead and refer me. I can always use a discount. Speaking of your quarters, does everyone sleep on deck three, including the performers?" *Is that where Rex has been staying?* She cleared her throat and added, "If you don't mind me asking."

Viv knew she'd put Tonya in a bit of a quandary. She assumed her interest in booking another cruise might make her more eager to share information.

"Like I said, we're not allowed to get too friendly with passengers." Tonya's eyes took a furtive look around the room. "It could be a problem for me. Some travelers get too close and try to fraternize. Not that you're one of them." She eyed Viv with an intense stare. "I don't want to be fired." She pulled away from the bar, turning her back, stepping toward the sink.

Realizing she'd gone too far, Viv took a sip of tea. *How am I going to recover this to get the information I want?*

"Oh, I'm not a fraternizing type," she said firmly to Tonya's back. "I didn't mean to give that impression. I'm just a curious woman who has a lot of free time to think about things."

Tonya turned back around and took Viv's empty cup. "I didn't mean to imply you'd be that kind of woman." She hesitated, inhaling deeply. "You can't imagine what I see on board. Older men and women using their money and passenger status to get their needs met. It happens all the time."

"I'm not rich," Viv said immediately. "In fact, I'm out of work at the present."

"What do you do?" Tonya looked curious.

Viv hesitated. *Do I make something up or tell the truth?*

"I run a doula agency, or at least I used to. I had some employee challenges this past year, which makes it difficult," she explained.

"I've never had children," Tonya said. "That must be rewarding work."

And then to her surprise, Tonya's eyes teared up.

18

VIVIENNE ROSE

Viv patted Tonya's hand, offering her a clean napkin from the bar stack to dab her tears.

"I lost somebody close to me recently. We had plans, you know, to start a family." Tonya turned to blow her nose.

Tossing the napkin away, she rushed to help another customer who had just approached the counter.

Viv felt bad for making her cry. But she knew she'd gotten past Tonya's reserve, which was her goal.

While Tonya helped another customer, Viv stepped aside and pulled out her cell phone. She remembered journaling and then trying to call Rex the day before. When the call failed she'd tried to text him, which turned out to be undeliverable. It only took one tap now for her to realize that the text still hung in limbo.

I really do need to check on this as soon as possible.

She turned off her phone. Then she turned it back on. *I don't have any connection at all*, she concluded.

"Excuse me," she called to Tonya. "I do have a question. It's about the ship's Wi-Fi." When Tonya turned, her face looked more composed. She came closer.

Viv continued to explain. "I think I've been disconnected somehow."

"We're in international waters. But the ship has its own Wi-Fi. You can go to the IT desk tomorrow morning. They'll help you right away."

"Are they open at— What time is it? Ten o'clock in the evening?"

"You can try. But they do close fairly early. Not like Crow's Nest. Plus it's time for the evening entertainment. That mentalist." She turned to the next customer, ending the conversation.

Viv slid from the stool at the coffee bar. She made her way to the elevator, frustrated. Waiting for the door to open, she really wanted to complain. And then she stopped. *Wasn't I just worrying about the staff hours and overworking? And now I'm the same person who wants service this very minute, no matter how late it is. Honestly, Viv.*

Watching Rex from the back of the theater, Viv knew something was wrong. *Probably because I couldn't send him enough info for the act,* she concluded. The longer she watched, the more nervous she became.

He's not himself. I know he has material he can use if he's in a pinch, but even that's falling a bit flat. The "pees outdoors" remark was beneath Rex's usual banter.

Once he invited Sandi to the stage, she felt a bit better.

Clutching Daddy in her arms, Sandi seemed genuinely upset.

"Why won't he talk to me?" she cried.

Leaning forward to hear every word, Viv watched as Rex smoothly comforted the young woman, talking in a low voice.

His tone assured her that he'd taken charge, giving her a minute to check the bars on her phone. *Still no Wi-Fi. If I don't get this fixed, Rex will be stranded for the two remaining shows while we're at sea.*

After Sandi spoke to Daddy again, she was safely escorted back to her seat. The audience applauded as Rex took his customary bows. Lights were brought up over the audience. Viv made her way to the exit. She was one of the first to walk toward the bank of elevators. Instead of heading to her stateroom, she decided to give it one more try.

Minutes later Viv stood in front of the IT desk. When no one appeared from the back room, her mind raced. *I bet someone's behind the wall, looking at me through a camera. There's one plainly visible in the corner.*

She'd read stories about secret surveillance in hotel rooms. *If Rex were with me, we'd check our rooms. He'd know right away if there was any silly business going on.*

Since meeting Rex, she'd found herself returning to some of her old habits. Expecting him to help her out. And to keep her company too. *I'm getting needy again,* she scolded herself. *I can check my own room when I get back.*

At that moment, standing alone at the IT desk late at night all by herself, she was aware of something more complex. An emotion she'd not felt for many years.

I miss him, she realized. *His smile and his laughter. The way he looks at me as if I were the most important person in his world. His arms around me when we embrace.*

Viv lifted her hand and waved at the camera. She turned and walked to the elevator, and the door slid open, revealing two staff employees.

The man's face dropped. "Excuse us, miss," he said. "We'll step off so that you can get on." He nudged the woman who stood next to him. They quickly exited the elevator.

She watched the doors slide closed as they disappeared around a corner. She glanced at the button panel reminded of as earlier conversation.

What was it Tonya said about staff quarters? All on level three. Okay, then. I'll head there tomorrow to find Rex.

19

REX REDONDO

Fortunately he didn't need to come up with any other readings before time ran out and his show was done. Rex rinsed the cold cream from his face with tepid water. As he patted his skin dry, a knock came at the door. His heart raced. *Maybe it's Viv.*

The door opened, revealing Cricket Hicks. Rex's heart dropped. *I forgot about that drink I promised her.*

Cricket wore a very short red sheath. The neckline plunged over her small breasts. The clinginess of the fabric made him avert his eyes. *A woman dressed like that thinks she's on a date. Or maybe not.* He realized he'd made an assumption that wouldn't pass the muster of #metoo.

Rex made room for Cricket to step inside. She passed close by, brushing lightly against his jacket. He left the door open.

"I brought you something." She held up a bottle of champagne. "The house's best." After setting it on his dressing table, she didn't wait for him to make the first move. Standing in front of him an inch away, she patted her hands up his white shirt. She kissed him full on the lips, her tongue lingering before she stopped.

He placed his hands on her waist to gently move her away. Instead of being rebuffed, she took his resistance as a game. Leaning in, she wrapped her arms around his middle. "This is what you wanted, right?" Her lips came toward his again.

Rex was not unfamiliar with attention from the female sex. He'd earned the nickname "silver fox" among many women for good reason. It wouldn't be that big of a deal to have a quick fling with this obviously besotted woman.

But what if Viv found out? he reasoned. No explanation would convince her that it didn't matter to him and that she was who he wanted to be with. Especially with their disconnect on the cruise. Plus he felt nothing for Cricket Hicks at this moment. In fact quite the opposite of attraction was what he felt. The idea of another kiss made him slightly queasy.

Rex pushed her back again, and this time he spoke with authority. "Actually, I am very tired. Even the idea of a drink isn't in the cards tonight. I want to go to bed. Alone." Before she could speak, he continued, "What I wanted to talk to you about is why you keep coming into my room, even though I left the Do Not Disturb on the handle."

Her lips tightened. She pounded his chest with one fist. "You're such a tease. I thought you wanted to have a good time."

He braced himself for a slap on the face. When it didn't come, he took another step backward.

She beat him to the door and huffed as she left his room.

Rex looked up and down the hall to make sure she'd really gone. He ran his hand through his hair with relief.

Not one part of him regretted his behavior, and that was at least a small victory.

He just hoped that no one saw her come and go. If word got back to Viv...well, she'd hardly forgive him, now would she. Viv being who she was: straightlaced and a woman known to speak the truth—nothing but the truth.

20

REX REDONDO

On the third morning of being at sea, Rex stumbled his way to the staff dining room. *If I didn't know better, I'd think I had a hangover. This headache is becoming a regular nuisance.*

The first person he saw was Cricket. She patted the seat next to her with a provocative smile of invitation. He felt slightly surprised but then decided, *I guess she's not holding a grudge.*

He returned her smile and pointed to the buffet table. "Save me a seat. Be right back." He spoke loudly enough to be heard over the hubbub of other voices.

Once seated, he spread his napkin on his lap, aware that he wasn't that hungry. The pause also gave him a moment to think about what he'd say to Cricket since their last encounter.

Rex took a bite of his scrambled egg. "Good to see you. I'm glad there are no hard feelings after the other night. I haven't been feeling well." He offered that as an explanation for his behavior and to give her an excuse for rebuffing her advances.

"I was wondering if it's possible to contact you on the employee portal." He tried not to sound too enthusiastic. The purpose of his question was to find out how employees communicated. He knew there must be a way besides whispering and sliding notes under doors.

"Give me your code and I'll unlock your phone," Cricket said lightly.

Rex felt a stab of guilt. He could tell by the tone of her voice that she might have misconstrued his intentions yet again. *I'm too tired to think like a lady*, he told himself, stabbing another bite of egg.

"I'll put it in myself," he told her firmly.

After he'd typed her number into his contacts, she said, "I can send you photos if you want. Of me. It might make your day go faster, at least until later when we can be together."

His stomach turned over. More from the food. But thinking about a naked Cricket hadn't helped. He also knew if he didn't shut this down quickly, he'd be expected to return the favor with photos of himself. He gulped. A long sip of water gave him a moment to think how to proceed.

Rex ignored her and started back in on his own goal. "Actually, what I'm really curious about is the Wi-Fi. Can staff text passengers, for example?"

"Oh no. Fraternization is against the rules," Cricket stated flatly. "We sign a legal statement as part of the hiring. And we have to take classes before our first assignment. And again every year," she insisted, "because we're not supposed to send any texts or email to cruise customers. Some of the higher-ups can access both portals, but not us."

Putting his coffee cup down, he knew he needed to cut to the chase. "So you're my room steward, right?"

"That's right. I come with benefits," Cricket teased.

"And you saw the Do Not Disturb on my door, right?"

Her eyes widened. "Oh, sweetie. I never pay attention to those signs. I knew you'd appreciate me once you got to know me. So I just walked in and made the bed."

Pure confidence, Rex concluded. *And maybe habit. Just barging into another employee's room may have gotten her perks in the past. No wonder the cruise line has such strict regulations with regard to passengers.* He pushed his chair back and stood. "I have some things to do," he told Cricket.

Her lips turned down in an exaggerated pout. "Like I said, I'm available later." She lifted her phone. "In just a second I'll be sending my first photo."

Rex felt his cell vibrate in his pocket. "Sure," he said dryly. "I'll check it out. Not here though. Too public." He wasted no time moving away from the table.

Back in his room he had to admit that Cricket was turning out to be a problem. And she had access to his luggage and belongings, which made it even more difficult. It didn't help that Sutton was slightly paranoid; over the years he'd learned to fiercely protect his privacy. She'd taught him that early on.

With his stateroom door securely locked, he sat on the edge of his bed. Feeling nauseous with the headache, he dreaded planning another show.

I'm having a lot of trouble concentrating.

Inhaling deeply, his throat caught and he coughed. *My symptoms are worse when I'm in my room.* A litany of "poor Rex" words ran through his head. *Poor old Rex. Your cruise tanked and your show is awful and you have no one you want to be with. No one to hand you tissues or pat your head. No one to pull the covers up around your shoulders at night. No one.*

Easing into self-pity wasn't that unfamiliar. He occasionally dipped a toe in that particular cesspool, and now he felt he deserved a brief swim after all he'd suffered.

Flopping back on the bed, Rex closed his eyes. Then he forced them open.

Come on, old boy. He began his self-talk again. *You're not dying. You've probably got one of those viruses people spread on cruises.* He rolled his head to the side to cough. *Now it's settling into my lungs.*

Rex held his hand on his brow to check for a temperature. Then he reached into his nightstand for over-the-counter pain relievers. An unopened water bottle had been left on his bedside table. He unscrewed the top and took a long drink, tossing back two pills.

That should do it, he thought. When he didn't feel immediately better, he grew impatient. *Maybe the ship's doctor has an antiviral medication. Maybe I can check into that.*

Unsteady on his feet, he groaned. *Come on, Rex ol' boy. Off to sick bay. The doc will give you some meds.* He made an effort to walk slowly toward the door without stumbling. Then he glanced over to where his planner lay open to his performing notes.

I'd better put that in the safe, he concluded.

Closing the door behind him, Rex made his way toward the lobby. Unlike the passenger elevators, the staff ones did not have a glass side nor an ocean view. As the elevator began to move he felt his stomach lurch.

It occurred to him that he had a chance to stop by Viv's stateroom on his way back from medical. *No one's stopping me from knocking on Viv's door. Once I have an antiviral, I'll be on the mend. I don't need to get too close to her. I just want to see her face.* He hit his palm against his head to unplug his left ear.

The smell of disinfectant met his nose as he entered the lido deck. Steam rising from the spa and the crowd of people around the pool area made the room feel uncomfortably warm. Rex wiped the back of his hand over his forehead.

He made his way toward the opposite side, passing people seated around the tables who still lingered from breakfast. A hacking cough brought him up short. *It hurts to breathe.*

He noted two people doing laps in the pool. The navy blue of cruise ship towels thrown over chaises caught his eye. A quick scan did not reveal Viv. The doors to the gym slid open. Once inside, he leaned his back against a wall to take a few shallow breaths. One glance revealed that the entire wall of ellipticals was occupied.

With his previous knowledge of ships, he knew he had a good chance of finding sick bay on the other side of the gym. But the way he was feeling, he needed to sit down to catch his breath before wandering around in his search and drawing any more attention to himself.

So he walked slowly toward the coffee bar. Three people sat at the counter. He took the only available stool. The server came right over. "You're that mentalist, right?"

"I am," he said pleasantly.

She looked him up and down, a slight smile at the corner of her mouth. "Don't you belong on the staff level?"

"I'm not exactly staff. I'm an entertainer," he explained. He knew better than to give her the entire sad story about being spotted on the passenger list. How they'd plucked him out of line and hired him on the spot.

"Why don't you get me a coffee and let me worry about

getting in trouble. I won't mention your name." He looked at her badge. "Tonya. That's right. I won't tell anyone, Tonya. I'll take the morning blend."

"I warned you," she taunted him, a flirtatious lilt to her voice.

Rex swiveled his stool around to observe the people in the room. He swiveled back right as Tonya placed a mug in front of him. "Since you don't have a tab, I have no way of billing for this." She lifted the mug and put a napkin underneath.

"How about we keep my coffee drinking to ourselves," he suggested, using his most conspiratorial voice. "You know you do this for other employees."

"I do not," she said hastily.

Rex raised his brows in disbelief.

Tired of verbally sparring with the barista, Rex pulled out his cell. He watched Tonya serve other passengers. The flirtatious guy on the end at the counter asked her for her number, but she wasn't interested. Just took his mug away with a pleasant nod.

He glanced up at the shelves above the coffee machines. Mugs with the ship's logo had been lined up. Some were for sale. The next shelf underneath held various containers filled with a variety of loose-leaf tea, all carefully labeled.

And on the lowest shelf, there were more mugs. Rex's eyes methodically moved from one to the next until a glint made him stop. He saw a glass orb, fitting atop a wood base. *That's not a mug.* He blinked. Not because he thought he was seeing things but because what he saw didn't belong with the others. *Maybe it's one of those tourist things that people buy. Shouldn't there be a hula girl at the center wearing a bikini and a lei?*

When the barista drew near, he asked, "Excuse me. Could you come over here for a minute?"

"You don't belong here," she mumbled. "I have real customers."

"I'll step behind the counter and wash my mug if that would help," he sarcastically responded. "And by the way, what's that doing there on your shelf? If I didn't know any better, I'd say that's either a tourist snow globe or a crystal ball."

Tonya turned slowly to look where he pointed. "It is a crystal ball," she said quietly. "A friend left it here with me for safe keeping."

"I think I know who that friend might have been," he said calmly. "Part of the trade, to have a crystal ball. I don't use one of course, but other mentalists do."

Tonya nodded. "Jon Jon Mulroy. He used it in his act."

"The guy I replaced?" Rex said.

"The one and only. I knew him pretty well." Her rueful smile made him suspect that she knew him quite well. *Quite well indeed.*

"Can I have a closer look? Professional interest." He opened his hand, letting it rest on the counter.

To his surprise she turned right around and lifted the ball off the shelf. Once he held the ball in his hand, he looked at it closely. It felt cool. The first sign that it was most likely not a tourist globe but the real deal. "Why do you have this exactly?"

"I kept it for sentimental reasons," she replied, although her answer didn't make sense to Rex. *Doesn't he need this for his act? Maybe he gave up that bit of his routine.* "But now I don't need it. I'm over him. Easy come, easy go." Her smiled didn't convince him any more than her words. "Why don't you keep it. Since you're the mentalist and all." She closed his fingers around the globe in an intimate gesture.

Confusion left him torn; he wasn't sure if Tonya was interested in him personally, or if she might be grieving an old flame.

Holding onto the globe, he said, "Thanks for this. See you later."

I better get out of here before another woman starts asking for my contacts and sending me dirty photos.

On the other side of the gym, he stopped to catch his breath, his fingers clutching the crystal ball. *I've stumbled onto a partial solution for my next show. I've never used this kind of prop but I've seen other guys work the territory. The ball may get me out of this slump. At least until the images come back and I'm feeling better.*

He slipped the ball into his pocket, covering his mouth with his other hand to cough. *I'll go to medical later. I need to get back to my stateroom and take some performance notes.*

21

REX REDONDO

Back in his stateroom, Rex removed the crystal ball from his pocket for closer inspection. He turned it in his hand, gazing into the spherical shape. He noted the wooden base.

I could drop this and it wouldn't shatter easily. It's not one of those expensive fragile kinds but authentic. Maybe I can conjure up the previous owner. What was his name? Jon Jon...something or other...

Rex lifted the ball toward the light right as the throb in his head turned into a bolt of pain. He focused on the sunlight beaming through the clear liquid, instead of how terrible he felt.

Once he set the ball down on the counter, he felt better. *Maybe not my thing. But it will work in a pinch.* He paused to stare at the ball again. *I need a name for that thing. Mentalists rarely call them crystal balls. I'm not a carnival sorceress gazing into her orb of light.*

He searched for words. Usually his mind felt over-crowded, what with both thoughts and images. Not now. Then he remembered a guy in Texas who had a special name for his globe. He called it a fortune globe! *That's it. I can weave a few stories around what I see in the liquid. And then I'll have a good prop to make predictions. The audience will love it.*

Since he didn't want Cricket to find the globe on one of her unwanted explorations of his room, he knew he had to put it in safe keeping. He made his way to the closet. Spinning the dial, he opened the door of the safe and put the fortune globe inside.

With that out of the way, he realized he no longer had the energy to find medical by himself. *I'm going to ask for help. Maybe someone will come along with me.*

On the way toward the dining room, he turned the corner, nearly stumbling into Robert Redford. "Oh, sorry," Rex said. "You're just the guy I wanted to see."

"What can I do for you?" Redford rubbed his arm, looking distractedly over Rex's head.

"It won't take a minute," Rex said. "I need to find the ship's doctor. Got something in my throat." Rex coughed with his hand in front of his mouth. "And a headache." He touched his temple. "And my stomach." He patted the front of his trim waist.

"That's not good." Redford took a step backward. "Let me take you right to sick bay. They can give you an antiviral. I haven't heard of any other cases on board. But we have to take every precaution. Or you'll be quarantined."

The last thing Rex wanted was to be shut up in his room. A target for Cricket Hicks being one good reason. Plus now he was eager to work with the fortune globe. It had been years since he'd tried a new trick.

Taking him by the elbow, Redford moved Rex along the corridor. "You can well imagine we keep a close eye on any possible virus going around. That's why we have all those hand-washing stations. You do that, right? Wash your hands a lot?"

Feeling more like a child being scolded than a grown man, Rex nodded. "Don't worry. I keep it clean," he mumbled.

Once they made it through the gym, Rex realized there were no passengers walking up and down the corridors. Everything seemed very quiet. He knew that the cruise line wanted to keep people's minds off of illness and that the placement of the sick bay was meant to be hidden from plain sight. But this felt like he was walking to nowhere, and it made him uneasy.

"Here we are." Redford turned the handle on a door marked Infirmary. "Give me a minute to check with the doc. He may be busy."

Rex shrugged. *He said the doc may be busy instead of with a patient. Since when is a doctor too busy to see a sick person on a cruise ship? Or an employee, for that matter. I wonder what he does all day...*

Minutes passed while Rex scrolled on his phone. *Still nothing from Viv.* He tapped the screen and held his phone to his ear.

"Sutton Drew," came his assistant's voice.

"I think we're several hours ahead," he muttered, "though in the middle of the Pacific, I'm not entirely certain. My phone's been acting up."

"So you called to interrupt me with tech issues? Isn't there someone on board who can help you with that?" Her voice didn't sound as harsh as her words implied.

"God I miss you," he moaned. "And I feel terrible. Must have picked up a virus. I'm standing in the corridor outside sick bay, waiting for the doc."

"Like the good ol' days," Sutton reminisced. "You and

me on board a Navy ship, heading to Southeast Asia without a care in the world."

"Except for that tiny thing called combat," Rex muttered.

"There was that," Sutton said. "But when I look back, all I try to remember are the fun and games."

"You don't mean that," he objected.

"I kind of do. I've put the bad memories behind me," she said. "We haven't talked about this in a long time."

He knew she referred to their military service together in Afghanistan. But he didn't want to think about that now. Or ever, if he were truthful. "You're taking care of the pets, I hope."

"I'm doing that and feeling quite useless, if you must know. Without you I have so little to do. No one to push around. Very dull."

"Aren't you dating anyone?" Rex knew his assistant had no trouble finding men.

"A couple of guys. One I really like. The brother of Viv's bodyguard, as it happens. How's Viv?"

"I haven't heard from her," he confessed. "There's some glitch with the phone."

Sutton explained, "The Wi-Fi on ships in the middle of the sea isn't that reliable. Plus phone companies charge extra for cell service on cruises. I got you that plan, if you remember. Before you left."

"I told that to Viv," Rex muttered.

"And?"

"I don't think she wanted to pay extra. It was such a rush at the last minute, she may have decided to leave it. Like I said, I can't talk to her now."

"Because she's hanging out with the paying customers," Sutton said. "I haven't heard from her either. No big deal."

"Damn right it's a big deal. This means she can't give me any intel for my show," Rex complained. "Both women in my life have abandoned me and now I'm sick." He coughed into the phone just to make sure she realized the dire circumstance he'd found himself.

"Stop sniveling!" Sutton commanded. "Nobody likes a wuss. Get your meds. Take a nap. And don't forget the clean socks."

Rex chuckled. The socks were a joke between them because they'd met in the Marines, and the docs there, no matter how sick you were, always recommended clean socks. Before he could continue his lament, the door to the sick bay opened. Redford stuck his head outside. "Just a few more minutes. He has a patient and then you'll be next."

"Gotta go," he told Sutton. Sliding his phone back in his pocket, he leaned his back against the wall. For a moment he felt a bit better. Maybe he wasn't really sick, just a bit lonely.

He inhaled, taking in the recycled air that didn't smell bad but didn't smell good either.

Not like home. The Mojave Desert, the early walks. He missed his morning chats with Viv as they walked Kevin in the neighborhood. And he also missed the sunshine. *I haven't been out of doors for two days*, he realized.

He closed his eyes, willing the images to return. *Nothin'. Like a blank in there. I hate being ordinary.*

The infirmary door opened again, revealing a smiling Redford. "He's ready for you now."

Once inside, Rex looked around. His eyes stopped at another door. *Okay, that explains it. I know my eyes were closed, but I would have heard the other patient leave. So there must be an exit out door number two.*

Rex took careful note of the wall on the left, lined with

charts. One laid out instructions with photos about hand-washing, another recommended ways to avoid coughing in people's faces.

Rex had never seen a "see something, say something" poster that was used as a medical warning. He felt a bit overwhelmed, as he often did when faced with a lot of rules and regulations. *Reminds me of the Marines*, he thought.

"I'll check in on you later." Redford made his way to leave.

"No worries. It's probably just the sniffles," Rex assured him. He wasn't convinced himself, but he didn't want Redford's excessive attention either. Now if it were Viv, that would be entirely different. He always welcomed her.

Thoughts of Viv fussing over him, bringing soup, ladling it into his mouth, wiping the dribbles off his chin, made him smile. He was pretty sure she'd never do that, ladle soup into his mouth, but he liked to imagine how that kind of care might feel.

She wore a nurse's outfit in his imagination. She'd put down the spoon and lean over to kiss his forehead using her soft lips to test his temperature. *Ahh, Viv. Where are you, love of my life?*

The doctor arrived through the other door. "Come on through," he said curtly. Once inside, he gestured for Rex to sit in a chair. He took out his stethoscope and listened to his chest. Then he touched his fingers to his wrist. Next came the blood pressure cuff.

None of this lived up to Rex's fantasies about Viv, so he tuned out.

When the doc stepped back to make notes, Rex asked, "What do you think? Am I the victim of norovirus?"

The doc looked up. "I know people think that happens because of cruise ship sanitation breakdown. But the truth is passengers bring it on board." His voice sounded defensive, so Rex searched for another question that would ease the tension. "Does that door lead to your private office?" He pointed to yet another door on the other side of the room.

He imagined the doc spent a lot of time out of sight, taking long naps.

"That's the infirmary." He didn't look up. "Is your stomach upset? That would be the first sign of noro."

"Mostly I'm stuffed up. Not that hungry or thirsty. And I feel really tired and achy." Rex looked toward the closed door. "Is anyone in the actual infirmary?" he asked.

"None of your business," snapped the doc.

Five minutes later Rex left sick bay with a small brown bag filled with several plastic bottles. Antihistamines. Decongestants. Pain relievers. He also had a plastic bag filled with cough drops. Two bottles of nose spray and extra packets of tissues were included. "Just in case," the doctor said.

When the doctor finished typing notes into his computer, before handing over the brown paper bag, he scribbled Rex's name on the outside with a felt marker. It looked more like a hastily assembled school lunch than an actual bag of medicine.

On his way to the door, the doc gave him advice. "Take the anti-inflammatories every four hours. Don't forget to hydrate." Then he closed the door before Rex could ask any more questions.

So much for bedside manner, Rex mused. *I feel worse than I did before the appointment. Maybe because he didn't tell me about the clean socks. That was always so comforting.*

When Rex stepped inside his stateroom, the sound of ambient jazz music came from the television. The rest of the room looked overly tidy and staged, as if ready for one of those advertising videos for the cruise company. Low light. Pseudo romantic music. Curtains partially closed. He exhaled slowly, knowing what was coming next. A slow turn revealed the woman in his bed.

Cricket had managed to let the sheet drop in an artful way, revealing her naked shoulder and the tops of her breasts. "I thought you'd never get here," came her sultry contralto. "There's room for one more." She pulled back the sheet.

His breath quickened, then he coughed. "I'm sick. Got medicines. You'd better stay clear or you might catch what I have."

He watched her smile fade as alarm reached her eyes.

It was a gamble. But he'd used what was at hand. Ill heath. He hoped Cricket didn't want to be around a sick person. And sure enough, she was already standing up, reaching for her clothing.

He felt slightly offended. *She could have acted a little more reluctant.*

Cricket, now fully clothed, bent over to reach under the bed. Waving her purse in the air she told him in a hasty voice, "I can't get sick. Don't breathe on me." She held up her hand as she walked past.

A rush of stale air from the corridor hit his face when the door opened. It wasn't until he'd pulled the chain across that he took a deep breath.

Climbing under the covers fully clothed, he smelled Cricket's perfume on his pillow. He sneezed and moved the pillow aside. *Note to self: ill heath works to keep the ladies at bay.*

Then he coughed three more times before falling fast asleep.

22

VIVIENNE ROSE

"Well that was a bust," Viv said aloud. She'd tried to reach the staff level on the elevator but then found she needed a special access card. To soothe her defeat and figure out the next move, Viv sat on the balcony enjoying her breakfast.

She appreciated the breeze on her face as the ship sliced its way through the international waters. Sitting outside was her preference, especially now. She'd plugged her nose on more than one occasion as she walked in the corridors. Smells she associated with public restrooms more than often assaulted her nose.

Plus the ship's loudspeaker system grated on her nerves. The captain sounded his whistle followed by announcements every morning. He shared information like the temperature of the sea and the speed they were traveling in knots.

None of that remotely interested Viv. She wanted to dismiss any thoughts of how the ship did its business, suspended in the water. Unfortunately she'd admittedly watched *Titanic* too many times. *Those icebergs. Leonardo dying. Ugh.*

As if the captain's announcements weren't enough, he was often followed by the ship's activity coordinator. Robert Redford would do his bit. He'd announce trivia quizzes in the library and lobster specials for lunch. "All the information is available on your app," he'd add with an upbeat delivery.

And then Viv would feel angry since her app and her Wi-Fi had not been restored. She decided at the light of day to do her best not to feel upset. She'd sit outside on her veranda and enjoy her breakfast in peace and quiet. Until...

A loud horn blow pierced her ears, followed by coded message: bravo alpha, star code. She had no idea who those announcements were for nor what they meant.

Yesterday she'd heard, "Mama gayo on the lido. *They speak a language I do not understand,* she'd conceded, taking an aggressive bite of her buttered toast.

Come to think about it... Viv paused to raise another piece of toast slathered in butter and strawberry jam to her mouth. *I overheard two crew members saying, "Don't get a banana." I know that's not meant for my ears but really? A banana? What could that possibly mean? Surely the staff has other things to worry about than tropical fruit.*

One of the things that annoyed Viv the most was that she couldn't do a quick search on her phone to answer any number of questions that puzzled her about ship life. And when she realized that, she was irritated once again.

Unless I want to spend another hour at the IT desk, she fumed to herself. *Or send more money to my cell provider. For what! I only have a few days at sea as it is.*

So to keep herself from being constantly annoyed, she decided to ignore the morning announcements and sit on her veranda. To her dismay, the heavy door that separated the room from the deck outside only blocked some of the words coming over the loudspeaker. As soon as she heard the click, she couldn't help but pay attention.

And then off her mind would go again. "Blah, blah, blah," Viv spoke to the wind and the sea. The food announcements were Viv's least favorite. "I don't even like lobster," she muttered. And then a glance at the vast expanse of ocean would bring back a sense of calm. The horizon reminded her there was an end to the journey.

Viv stood to glance over the rail to the decks below. Her eyes drifted to the lowest deck, where lifeboats had been stacked on racks. Her throat caught. Back to the *Titanic. I can swim at least*, she assured herself.

Visions of the movie *Titanic* rose in her mind again. The dramatic shots of the ship sinking and everyone scrambling for safety felt so real. People in the water clinging to icebergs. *Just stop it, Viv*, she told herself. *You're not going to sink.*

Even Leonardo DiCaprio isn't enough to distract me, she told herself wryly. *The last photo I saw of him did not resemble that young man in the nineties film. He was so good-looking back then.*

She realized no matter how hard she tried to talk herself out of feeling afraid, the whisper of panic still lurked in the back of her mind.

She doubled down on her self-talk, her mental life raft in times like this.

Okay, Viv. Don't think about the ship on the water. Think about this delicious chocolate croissant and pour yourself another cup of coffee.

When Viv was feeling better, she wondered if anxiety was the price of aging. *When I had more estrogen I was not bothered so much.*

Viv savored the last bite of croissant. *Maybe that's my*

takeaway from this cruise. There's such a thing as too much time on my hands. Cruises may not be my thing. If it weren't for Rex I wouldn't be here. And then, because she couldn't stop herself, her mind slid up and down like a yo-yo, as she made note of the pros and cons regarding cruises.

Viv shuddered. She begged her mind to relax. *Stop catastrophizing! Be like everyone else. Be a person who keeps eating croissants and lobsters. Who dismisses all other concerns to enjoy the pampering and luxury.*

The sound of a chair scraping came from the direction of the veranda next door. Despite her previous decision not to spy, she stood and hung over the rail as she tried to catch a glimpse of who'd made the noise.

With two thousand passengers and all of the crew, Viv wasn't surprised that she'd not run into her neighbor in the corridor. Though the Old Lady of the Sea managed to pop up on a regular basis. And so did Sandi with Daddy under her arm.

She only needed to walk to the lobby in front of an elevator to run into either of them.

Maybe the person in the room next to mine is someone who values their privacy. Another single traveler perhaps. She leaned over the railing again, her head turned to the left to catch a glimpse. All she could see were two bare feet hanging over the end of a chaise lounge.

Another scrape and the chaise pulled from sight, taking the bare feet with it.

Maybe they're hiding, Viv thought. *Or just terribly shy.* The ocean's water splashed past the hull of the ship, a slight spray hitting her face. Pushing herself away from the rail, she walked indoors. The heavy door closed behind her.

Once dressed in her resort-wear ensemble, Viv

wondered about the time. *It's hours until lunch. What am I going to do until then?* She picked up her room phone.

Two rings and a voice spoke. "Yes, Ms. Rose. How can we help you today?"

So polite, Viv thought. And again her mind went to what that person might be feeling. *I'd be slightly impatient with people's requests. Good thing I don't work on a cruise ship.*

"Would you send someone with a fresh pot of coffee? I'll be staying in my room a bit longer." She hung up the phone, feeling slightly guilty. *Everyone on staff is very nice, but they must get tired of waiting on people.*

She returned to the veranda to sit and contemplate what she'd do on her third day at sea. Wistfulness came over her. *I miss walking Kevin in the mornings and my routine at home. Oh sure, it's nice that all the food prep is done for me, and I do love fresh towels every morning. But I don't think I could do this cruise thing all the time.*

To be truthful, it's kind of boring.

She made an effort to keep her thoughts calm, staring toward the distant horizon. The sound of slapping water against the ship's hull helped soothe her nerves.

A tap against the glass door startled her. She jumped. A man stood on the other side of the door. *He must have let himself in. I forgot I ordered coffee...* Exasperation came over her. *I like being waited upon but I don't appreciate the lack of privacy. Maybe all those rich people in Downtown Abbey aren't as enviable as they looked.*

Be polite, Viv, she corrected herself.

He smiled, holding a tray balanced with one arm.

"Good morning again, Ms. Rose." He quietly placed the tray on the table and then slid a plate holding four small macaroons closer. Then he picked up the dirty dishes from her previous tray. "Is there anything else?" he asked politely.

Viv shook her head and admired how effortlessly he hoisted the tray to his arm and made his way out the door without assistance.

This is the life, she told herself. But she knew she was pretending. The contrast of living in such luxury without the reason for the cruise, Mr. Rex Redondo's company, had become crystal clear over the past days. *I wouldn't have time to be thinking about all of this if he were here.*

Now that is sad, Viv scolded herself. *You've got all of this luxury at your fingertips and you can't be happy with your own company.* Her gaze drifted to the sea once more.

Minutes later she realized she'd been lulled into forgetting one thing this morning. The guy on the lido deck. *What about him? Have you given up your investigation, Vivienne Rose?*

She left her napkin on the tray to make her way back inside the room. Reaching for the pad of paper on the counter, she clicked the pen. *Time to line things up in writing. Before I forget the details. What have I found out so far...*

First of all, the man fell off the elliptical. Hit his head. I turned my back, and when I turned around his body had disappeared. No one admits there was a guy or a body. What am I, some old lady in a Miss Marple movie? So old that I'm to be ignored? Why has there been no announcement that one of the passengers is ill? Or dead? He could be dead! Someone must be wondering where he went by now.

She left her pen on the pad. *If only I could communicate with Rex. We could sort this out together. Is there a connection between my Wi-Fi break down and the guy falling off the elliptical?*

. . .

Leaving her stateroom Viv strolled through the dining area looking for a place to sit and eat lunch. The tables were already occupied by people who made early arrival to their meal a priority. Larger groups sat toward the center of the room. Individuals and couples looked out at the sea from tables placed closer to the windows.

Many people held phones in one hand, taking bites while they stared at their screens. Two people actually held a paperback book in one hand. She spotted an empty chair across from the Old Lady of the Sea.

"Is this place taken?" she as

"By you, dearie." The woman's eyes crinkled at the side when she smiled. She took charge. "I'll have them bring you water while you get food. Would you mind picking up a slice of that delicious-looking chocolate cake for me? I'm ready for dessert."

"Of course," Viv answered.

Finally I'm making myself useful, helping an old lady. She chuckled. *At least one older than me.*

She returned with a seafood salad and a piece of cake for her companion.

Napkin spread on her lap, Viv began the conversation. "I heard that you've been traveling on this cruise line for quite a while. I think you're a legend."

"I have, my dear. Traveled for decades on the Aloha line. I have my own cabin on the starboard side of deck three. It's been set aside for me. After all of these years I feel like one of the Aloha family. I've come to know the new captain of this particular cruise, and I've come to know all the other previous captains as well. A fine bunch of seaworthy gentlemen. No ladies yet, but I'm hoping."

She took a forkful of cake, slipping it demurely past her lips. "How are you enjoying your cruise so far?"

Maybe because Viv was tired of her own company, or maybe because the woman sounded genuinely interested, she decided to open up. "I'm not sure cruising is my thing. I'm only here because my..." She hesitated because she didn't know what to call Rex.

Viv usually felt stumped when it came to describing Rex Redondo. Once she'd hit a certain age she hesitated to call men she was seeing, "Boyfriend." Plus Rex wasn't even that. He was her neighbor. The old woman must have noticed her hesitation because she began to chuckle.

"You're stuck on what to call your companion, aren't you?"

"I am," Viv admitted.

"Don't worry, dear. Over the years I've seen everything on this ship. I don't judge." The smile made her eyes light up.

"He's actually my neighbor. A Palm desert community. He lives next door to me. He invited me on this cruise. It's my first."

"I learned once I turned a certain age to call my friends by their name. Who is this mysterious companion of yours? I don't see you with him. Or is it a her? Not that there's anything wrong with that."

Viv felt completely beguiled. She was eager to talk to someone about Rex, and this woman sounded like she'd be the one person who might understand her feelings. She leaned over the table to confide. "Rex is the name of my companion. He's six feet tall. Very full head of wavy gray hair. Good build. Beautiful smile. Very fit, especially for his age. Wears his clothes like Cary Grant. He still looks great in a pair of jeans even at his age."

The older woman chuckled. "Sounds like you're describing that mentalist fellow. The staff calls him the silver fox."

"That's him," Viv said. It was such a relief to tell someone.

"But he's on the staff. And you're a passenger." The woman's voice dropped. "Does that mean you're getting together at night? Hopefully that's true. I'd hate to think you're all by yourself on a cruise to a tropical paradise like Hawaii."

Viv couldn't help herself. She laughed. "But I am. All by myself. That's not what we planned. It was supposed to be a getting-to-know-you week. But Rex filled in for the mentalist who didn't show up for work. A last-minute switch leaving me on my own. At least until we arrive in Honolulu."

Pushing her plate to the side, the old woman chuckled. "Call me Bertha. I don't give everyone my name, but I like you already."

"Okay, Bertha." Viv nodded in return. "I'm Vivienne. Would you like anything else from the buffet? I'm going to get a piece of that cake for myself."

Viv tried to push her chair back but was nearly knocked over by a woman who stood behind her. "Excuse me," the woman muttered, coming around the table to speak. "I'd like to have a word with Ms. Alcott."

As she turned away, Viv looked her over.

Dressed in an Aloha Cruise staff officer's uniform, she'd combed her dark hair back in a bun. An enormous pair of square-shaped glasses didn't disguise her bright blue eyes. Her makeup, applied simply, only added to her youthful elegance.

Once she'd finished whispering in Bertha's ear, she

turned to Viv. "I heard you're having trouble with your Wi-Fi service."

The cheery comment and the sheer perfection of the woman together with her chipper voice hit Viv's last nerve. *She makes me want to disagree just for the sake of disagreeing.*

"Who told you?" The words passed her lips sounding indignant and accusatory. Looking more closely at the name tag, Viv realized they'd already met. *Allison Thompson. She checked me in before I boarded the ship. And she was the one to tell me I'd been seeing things and that there was no guy falling off the elliptical.* That *Allison Thompson.*

"I'm the information technology senior manager. So it's my job to follow up on all complaints," Allison explained.

Viv cleared her throat. "How soon can you do that? Fix my Wi-Fi." She glanced out of the corner of her eye toward Bertha. The older woman leaned forward as if fascinated by the unfolding bit of drama.

"Bring your phone down to deck three, to the IT desk. I'll take care of it," Allison said quickly. As she turned to leave. Bertha touched her elbow.

"Allison, dear, stay and talk. How are you and the children? They must miss you. I imagine Maine seems very far away right now."

Perhaps flustered at the personal questions, Allison seemed at a loss for words.

Bertha didn't wait for Allison to answer. Instead she turned to Viv and kept talking. "Allison and I are old friends. She has two children and a husband. They live in a small bungalow in Maine. You can image how challenging it is for a family to be separated." She looked at Allison again. "You're heading to the tropics and they're stranded in all that snow." The Old Lady of the Sea shuddered.

Allison reached to tap Bertha's shoulder with her finger. "Fear not, Ms. Alcott. My husband and I spoke last night for nearly an hour. And the children have school and after-school sports. He's a bit frazzled but happy because I'm bringing home a paycheck."

Allison turned back to Viv. "Like I said, when you're finished I'll meet you at the IT desk. We'll iron out the problem."

"I'll go with you," Bertha promised.

Viv sighed, wishing she'd kept track of how many hours she'd spent standing at the IT desk already. *Will this cruise ever end?*

23

VIVIENNE ROSE

An entire hour at the IT desk did not fix Viv's problem. Allison tried her best but then had to call Redford in anyway. No matter how often they turned the phone on and off and clicked buttons on the desktop computer, nothing worked.

Viv held back her frustration, observing their comedic play unfold. *It seems the actors know their lines, but they aren't quite connected to the plot.*

Though Bertha had promised to stand with her, she'd given up after twenty minutes. "My knees are barking," she'd explained. "I'm heading to play a game of gin rummy on the lido deck. Feel free to join me when you're done." The Old Lady of the Sea hobbled away, using her cane for support.

"I'll take the phone to the back room," Redford finally offered. Perspiration beaded on his unlined forehead. *Serves him right*, Viv thought.

When he returned, he smiled. "I think we've got it this time." His confident grin aside, Viv took her phone from his hand. She'd grown tired of standing with all the people behind her fussing and fuming about getting their turn.

"Thanks," she mumbled and then hurried away. It wasn't until she stood outside the sliding glass doors leading to the lido deck that Viv thought to text Rex and reconnect.

My phone's been out of order.

She pushed send, hoping she'd finally fixed one problem. At least Rex would know why she'd been out of touch.

Undeliverable, her phone told her.

Viv felt her gut churn. Not only had she wasted over an hour and pretended to be grateful at the IT desk, they hadn't done one thing to improve her connection. *A waste of time*, she thought. It was then and there she made up her mind.

I'm taking things into my own hands. First I hunt down Rex. He's the reason I put aside my better judgment and agreed to this cruise. So he gets to hear how I feel. Even if they arrest me and put me in cruise jail for breaking the rules. Abandoning the plan to catch up with Bertha, Viv pocketed her phone and turned back to the elevators.

In her room, she concocted a more specific plan to reconnect with Rex. *I'll sneak down to deck three. Then I'll figure out how to take the wrong turn on purpose to the staff area. But first I have to get out of this poolside getup. If I wear this outfit, I'll be spotted as a passenger right away.*

Glancing at herself in the mirror, she assessed her ensemble. The pair of pink sandals that coordinated with her nail varnish was the most obvious clue that she was a passenger.

Viv returned to the bed. Bending down, she pulled out

her suitcase, rummaging for the travel clothes she'd worn three days earlier. Unfolding her jeans, she held them up. *Wrinkly but not terrible. Those will do.*

Then she stepped closer to her closet to search for a top. *I have that black t-shirt. It's not a perfect selection, but at least I'll have ditched the Aloha-esque apparel. And I won't be looking quite like every other passenger on this boat—I mean ship. Rex told me that it's called a ship.*

Sadness came over her unexpectedly. *What a mess this cruise has turned out to be.* She took off the caftan and her bathing suit and then pulled on her jeans and tee.

Then she tossed her sandals into the bottom of the closet, replacing them with her worn black sneakers. *Good-bye, cute toes... And the most expensive pedicure I've ever paid for.*

Now all she had to do was make her hair disappear. Digging back into the suitcase, she found her black baseball cap. *This will do.* She tugged on the brim to pull it down over her eyes.

Now that I've changed, what's next... "Score a staff elevator keycard," she told herself aloud.

Easier said than done. She sat back on the edge of the bed.

Viv considered her options. The one place she hadn't been yet were the shops. *I could get a look around and engage an employee in conversation. And then maybe they'll get distracted.*

The waft of sadness returned, settling over her spirit, bringing her close to tears. *Who are you, Vivienne Rose? You're turning into such a sneak, planning to steal an elevator access card.*

With exasperation fueled by guilt, she looked down at her clothing. *This won't do for shopping. It's for sneaking about.* Viv stepped out of her clothes again, leaving them folded at the end of her bed. It took a few more minutes for her to get back into her resort wear. She replaced her cap for her straw hat as a finishing touch.

That's good. Time to go shopping, old girl. You've finally got a plan!

Several women browsed the boutique apparel shop when Viv sauntered inside. She didn't recognize anyone. Taking a moment to pretend to admire a blouse on the sales rack, she looked around for an obvious employee. Only the man behind the counter seemed to be available. And he was busy handing out tickets to two women who giggled at his jokes.

She drifted to the next rack. Lifting the price tag, her jaw dropped. *One hundred bucks for a thin tee that will probably disintegrate after the first wash.* Pushing that aside, she inspected a pair of wide-legged pants. That sales tag inspired another near gasp. *People on cruises probably buy lots of stuff at these shops because they're plain old bored, too much time on their hands.*

She felt a rumble come from her purse. Her heart quickened. She hadn't given up that Rex would somehow get in touch, and she longed to hear his voice. Have him tease her into a better mood.

Stepping to the corner of the shop, Viv held the phone, pretending to inspect the small section with laxatives and sunscreens. Once she was alone, she checked her messages. Her heart dropped.

Not Rex. It was her phone service pinging her with another offer. *Oh sure,* they *have no problem getting ahold of me.*

Viv tapped on the text. Anger flamed in her cheeks. *The nerve. As if I hadn't already figured this out. Somehow they know that I'm in international waters. I can't get ahold of Rex on this ship, but they can contact me from who knows where.*

Her head felt like it was ready to explode. *It's not too late to sign up for the international plan for a small fee. Really! You know what you can do with your fee...*

Clicking her phone to silent, she shoved it back into her purse. After a deep breath, Viv knew she might be overreacting. Just a bit. And that on some level, this disconnect was all her fault.

She'd not researched special cruise phone plans before she left Palm Desert, and now she'd have to pay three times the cost if she wanted to update her coverage. Plus Rex had warned her. But she'd dismissed his advice out of hand.

With a deep sigh, Viv lifted a bottle of cough medicine to stare at the price. *Too much.* She replaced the bottle to inspect a stool softener. *That's two dollars less and I can put it to good use.*

As she waited at the end of the line, she did her best to listen in to the conversation of the couple ahead.

"The mentalist was off his game last night," the woman in a bright pink shirt complained.

"He didn't seem that alert," her companion agreed. "Anyone can feed a dog. You don't have to be a mind reader."

"I thought that part was pretty cute." The woman's tinkly laugh made Viv flinch.

"I hope he comes up with something better tonight." Her companion moved forward in the line. Viv took an extra step to stay close. But then she felt a tug at her elbow.

"Hello, dear, I thought we were meeting on the lido

deck." Bertha tapped her cane. "Do you mind if I step in line with you? I need more cough medicine." She held up the bottle and waved it in front of Viv's eyes. Viv recognized it as the brand from the shelf.

"I'll get that for you. I can bring it back to the lido deck if you'd like." She took the bottle from Bertha's hand.

Viv hoped the offer would convince the Old Lady of the Sea to go away. Viv didn't wait for Bertha to agree. She turned her shoulder slightly as a further message.

"You can bring it later. Maybe during cocktail hour. I'll be at my place in the level four bar," Bertha said crossly.

"You mean the one outside the casino?" Viv clarified.

"That's the one. See you later, dear." To Viv's relief she ambled away.

The woman ahead of her moved aside, having finished her transaction. Viv reached into her purse for her wallet, realizing she'd be paying for the expensive cough syrup despite her intention.

"I'll take those." The employee behind the counter looked quite crisp and efficient with his hair slicked back. He held out his hand, and Viv gave him her two items. "Anything else?" he asked with a quick nod to a display next to the counter. "Our cruise shirts are half off this afternoon. I can add one to your tab. Size medium, right? And don't forget to put this ticket stub in the raffle jar. You can win a gift certificate for the jewelry event and a discount when you book your next cruise."

Considering I'm spending nearly twenty bucks on a laxative and a tiny bottle of cough syrup, I'm gonna pass on the t-shirt. When Viv reached for the cash in her wallet, the salesperson interjected.

"I'll put it on your room charge. You can pay the bill before debarking. We don't handle cash at the shops."

She handed him her room key, striking up a casual conversation. "Have you worked for Aloha Cruises long?"

He carefully watched as she tapped the machine. When he didn't answer, she asked, "There are so many people and a lot of crew members on this ship. How do you not get lost? All the decks and rooms look the same to me."

"It takes a couple of weeks to get used to it." He pulled out a small plastic bag with the blue Aloha label printed on the side. "Senior staff are helpful. Plus there's a map on your phone app."

"I bet staff has their own phone app, separate from the passengers."

"Employees have their own portal, if that's what you're asking." He reached into his pocket to show Viv his screen. "This holds everything, including my room key." He took his phone away quickly before she could get a better look. Then he handed her the bag with her items.

"Thanks," she mumbled.

Stepping to the side, she let the people behind her come forward. *That didn't work. Not like I can dig into his pocket for his phone. Not like I know his code. Not like I'm an actual pickpocket...*

Frustration accompanied Viv down the corridors. Getting access to the employee elevator was proving to be more difficult than she'd hoped. *Stealing a phone isn't like stealing a card*, she told herself grumpily. *Phones are personal. Even if I took their phone, I'm not tech savvy like Sutton or Rex. I'd have no idea how to get access without a PIN.*

She strolled past shops with windows decorated with shiny jewelry and expensive leather bags. Viv clutched her crossbody purse to her side, determined not to be lured into buying what she didn't really need.

She ducked her head and kept walking. Her nose was assaulted by the smell of expensive heavy cologne. It poured out the door into the corridor, coming from the last shop before the lobby.

Viv hurried past, heading toward the elevator. A familiar passenger waited.

Sandi held the box of Daddy's ashes tucked under one arm. She was speaking to Robert Redford in an assertive tone. "I expect to invite more guests than I originally planned," she insisted.

"You've already included twenty-five people." Redford looked grim.

"I've made so many friends on the cruise. Everyone wants to help me say goodbye to Daddy." Sandi turned her head, her eyes held shut as if warding off tears. Then she opened one eye and caught sight of Viv.

"Oh hello. I've been looking for you." Without a backward glance, she moved away from Redford to approach. "I'd like to invite you to Daddy's memorial tomorrow. It will be catered. The service will be in the small dining room, which is on the third deck on the staff side. I have a special pass if you're interested." Sandi handed her a small paper.

"I am honored to be invited," Viv replied.

"There's a QR code for you to donate to Daddy's favorite cause." Sandi pointed to the symbol on the paper. You only need to use your photo app—"

"Thanks again. I know about QR codes," Viv interrupted. "See you tomorrow."

"One o'clock," Sandi called over her shoulder. She turned back to Redford, picking up where she'd left off.

"Make that twenty-six people," she told him in a loud voice. "And get the captain to disburse the ashes. I've told everyone that he'll be there to give Daddy the most amazing send-off."

Sandi's voice cracked, giving way to a rush of tears.

Viv decided to take another elevator. Clutching the paper in her hand, she realized, *I can use this to find Rex. It's my ticket to ride right over to the staff side. And I didn't need to snatch a phone and turn to a life of crime.*

24

REX REDONDO

Rex awoke with a start. He reached for a tissue from the box on the bedside table to dab at his runny nose. Despite swallowing down the medicine and sleeping, his head ached.

Staring at the ceiling, he felt sorry for himself. His hand reached over to grab his cell. *Maybe Viv called.* One glance brought him upright in bed. *I only have an hour to show-time. Must have forgotten to set my alarm.*

Rex felt great pride about his timely way of going about business. He'd never missed a scheduled performance. In fact he'd never even been late. A well-disciplined mentalist, he didn't believe in leaving anything to chance. He planned ahead.

And don't forget what they told you in boot camp, he cautioned himself. "If you're not fifteen minutes early, you're ten minutes late." When he tried to explain why that didn't make sense and do the math with the sergeant, he'd been severely reprimanded.

"Redondo, you need to have your butt in the chair fifteen minutes before the senior officer enters the room. Is that clear enough for you!"

Even the way he walked on stage had been carefully choreographed over the years. *An entrance is everything,* he'd told Viv. He knew the audience judged his first appearance, making up their minds then and there whether to believe that he was the real deal.

An hour was barely time enough for him to get ready. Just his makeup and getting dressed took some attention, no matter how familiar the routine. And he needed to go over his act to include the crystal ball. *I mean the fortune globe,* he corrected himself.

Shivering in the cold shower, he carefully planned what to do. Shaking himself off minutes later, he grabbed a towel, running it along his back to stop the water dribbling down his spine. Still shivering, Rex realized, *I may have an actual temperature. The doc claimed it was normal, but maybe since the nap...*

His shoes polished and bow tie in place, Rex walked to his closet. Reaching inside, he used his code to open the safe. With the fortune globe in his pocket, he took a brief glance into the mirror and then stepped into the corridor.

Turning to the right, he nearly tripped over a wheeled hamper, which partially blocked the door. He moved around, thinking maybe they'd leave him a clean set of towels.

"Good evening, Mr. Redondo," Robert Redford greeted him at the end of the corridor. "I hope you're enjoying your cruise." Redford was dressed in an Aloha uniform complete with cummerbund. Another reminder of the formal-wear evening planned by the ship's activities director.

"I don't have any hot water," Rex complained. "I meant to pick up the phone and tell maintenance but got waylaid and then I forgot. Until I stepped into the shower and nearly froze."

Self-pity came over him, his voice grumpy. *I don't have the energy to play nice.*

Redford adopted a concerned expression. "I'll look into that. Anything else?"

Rex shrugged and moved past. "I'm late, I'm late. For a very important date," he quoted the White Rabbit from *Alice's Adventures in Wonderland* under his breath.

Determined not to stop in the staff dining hall, he made his way toward the sliding doors on the other side of the room. A muffled voice called his name. He pulled on his ear.

Despite not being able to hear well, he heard someone call his name. "I don't have time for conversation," he quickened his pace.

"Rex Redondo," came another call. Because he was basically a polite person, he finally stopped and looked around.

The Old Lady of the Sea waved from the far corner of the room. Her table was closest to the exit. He didn't like to be rude, especially to old ladies. And she obviously wanted to have a word with him.

"Come over, dear. I have news for you." She smiled.

His eyebrows rose. *What's she doing in the staff dining room? Why isn't she eating with the rest of the passengers upstairs?*

Can't think about that now, he reminded himself. *I'm late and need to get backstage.* But because he never left a lady in a lurch, he edged closer to her table.

"Can't talk right now," he hollered. When she looked surprised, he realized he'd spoken too loud. "Got a show," he added in a quieter voice.

"I'm not deaf," she told him, her mouth pursing in disapproval.

"I'll catch up with you afterward." He hurried away toward the elevators.

As the door slid closed, Rex touched his temple with his forefinger. *Maybe it's the medicine,* he thought. *I can't hear well and I do feel dizzy.*

Shaking his head to clear the spacey feeling, he reached into his trouser pocket to connect with his prop. *Okay, fortune globe. I hope you've got the magic. I'm going to need a real vision for the show tonight.*

25

REX REDONDO

He had five minutes to spare until showtime. Rex looked in the mirror. *I'm not sure I can go on.* Blinking at himself, he groaned. Then he spun his chair around so that he had a view of the rest of his small dressing room.

The glare from the lights overhead made him repeatedly blink. Slumping back into his chair, he lifted the fortune globe for another look.

He shook the globe, waiting for an image to be revealed inside the clear liquid. Nothing happened. Then Rex tried to remember something he'd read about scrying from other mentalists who posted online. No luck.

He shook the globe again, laughing at himself. *It's not a dime-store snow globe, you fool.* He put the globe down on the counter to vigorously scratch at his forearm through his shirt. He rubbed both hands over the sleeves, hoping to calm his nerves.

Rex felt defeated. *I'm just a mess. Getting old, I guess. Maybe I'd better take this aging thing more seriously. The next thing you know, I'll need hearing aids, and then it will be cataract surgery.*

He made a list in his mind of all the things he associated with older people.

And I'll need a wheelchair for those bad days when my trick knee gives out.

He rested his head in his hands, overcome with gloom. *My youth. Where has it gone!*

A tap came to the door; a voice outside announced, "Showtime, Mr. Redondo."

Rex stood. Reaching for the fortune globe, he lifted a clean handkerchief from his pocket. He held it to his nose. *Smells like home—like Palm Desert.*

I wish I were sitting by the firepit with Kevin, watching him paw at the fence. Rex sniffed back his unhappiness. *Viv would be on me for feeling sorry for myself. Get a grip,* he told himself, using her tone of voice.

Taking the handkerchief, he carefully wiped the globe, removing any lint from his pocket and smudges left by his fingers. He held it up, gazing through the ball toward the mirror. A white film formed as the clear liquid gradually turned murky. The liquid began to swirl, moving in a counterclockwise circle.

That's more like it. Maybe this thing will work after all, he concluded.

He wrapped the handkerchief around the globe and slipped it back into his pocket. Then he checked the other pocket to make sure the dog treats were where he'd left them earlier.

He'd been caught off guard the night before, using salmon. It wasn't until later that he realized the fish might have stunk or made the dog ill. But then he rationalized it was most likely smoked and preserved. Not willing to take that chance again, he'd remembered an old packet of Kevin's beef-flavored snacks in the zipper compartment of his suitcase.

Finally Rex opened the dressing room door to the hallway. He took a deep breath and headed toward the stage.

He waited in the wing while the announcer spoke. "And now, ladies and gentlemen, we have the one and only Rex Redondo!"

Rex pasted on a gleaming smile and strode onto the stage.

Scattered applause met his ears as he turned to face the audience. Heat from the intense overhead lights made Rex feel even more dizzy. He took a moment to catch his bearings by mentally distancing himself from the crowd.

He didn't want to be affected by the applause, whether it be light or thunderous. He had a job to do. And his imagination to use.

After he spent twenty minutes warming up the audience, perspiration dripped from his forehead. He'd known since the night before that working with the dog had made people responsive. He would use that bit again.

He rationalized to himself that every mentalist had "low-hanging gags" in their act. The tricks that always worked. Plus the two poodles in the front row begged for attention. He couldn't disappoint them.

The dogs ate Kevin's beef treats without complaint. But now the audience had grown restless.

They wanted more. And Rex was hoping he could meet their expectation. He brushed his finger across his nose, which was the sign for the light guys to illuminate more of the audience.

This provided enough distraction for Rex to pull out the fortune globe and hold it in the air. Once people focused on him again, he removed his handkerchief with a flourish.

"Ladies and gentlemen, I want to share a secret with you. I rarely bring the fortune globe to my shows. But you've been so special during my performances, I've grown to trust you. I know you can support the energy of the globe and that you'll keep our secrets after you leave. Can you do that?" He lowered the globe in front of his waist. He wasn't disappointed. The applause was instantaneous.

"Just as I thought." He touched his finger across the bridge of his nose again. This time the lights dimmed. He brushed his finger against his nose again and they dimmed further.

Darkness descended over the audience. Only a single spotlight focused on the globe, which Rex extended in both hands.

He stared into the gleaming liquid. To his relief, the white cloud he'd seen in his dressing room began to form and then swirl. This time moving in a clockwise direction. He rubbed one hand over the globe, barely touching the glass surface.

He did this to assure the globe that he was watching.

Time to start my patter, Rex thought. "I'm seeing formations in the globe," he announced into his microphone. Then he paused, knowing that timing was everything in his work. The pauses were as important as the speech.

Plus it was a practical matter. He knew that if this conjuring part of the act went too fast, time would run out and he'd have to come up with another act to fill in. If he went too slow, he'd lose the audience's attention. *An amateur mistake.* So he counted to ten slowly in his mind.

Holding the fortune globe to his forehead, he waited. The spotlight engineer knew exactly what to do, focusing the lights on the globe. Lasers of reflected light shot from the glass into the darkness. The audience gasped.

Rex walked the stage from left to right, forward and back. He held the ball aloft as the beams of light increased.

For a moment he was distracted. His eyes scratched. The glare from the fortune nearly rendered him blind.

Finally a white cloud appeared in the liquid followed by a dark spinning mass. The bubble of darkness bumped along and then reshaped. Then it split in two. An image appeared.

The audience watched with fascination. Rex partially shielded the ball with his outstretched hand. He opened and shut his eyes over and over. No matter how often he blinked the image would not go away.

There was a man on an elliptical, his arms moving back and forth, his feet on the pedals. Arms and feet moved faster and faster until... He fell over, tumbling toward the ground, his head banging against the handlebar of the machine nearby.

Rex blinked and the image finally disappeared. The liquid, still dark, began swirling again. He looked out at the audience, the spotlight preventing him from seeing anyone's face.

He struggled to make sense of the image, knowing full well it was a confirmation of Viv's story. *But how do I make this important for the audience?* he wondered. *I only have a second before they get annoyed.*

"Ladies and gentlemen. I've seen a vision of the ship." He paused to make certain he had their attention. "And all I have to say is..." Again the pause, while he figured out his next revelation.

Rex gulped. He spoke in a conspiratorial tone. "The globe's wisdom wants everyone to know. Stay away from the gym. Wait until you get home to lose those extra pounds. Now it's time to party."

For a moment he thought his joke wouldn't hit the mark. But then a titter began from the front row. Then an actual chuckle. Finally people began to laugh aloud, giving Rex the chance to glance at the globe again. The liquid had reversed its spin, revealing another image.

The shock reverberated up his spine. *I can't deal with this right now.* He covered the fortune globe with his hand-kerchief and slipped it back into his pocket, right as the stage lights came up.

This time people gave him a standing ovation with wild applause. Rex wasn't sure why exactly. The fortune globe act had been lame at best.

But he wasn't one to take an accolade of applause for granted once the show was over. The audience always knew best. It was his job to keep them entertained, and apparently he'd done that. *Only one more show to go*, he told himself, hurrying off stage.

As the clapping continued, Rex's knees began to shake. Doubts filled his mind. *Okay, that may be jeering I hear. Maybe the audience thinks I'm a fraud. They just wanted this show to end, so they applauded to get rid of me.*

The feeling of defeat followed him back to his dressing room. He opened the door, expecting to be alone. Unfortunately, the Old Lady of the Sea sat on the small love seat.

"Good show, Mr. Redondo," she said. "I've been speaking to Vivienne, and I've heard all about your canceled plans. I can see you're surprised I'm here. May I call you Rex?"

26

VIVIENNE ROSE

The early dinner seating made it difficult to see, let alone move around. Finally Viv found an empty spot across from Bertha Alcott. The waiter leaned over to pull the bottle of wine from the bucket and refill her glass.

Bertha had consumed most of that bottle before she'd arrived. Viv took a sip of water. She'd learned over the years not to drink with other people. It turned out that she was kind of a lightweight when it came to alcohol. Plus she hated feeling sluggish the next day.

Of course, people who didn't like to drink alone would scoff once they caught on. At least that's what her ex told her right after they'd separated. When the truths, the ones he'd hidden for so many years, came spilling out.

"You don't drink enough," Laurence had complained. "I need to get out more now that I've turned fifty. You aren't fun anymore, and you're not even trying to keep up."

At the time Viv didn't argue. She was too busy coping with her own life changes. The new body that felt clunky and as if it required lubrication. Like the Tin Man, she'd tell her doula friends. Then she'd turned to yoga and more supplements to make her joints move more effectively.

But after they separated, she'd realized Laurence was probably right. In many ways she'd never enjoyed drinking as much as he did, and she didn't like parties either. In fact, her idea of aging wasn't his at all.

But now Viv shifted her thoughts back to the woman sitting across from her. The Old Lady of the Sea had certainly adjusted to her aging. *Just look at her.*

Has Bertha always been this way, the center of attention? Viv observed her companion more closely. The older woman had plenty of wrinkles, and not just around her eyes and mouth. Deeply etched lines on her cheeks, indicating a life spent in the sun. Viv appreciated that she wore her wrinkles with some pride.

She suspected that Bertha smoked. Maybe not now but years ago. Not surprising really. She'd been young in the fifties, and more women smoked then. If Rex were here, he might recommend his dermatologist-to-the-stars to the older woman.

Viv hid a slight smile behind her napkin.

She'd done the same a couple of months ago when Rex explained about his extensive skin routine. How the quarterly hot spring treatments helped to restore balance with some kind of peptides.

She'd relented and gone on a rejuvenation retreat with him. But the whole idea of spending thousands on her skin made her slightly uneasy. She loved her aging body for all of its demands.

I'd rather just wear a hat and my wrinkles with pride, she'd told him later.

By now Bertha had finished her meal. The waiter took

away her plate. "May we have the dessert and digestif menu?" Bertha asked in her gravelly voice.

"Certainly, Miss Alcott." The waiter turned on his heel.

Bertha leaned over the table to speak in her conspiratorial tone. "Everyone knows my name on board. It makes me feel so young."

A Sinatra song floated from Viv's memory. "Isn't that a song by Frank Sinatra? 'You Make Me Feel So Young'?" she asked.

"Yes, it is. I didn't expect anyone your age to recognize it."

Viv knew anything she said would only play into their age difference. She was sixty and Bertha in her nineties. So she moved past the reference to ask another question. "Do you have a favorite dining room waiter?"

Viv wondered just how close Bertha was to the staff. Maybe she would drop some gossip that would be helpful with her investigation.

"Not a favorite waiter, but I do have staff members who might call me family." Bertha nodded. "This is my favorite cruise itinerary. Unlike some cruises that dock in port every day, where people debark for daily excursions. This particular route spends more time at sea. I find the ocean spray, the sound of water against the ship's hull, the horn blaring into the fog exhilarating." She looked out the window into the night before continuing.

"I get to share the peace and quiet on board with the staff. We are just like family," Bertha repeated. Then she added, "Another song, I believe."

"'We Are Family,' Sister Sledge," Viv said.

In the silence that followed, Viv recognized a sense of uneasiness. Calling people she'd found along the way her family had been her downfall in the past. Just recently, in fact.

"Family can be complicated," Viv quietly added. "I've had friends who I thought were family and then they weren't. It turned out to be kind of messy, actually."

Bertha nodded and picked up the dessert menu.

Viv did the same. "Have you had the cheesecake?" she hoped to ease any awkwardness about family that she'd inadvertently created.

After they both ordered, Viv broached the topic she'd been wanting to ask all evening. "Bertha," she began, "in that you know a lot of the staff and they treat you like family, would you be able to get a message to Rex? My phone is still not connecting to the Wi-Fi."

By now Viv was accustomed to Bertha's indirect conversation style. How she rarely answered a question when asked. Instead, Bertha preferred to tell a story about something relating to the question. This time was no exception.

"I've found cell phone communication a bit difficult on ships," the older woman began. "The international waters are the main factor. The staff helps me out on occasion. I've found tracking them down works best.

"As for my other friends, I find emailing at certain times of the year effective. I tell everyone about my traveling experiences. But aboard ship, when I can't use my phone, I'm at a loss. That must be frustrating for you." Bertha sipped her water as the waiter delivered their desserts, a cheese platter, and Bertha's after dinner drink. Before Viv could launch another question, she continued.

"I remind myself that there's an addiction to staying in constant contact with people, whether they be family or friend. What with the constant texting and FaceTiming. It's not healthy." She took her fork and carefully cut into the cheesecake.

"I may be addicted," Viv admitted, "but I don't want Rex to worry. Would you give him a message for me?"

"So tasty." Bertha licked her fork. When she'd finished swallowing, she took another sip of wine.

"I wish I could help you, but that would be impossible. Aloha rules, you know. My special status might be revoked."

What with Bertha's delayed responses and the lecture about texting and cell phone usage, Viv concluded that she wasn't going to be much help. Plus she didn't want to get the older woman in trouble.

Bertha paused over another sip. "The stairs might work, if you want to go staff side. But may I warn you? The staff section is carefully blocked off behind private doors. I haven't tried myself"—she reached for her cane next to her chair—"but I've heard from others."

"I see," Viv sighed. She tried one more time. "Would you be willing to take a note to Rex?"

Bertha held her cane in one hand and raised the other to snap her fingers. "Let me get the attention of the waiter and I'll consider your request."

Bertha balanced her cane against the table and settled back into her chair to wait. She took her time, fidgeting with her napkin on her lap. After glancing at the cheese platter, she took the remaining slice. "I suppose we're in no hurry. It's good to end a meal with a savory."

Viv made an effort not to look as disgruntled as she felt.

Finally Bertha addressed her concerns. "I will take your message, but on one condition. That you don't make a habit of this. He can afford to wait. I think the man is a bit over-confident. No use chasing him." Her voice sounded tart.

Anger swept over Viv. Tempted to get argumentative,

she stopped herself with a swallow. She didn't disagree with the older woman's assessment of Rex; she also thought he was overconfident, often a bit arrogant even. But Viv didn't appreciate Bertha pointing this out. It wasn't until her irritation waned that she managed to mumble, "Thanks for your advice." She kept the word "unsolicited" out of her sentence.

As Viv ate her dessert in silence, she wondered if she dared broach another topic, the one she'd been keeping back. Once the table had been cleared, she took the plunge. "Bertha, I have another problem that you may be able to help with."

The older woman nodded. "Yes?"

"The first day, when people were boarding, I saw a man fall off an elliptical in the gym. His head banged against the machine next to him and he collapsed. I reported the incident to a staff employee. But when I tried to show her, the man was gone."

Bertha lifted her chin, her expression registering interest. Viv continued.

"When I mentioned the incident to Allison Thompson, she told me I was imagining things. That maybe the glare from the window distorted my view."

Eyebrows raised, Bertha put down her glass. "What an alarming story. And then to be told you were seeing things... Has anyone followed up?"

"Not one person. It's as if it never happened. Allison told me she'd make inquiries. I know what I saw. There was a body."

Bertha's lips pursed. "I so hate it when people dismiss me like that. An ageist thing, don't you agree? Young people." She sighed.

"I do agree," admitted Viv. "It's been happening more and more over the years, being dismissed. But my feelings aside, I want to find out who that man was. And for that matter," Viv swallowed as her voice began to rise, "if he's dead."

"Could have tossed him overboard." Bertha flicked her fingers. "Just like that. I've heard lots of stories over the years."

"Oh no. That wouldn't happen." Viv shuddered. "The cruise line wouldn't do that."

Bertha raised an eyebrow. Then she leaned forward. "Lower your voice," she insisted. "And yes, it could have happened. Why a year ago, there was this young honeymoon couple and what a ruckus they caused. A big fight on the promenade deck, and the next morning they were shouting over their eggs Benedict.

"The next evening he was eating alone in the dining room. After that I only saw him, never her. When I asked him where she was, he told me that she was feeling ill and staying in their stateroom. So I mentioned the situation to a staff member. I was told to mind my own business. My assumption is that the husband pushed her over the side late at night." Bertha nodded emphatically.

Viv's eyes widened. "Don't they have cameras on board?" She began to explain, "I've worked on a couple of cases, murder investigations, with Rex. And surveillance cameras are everywhere nowadays. Surely the ship—"

"The cameras aren't always operating," Bertha said. "Like your Wi-Fi, just because you have a system in place, that doesn't mean it's up and running."

"Will there be anything else, Miss Alcott?" The waiter stood next to their table.

Viv realized she'd been so agitated with Bertha's news that she hadn't paid attention to his whereabouts. *He might have been eavesdropping.*

"We're done with our meal." Bertha held out her hand for the waiter, who helped her to her feet. She grasped her cane for balance as he pushed her chair back under the table.

"See you tomorrow evening, Miss Alcott," the waiter said. "Don't forget we're having lobster to celebrate our next-day arrival in Honolulu."

Bertha nodded, thumping her cane ahead, taking each step one at a time.

Viv rose to her feet and followed from behind. Every time Bertha stopped to speak to someone, Viv stopped. Finally they made their way through the restaurant.

The Old Lady of the Sea gets plenty of attention, Viv concluded. *And she seems to enjoy every minute.*

27

VIVIENNE ROSE

Viv and Bertha stood side by side in the lobby. Viv felt exhausted. She'd hung back, serving as Bertha's escort as the older woman made her way through the dining room, waving and stopping to talk to everyone who called her name.

She was ready to excuse herself when Bertha spoke first. "We have time for tea before the show." *What about my investigation?And when did I start calling it my investigation?*

Not wanting to appear rude, she made a hasty decision. "Wait for me, I need to use the restroom."

"Oh no, dear. I need my tea." Bertha stomped off, leaving her on her own.

Tucking away in an alcove to avoid the crowd, Viv leaned against a wall. When she looked over she saw people standing in front of a camera. A photographer coaxed them to smile.

"One, two, three," she said. "Look at me!" And then the camera clicked.

A quick glance explained. The sign read, *Formal night*

photo packages. Capture your idyllic week in a professional setting to send to all of your friends.

This feels like a high school prom. Viv chuckled to herself. *But without the wrist corsages.* Her thoughts wandered back to her own high school days. She was a senior, and her date arrived at the door with a corsage in his hand. He'd tried to pin it to her dress, his fingers lingering over her right breast.

"It's got elastic," her father shouted from across the room. "Do you need help finding her wrist?"

At the time, Viv knew she was supposed to feel insulted. Or at least pretend she had no idea what her date was up to. But now she appreciated the moment.

She also remembered telling her girlfriends the following Monday about her father's overly protective attitude. *And that girl talk brings me back to my conversation with Bertha.*

She talks about everyone on board, the entire ship, all the passengers. I wonder if she has special girlfriends, maybe boyfriends too. Staff. People who would appreciate her stories about the passengers. Gossip bonded people, made them feel connected, Viv knew. *That doesn't mean any of it is true.*

To her surprise, Bertha rounded the corner. Apparently she'd changed her mind. "What about that cup of tea?"

"A tea sounds perfect." Viv realized she'd made her decision. *I may still get Bertha to talk about the guy in the gym. I'll push a little harder.*

Bertha weaved her way through the crowded corridor, waving her hand in the air as people called out. Just like in the dining room, her hand waved in a circular motion from the wrist. *She greets passersby like a queen of England.*

Viv followed in her wake right onto the elevator. "Press the button for the lido deck," Bertha prompted.

Viv followed orders. *It seems, without knowing, I've become the handmaiden to the Old Lady of the Sea. What would Rex say?*

When they exited the elevator, Viv made a right toward the coffee area.

"Oh no, let's go to the coffee bar in the gym," Bertha advised. "It will be less crowded this time of the evening." She thumped her cane for emphasis and then turned left.

Allowing herself to be directed, Viv had to admit that in this case, Bertha did know best. Only one other couple sat in the gym coffee area.

"Why don't you order me an herbal tisane and I'll get a table," Bertha said. She didn't wait for Viv to agree.

Viv didn't order right away. She took a moment to observe Tonya. The slope of her shoulders made Viv conclude, *She's too young to look so defeated.*

Viv understood how some women got caught in dead-end jobs and then had to rely upon a less than adequate wage. The demands of that job made searching for another job nearly impossible. They showed up for work, but their heart was somewhere else.

"What can I get for you?" Tonya asked in a curt tone.

"Miss Alcott would like an herbal tisane and I'd like a peppermint tea." Viv looked around. "You don't have a lot of business tonight," she observed.

"Never do on fancy dress evenings." Tonya pulled a glass container from off the shelf. She removed a tea bag, placing it in an empty mug. Then she turned to add steaming water from the spike of the industrial machine.

"Bertha likes a lavender mint blend with a touch of passion flower," she explained.

Viv watched the steam rise before speaking. "When I was here earlier, I meant to ask you something." She took a deep breath, reiterating what she saw in the gym. "I'm still waiting to hear about the man who fell from the elliptical."

Tonya turned to avoid Viv's stare. But not before Viv observed a micro expression of fear cross her face.

"Did I upset you—bringing it up again?" Viv asked.

Tonya turned back around, her face composed. "Not at all. I wasn't working at the time. So I don't know anything. You'll have to ask management."

It was the tone of Tonya's response that alerted Viv. The way she spoke in short sentences. The firm set of her jaw, how she nervously averted her eyes.

Viv shivered, apprehension creeping up her spine.

For the second time that evening, she thought of Rex.

I wish he were here. He'd know what to do.

28

REX REDONDO

Rex fidgeted. Finding the Old Lady of the Sea in his dressing room had been quite the shock. After the unprecedented performance with the fortune globe, he was a bit woozy.

He straightened one cuff of his white shirt, then tugged on the other. *Deep breaths, Rex,* he told himself. *And don't forget a pleasant smile.* Then he admitted, *I don't trust this old lady. She's everywhere all the time. Plus how did she get into my dressing room?*

"What a delightful surprise." He made every effort to sound convincing.

A smile played at her lips. She seemed pleased.

That was the bait, Rex told himself. *And here's the switch.* He lowered his voice. "How did you get into my room?"

Rex hoped his direct question might ruffle the old woman's feathers. He'd noticed the queen's wave and the thump of her cane as she made her way through public rooms. Upstairs or downstairs, this woman had aplomb. Very confident. And not necessarily in a good way.

He prided himself on his quick assessments of the female gender. Age didn't fool him one bit. No matter how old a person, their true personality showed through.

"Don't get smart with me." Ms. Alcott's smile vanished. "You know I have the full benefit of staff and passenger status. I have freedom to come and go anywhere I please. Now tell me, Rex Redondo, have you heard from your paramour?" Ms. Alcott glared, watching his reaction.

She reminded Rex of his third-grade school teacher, Sister Gwendolyn. She tried everything in her power, including her relationship with the Almighty, to provoke him into a confrontation. It was as if she despised his very nature.

His parents thought Catholic school might cure him of his attention-getting behavior. By second grade, he'd spent more time in the principal's office than in class. By fourth grade, he was back in public school, having failed to meet Sister G's high expectations. To his credit, his grades were excellent, top of his class.

The word paramour hit the intended mark. Rex felt his hand tingle, nearly crossing himself out of habit. His smile slipped, exposing his irritation. "If you're referring to Vivienne Rose," he said, "then you can call her my partner. We're partners. Actually neighbors."

"Except for one thing," the Old Lady of the Sea added. "Someone will tell you soon enough, so it might as well be me. In your absence, your so-called partner has been playing footsie with another neighbor. He's right next door. They share a veranda.

"Some women," Bertha continued, "have a certain penchant for men who cruise. Disgusting. At my age, I know a thing or two about free love. Back in my day we may have rabble-roused. The sex was a side dish, not the main course. Oh sure, some of us were partygoers, but the serious ones, like Bella, Gloria, Hillary. We knew our true purpose. It wasn't just for sex!" The distaste in her expression made Rex cringe.

Once he got ahold of himself, he shrugged. "Women have the right at any age to determine what they do with their bodies." He deliberately avoided saying Viv's name.

Ms. Alcott ignored Rex's declaration. "I see people on this cruise every day. It's so convenient. A little roll in the hay and off you go, back to your own stateroom. No muss, no fuss. No one need know. And there's no messy showering in someone else's domain. And then the week is over, and what happens on the cruise stays on the cruise." Her lips formed a straight line of disgust.

Rex wanted to reason with Ms. Alcott but knew it was out of the question. Plus he still felt terrible, his headache pounding in both temples with a vengeance.

That old lady is trouble, he concluded. *She's a fiery, opinionated gossip with a lot of access to staff and passengers.* He realized that he was on to something, but his head was so befuddled he didn't know exactly what.

If she'd not mentioned Viv I might have admired her. She's quite a confident and opinionated old... He cleared his throat.

"Who's to say I'm not having a bit of fun on the side myself? It's pretty easy living down here with staff. Just yesterday I found a naked woman in my bed. How's that for women's lib?"

As Ms. Alcott's eyes hardened, Rex wondered if she'd be just like Sister Gwendolyn and send him to the equivalent of the principal's office for his disobedience.

Her arms came up, folded across her chest, as she scowled.

I suspect that she's annoyed because I deflected her attack on Viv. And I ignored any comment about her name-dropping of legendary feminists.

I don't have to be psychic to see she's got some kind of ulterior motive for showing up in my dressing room that has nothing to do with Viv and the guy next door.

Keeping his face relaxed, he waited her out.

Despite not feeling well, Rex loved a good poker game. *Ms. Alcott came into my room thinking she had all the cards. Somehow I was able to ante up. Okay, Old Lady of the Sea. Show me what you've got.*

"I am not a feminist," she finally said.

Making her way across the room, she played her last card. "Maybe I'll have a word with your lady friend about your activities below deck. That should make for an interesting conversation over dinner."

Behind the closed door, Rex listened for the sound of her cane as she made her way down the corridor. One thump then another. Finally when he was convinced she'd left, he opened the door to peek out.

She's gone. Hopefully she was bluffing and not going to tell Viv what I said.

He closed the door and sat down in front of the dressing table mirror. He reached for the jar of cold cream. Smearing it on his skin, he stared at his face in the mirror. Itching caught him by surprise.

Scratching his skin with his nails, he felt frantic. *When will this stop?*

I can't think straight. Maybe the medication from the doc is making me worse. Rex stopped to remember what the man had told him. Then he corrected himself. *No, that's not right. I think he gave me that pill to stop the itching.*

These symptoms feel all over the place. Headache to cough. Then stuffed head to plugged ears. My skin on fire. And now I don't know which pill to take for what.

Rex glanced around the room and then turned his gaze back to the mirror.

He thought about Viv. Her smile, for one. Then his thoughts skipped to Cricket. How she entered his room despite the Do Not Disturb. And she was naked. "Boundaries," he shouted to the man in the mirror with a growl.

I hope no one's listening outside. They'll think I am insane. Am I?

I don't even like Cricket, he remembered. *But I'm beginning to wonder if I've been misdiagnosed. This has to be more than the sniffles.* He coughed into his elbow.

And now, as if my problems aren't complicated enough, I get that Alcott woman showing up in my dressing room uninvited. The sudden wave of self-pity caught him by surprise. He ducked his head in his arms to ward off tears.

Waiting for the feeling to pass, Rex lifted his head to take a swipe with a tissue at the makeup on his cheek. Then he remembered.

He removed the fortune globe from his pocket. Holding the globe toward the mirror, he stared into the glass. *This thing is more than a prop*, he concluded.

Once I'm feeling better, I could work the globe into my regular act. I used to love snow globes when I was a kid. He shook the sphere in his hands and watched the liquid shift. He held it to his forehead. After a minute he lowered the globe. To his surprise it turned cloudy and then black. He blinked. *What, another image?*

Not a new one but the second image that he'd managed to ignore on stage.

He'd not told the audience because he wasn't certain what to make of it. Plus he wasn't thinking clearly enough to interpret in that moment.

He saw a pair of panties. Just like the ones he'd found in his safe. But not just one pair, there were seven distinct panties, obviously a set. Each had similar lacy decorations. And each one had a day of the week. Monday through Thursday's letters stood out plainly. But Friday through Sunday were barely visible behind them.

Rex drew the fortune globe closer to his eyes. The image of the panties evaporated immediately. He placed the globe back on the dressing table, his fingers icy cold.

Then he closed his eyes, trying to recollect the pair in his safe.

Could I possibly have one of the set?

A giggle started at the back of his throat. He turned his head to cough, gasping for a breath.

You're really a mess, Redondo. Better get some sleep.

29

REX REDONDO

By the time Rex returned to his stateroom, it was nearly midnight. He stored the fortune globe in the safe, stripped out of his clothes and put on pajamas, and slid under the sheets. Pulling the comforter to his chin.

Despite his fatigue, Rex had trouble falling asleep. He opened his eyes when he heard a ping come from his phone. Reaching over, he pulled up his screen. Still nothing from Viv. Did I hear a ping or imagine it...

Rex put down his phone. *Something's not right.*Before he could figure out what to do, his eyes began to droop. He fell fast asleep, his phone upside down on his chest.

Rex rolled over on one side, forcing his eyes open. He raised his hand to pick up his phone. *I can't lift my arm. Too heavy. Too much trouble.* He groaned. *Just want to sleep.* His eyes fluttered closed again.

The skin on his belly itched him awake. Rex forced his eyes to stay open. Unable to lift his arm to scratch, he felt trapped. Then a click came from the stateroom door, followed by the sound of his wardrobe being slid open.

Heaving his body to a sitting position, he lost his balance and fell back onto the pillow. He tried to form a question on his lips, but he coughed instead.

His eyes fluttered closed as he drifted back to sleep.

30

VIVIENNE ROSE

"Tonya's having a difficult night," Viv told Bertha Alcott. Holding the cup of tea by the handle, she took a sip.

"Oh, Tonya often has difficult nights. She's been known to get quite bored and then make a fool of herself." Bertha sounded like a disgruntled mother.

"You seem to know her quite well," Viv said.

"She's a staff person that I've come into contact with on a frequent basis." Bertha lifted her teacup for a sip. "But you don't need to know about any of that. I'd like to hear more about our previous conversation. The one concerning that mentalist. He's obviously a ladies' man."

Viv felt her stomach clench. *Everyone's so chatty on these cruises. I could say anything about myself, and then the ship docks and off you go, never to see the same people again.*

The truth isn't a priority when traveling the open sea, she decided. "Rex is a good person at heart," she said firmly. "And he's an excellent neighbor. You would love his dog, Kevin." Before Bertha could object, She began a story about walking in the morning with Rex and Kevin, just to avoid any more personal questions.

By the time she finished telling the story of Kevin running through the golf course and disrupting everyone's game, Bertha pushed back her chair and reached for her cane. "That's nice. But I have to go now. Maybe we'll catch up later."

It worked, thought Viv. *Bertha has no time for anyone else's stories but her own.* Viv felt slightly guilty as she watched the older woman make slow progress toward the door. *But at least I defended Rex,* she stoutly reminded herself.

Out of habit she glanced at her phone to see if she had any messages. Only to sigh and click the screen closed. *I know we're in the middle of the ocean, but it would be nice to know the time. I didn't bring a watch. I bet I'm late for Rex's show.* She quickly rose.

Picking up her empty cup along with Bertha's, she placed them at the end of the counter. "See you tomorrow," she called to Tonya.

"You don't have to do that," Tonya replied. "I'm supposed to pick up and clean all the tables."

"I know," Viv responded. "I clean up after myself out of habit—can't get used to all of this service. It makes me uncomfortable."

"I see." Tonya's tone was skeptical, but the look on her face convinced Viv of the opposite. *Tonya doesn't see at all.*

The elevator door slid open.

"There's room for one more." Sandi edged her way backward to make space. Viv stood next to her as Sandi continued to speak.

"Daddy and I hope to get called to the stage again," she told her.

"That would be fun," Viv answered in a noncommittal tone.

The door slid open; Viv was the first to step into the bustling lobby.

To her relief Sandi made a beeline straight toward another person, leaving her to find her own way.

Sitting in the back row, Viv admired the theater. As people in the audience murmured, she nervously glanced at her phone again. Tucking it back in her purse, she looked around.

The loudspeaker background music faded away to the voice of the announcer. "Ladies and gentleman, Rex Redondo!"

From the way he came on stage, Viv knew something wasn't quite right. He nervously blinked and absentmindedly rubbed his right palm over his left sleeve. She let go of her concerns as Rex began to speak. Feeling herself begin to smile at the sound of his modulated and deep tone.

Like everyone else in the audience, she was mesmerized by his confidence. The way he spoke to the audience as if they were all his best friends. And then his self-deprecating humor and how he chuckled at himself.

Viv loved the part when Rex fed the poodles a treat. It wasn't until he reached into his pocket and dramatically pulled out a globe that she realized he was trying something new.

I don't think I've ever seen him use a prop before. I suppose he had to do something. With my dud cell, I can't get him the information he needs, so he's improvising. But where did he get that thing? I mean, is it even real?

"Excuse me, excuse me." Sandi stood in the aisle. When she caught sight of Viv, she moved past the knees of people in the row to come sit in the vacant seat next to hers. "I got stuck talking to Robert Redford," she whispered in Viv's ear. "He's supposed to be arranging for Daddy's memorial tomorrow and he's dropped the ball. I asked for catering weeks in advance, and now he claims he never read the email." She shoved the wooden box under her seat, kicking it with the heel of her foot.

Viv suppressed a giggle. "You can tell me all about it later," she whispered. "I don't want to interrupt the show."

Sandi stopped talking, settling back in her seat.

Viv watched Rex as he lifted the ball over his head to show the audience. She felt her stomach clench. *There's something kind of eerie about that ball. The way the lights play off of it and how clear the liquid looks, even from here. Wait a minute...*

Even from her seat at the back of the auditorium, Viv could see a white cloud begin to swirl inside the globe. As the audience grew quieter, she realized she wasn't the only one.

Rex's voice dropped away as silence overtook the room.

Up until that point, Rex had convinced Viv that he was not one of those people with magical skills. In fact, since they first met, she'd heard him, on a number of occasions, play down the whole mentalist label. Especially to anyone who thought he might be psychic. In a private moment he admitted to Viv that he could see pictures behind his eyes. "But that's different than being psychic," he'd assured her.

According to him, the images in his mind required inter-pretation. Which is why he'd made many mistakes over the years, thinking they meant one thing when they actually meant another.

• • •

Focusing on the performance, Viv watched as Rex raised the globe to his forehead. Within seconds the inner essence inside the globe began to spin faster and faster. The liquid gathered momentum, turning white. Her mind whirled too as she thought back to Rex's insistence that he wasn't a psychic.

Maybe he doesn't want people to realize the extent of his powers. She shuddered with anticipation, watching the man and the globe intently.

The liquid essence swirled, losing the white opaqueness, turning into a dark gray mass. Finally he drew the globe closer, breaking the silence with an unfamiliar voice she'd not heard him use before. The tone sounded lower and very deliberate. The best word she could use to describe Rex's tone was otherworldly.

"The fortune globe has something for us tonight, ladies and gentlemen. Just look right here." He held it above his head again as the lights from above followed.

Rays from the spotlights bounced off the crystal, shooting sparks of light toward the ceiling. Heads from the audience tilted backward to get a better view.

To Viv, it looked like a meteor shower. One she might see in the night sky from her backyard.

After the last round of applause, the lights in the auditorium came up. People began to make their way up the main aisle. Sandi leaned closer. "Gosh, he's really something."

Viv moved her knees back to let people get past. "He's good," she agreed.

As Sandi reached under her seat for Daddy, Viv suggested, "Let's sit here for a minute. Let everyone else go first."

"Sure, I don't mind." She hugged Daddy to her chest, then put the box down in the empty seat next to her. "You're coming, right? To his memorial."

Viv responded immediately. "Yes, I plan on coming. I've never been to a burial at sea."

"I've been to several, and I know you'll love the captain," Sandi said.

"I've only heard him on the loudspeaker," Viv admitted. She paused for a moment and then launched into her plan. "Will you be inviting Rex Redondo to the memorial? I'm sure after that first show that he'd be glad to attend."

Sandi's lips curved slightly. "I got his room number and left a message on that phone."

"Did it go through?" Viv felt slightly miffed. Only because everyone could text and talk to Rex but her.

"He didn't respond," admitted Sandi. "But then he's not supposed to—what's the word?—fraternize with the passengers."

"So you don't know if he's coming..."

"I'm going to ask someone to take him a message," Sandi said. "Now that you think it's a good idea, I'll make it happen."

"Oh, I do think it's a good idea," she assured her.

Once the crowd shuffled past, Viv stood. "I think we can go now." She made her way toward the aisle as Sandi followed. "You forgot Daddy." She pointed to Sandi's arms.

"He'll be so mad at me!" Sandi scooted her way back to the place they were sitting to retrieve the wooden box.

Later she bid Sandi goodnight in the lobby. Then Viv made her way down the corridor to her stateroom. She opened the door and sighed. A soft light illuminated her pillows; the bed had been turned down. A mint lay on her pillow.

A fluffy bathrobe rested at the end of the bed, along with her nightgown and slippers. A note had been placed on top of the bathrobe:

"We hope your stay has been enjoyable aboard *The Legend of the Sea*. Please let us know if there's anything we can do to make your voyage even more pleasurable on the last full day of our cruise. If you go online to the gift shop, you'll find a twenty percent discount coupon that can be used in any of our luxurious shops. Mahalo from all of your staff. It's been a pleasure to serve you."

Underneath the message someone had signed, Cricket.

Ready for bed, Viv slipped into the cool sheets. *I like the turndown service*, she thought. *Of all the luxuries, that's my favorite. I wish someone did this for me at home.* She pulled the comforter up under her chin as her eyes began to flutter closed.

31

VIVIENNE ROSE

The next morning, Viv dressed in her swimsuit with the flowing cover-up. She remembered how excited she was to purchase both items before her cruise. Her friend Jason Knew, the owner and proprietor of Out of the Closet Consignments, had helped.

"Viv, darling, you'll look sensational in this one-piece. The cobalt blue will shimmer underneath the white gauze of the cover-up, giving a hint of seduction. You are going with Rex, right?"

At the time, she'd assured Jason that she was traveling with Rex and that the ensemble he'd chosen was perfect.

"Will you be sealing the deal on this cruise?" Jason asked, his tongue in his cheek as he wrapped up her purchase.

"That's a bit personal, even for you," Viv retorted.

"You have no idea how important I am to your love life. Those who dress others keep their fingers on the pulse of each customer and their lives. I know you're ready, and I'm the man to keep the silver fox interested. Just look at these."

He'd crossed the store to pull up a pair of lace underwear with a matching bra.

Viv shook her head. "I don't think I'm there yet. It's been years since any man has been close enough to observe my underwear."

"You'll get there. Mark my words." Jason smiled. "And don't forget, your man has earned the title of silver fox. He's certainly an appreciator of ladies' undergarments."

On the cruise, having walked through all of the over-priced shops, Viv missed Jason and the familiar feeling of stepping into her favorite boutique. No matter how interesting the shops were on board, she had to admit she preferred the familiar. Glancing around her stateroom, her eyes fell on her straw hat, another of Jason's ideas. *I'll come back after breakfast to pick it up.*

One more day and I'll be back on land, Viv mused to herself. In the corridor, she glided into the throng of passengers like a minnow swimming upstream toward the elevator lobby.

The dining room buzzed as people stood in lines ordering their breakfast. In just a few days, Viv knew the routine. *Get a table first; food comes afterward.* She walked slowly around the dining area, eyeing people and their tables.

Seeing one man preparing to leave, she hovered close by. Then a waiter came and refilled his coffee, so he sat down again. *Everyone appears to be lingering over their meal this morning, getting their money's worth of food and service.*

Get that one! She hurried toward an empty table for two in the corner. By the time she reached her destination, a staff person held out a chair. "Would you like coffee and water?" he asked politely.

Slightly out of breath, Viv sat down. "I would like both," she told him. She left her napkin on the table, the cruise ship cultural sign that someone would be returning.

When Viv got back to her table with fruit and an English muffin, her coffee had been poured. Even the water glass contained fresh ice. She sat down and began to butter her English muffin, reflecting on her conversation with Bertha the night before.

Was the Old Lady of the Sea buttering me up to get information about Rex? Not so unusual. A lot of women, no matter what their age, seem interested in him. Even Jason liked to bring Rex into their conversations, she realized.

But the thing that stuck in Viv's mind, as she smeared strawberry jam over the butter on her English muffin, was that Bertha's previous interest may have waned.

In fact, she changed the subject and they never got back to discussing what happened. "Ouch!" Viv held her mouth open. She'd bitten her tongue along with the English muffin. Easing a piece of ice from the water into her mouth, she held it against her tongue for relief.

Bertha didn't just deflect my concerns, she told me that they threw bodies overboard all the time. She implied it may be a common practice.

Lowering her glass, Viv took a bite of her English muffin, still ruminating about the conversation. *Okay, so no one on this cruise, including the Old Lady of the Sea, wants to hear about what I saw.*

Just like that old woman in one of the Agatha Christie books made into a movie. What was the title again...

I remember! What Mrs. McGillicuddy Saw. *That's the name of the movie with Miss Marple. She was the only one to listen, one older woman to the other. Then she tracked down the murderer. I need Miss Marple,* Viv thought, lifting a slice of pineapple to her lips.

I only have one more day to get the bottom of why that man fell off of his elliptical and what happened to him afterward. And I refuse to leave this ship—I won't find myself trotting down the gangplank, packing a list of lies and unresolved circumstances along as a souvenir. Wiping her sticky fingers on the napkin, she knew what she had to do.

Viv pushed back her chair and stood. Making her way to the server station, she tapped the elbow of the man who'd brought her coffee and water. "Excuse me." She gave him a chance to turn around. "Thank you for the coffee. Have a good day." She looked at his name badge. "Have a good day, Juan," she repeated.

His look of surprise made her smile. "You too, miss. Have a good day," he said in a slightly mystified voice.

Viv stopped at the handwashing station near the exit. Soaping each finger carefully, she came up with a new plan. *I'm going to track down Robert Redford. And I'm going to stick to him until he tells me what happened to that guy in the gym.* She dried her hands under the stream of hot air and then marched away.

Only three people stood in line at the IT desk. *There must be back offices through that doorway,* she assumed. *And there's a camera right in the corner that can pick up people coming and going.*

"We want to speak to your manager," demanded a man at the counter. "My phone hasn't worked since we left the shore. My wife has a strong connection, but I don't. I can't text her, and that makes her mad. Plus I can't even access the cruise website." Viv noted the shade of red creeping up the back of his neck.

Allison Thompson shook her head, adding a stern voice. "Sir, we'd appreciate you keeping your voice down. Give me a minute." Allison lifted her phone to her ear. "Mr. Redford, there's a passenger who wishes to speak to you. Right now."

Robert Redford came from the back, walking briskly toward the counter. "Please come this way," he invited the man. They both disappeared down the hallway.

"May I help who's next?" Allison's voice chirped. The man in front of Viv stepped closer. After a ten-minute exchange, he huffed his way past Viv, carrying his phone and what looked like Aloha cruise coupons.

One look at Viv and Allison Thompson spun around to disappear down the hallway. Another employee took her place. Viv steeled herself as she stepped to the counter. "I'd also like to speak to Mr. Redford," she announced in a firm voice.

"Maybe I can solve your issue first," Dylan replied.

"This is my fourth time at this counter. My phone still isn't connected to Wi-Fi. And if something isn't done, I may have to stand on the pier in Honolulu and write up a scathing review of the cruise line."

The people standing behind her in line stopped talking. The employee's face grew pale. They picked up a phone to speak in a nervous voice. "Could you come to the front desk?"

Robert Redford returned with a grim look on his face. Pushing the employee aside, he reached across the counter. "I'm Robert Redford—no relation—the ship's customer service coordinator. How can I help?"

"We've already done the introductions," Viv replied. "Days ago, as a matter of fact."

Redford stared into her face before a look of recognition dawned. "Of course. Ms. Vivienne Rose. Why don't you step back into my office and we'll find a solution to your problem."

Viv followed as Redford escorted her behind the desk. Holding open the door to the last office at the end of the corridor, he said, "Have a seat."

Viv took note of the photos on the wall beside her chair. Most showed Redford shaking hands with men in uniform with stripes on their sleeves.

"Which one is the captain of this cruise ship?" Viv asked.

"Oh, Captain Barclay isn't in any of those photos. He's a bit new to the line. This is his first cruise with Aloha. He gave his notice to Mardi Gras Cruise Lines and came to us with glowing recommendations."

Viv had heard of that line. Known as party ships, where single people drank all day and made their way from one bed to the next.

"Captain Barclay," she repeated, making a point to sound like she cared.

"He's already made an impact, getting us back to a ship-shape routine," Redford assured her. "Barclay is a stickler for rules. Now what exactly is wrong with your phone?"

"Like I've been saying for days, my cell won't connect to the Wi-Fi," Viv quickly explained. "But that's not why I'm here. I have another problem I want solved. I used my cell as a ruse."

"Oh really..." Redford's right eye twitched.

Viv continued, "The man who fell off that elliptical in the gym—is he alive or dead? And don't try to put me off this time. I want an answer."

Redford began nervously pushing a pen around his

desk. His cheeks were flushed. When he refused to give her eye contact, Viv knew she'd gotten his attention.

Finally he looked up. "Are you sure you want to disrupt the last day of your cruise with what you think you saw? I know you're sad that Mr. Redondo took the job and left you alone. But a man falling from an elliptical? Honestly, that's just crazy talk. But then," he continued, shaking his head sadly, "it's not that uncommon for a woman of your age to think she's seeing things."

Just like Mrs. McGillicuddy, she thought. She ran her tongue over the sore spot, gathering her indignation, her mind shifting to another one of her favorite late-night movies. "I don't like being told that I didn't see what I actually saw. Right now, you're reminding me of my ex-husband. Have you seen that film with Charles Boyer and Ingrid Bergman? Directed by the late and great George Cukor. It's fabulous, by the way. Of course only women of my age would know such a film."

She gave him a moment and then kept talking. "*Gaslight* is the film. Are you familiar with the term? It's one arrow in the quiver of all good manipulators. Politicians and corporations think they can manipulate anyone and everyone into believing they are the problem.

"Gaslighters pretend something didn't happen when they know full well it did. So let me make myself clear: your condescending manner won't work with me. I saw a man fall off an elliptical in the gym. I'm not crazy or lonely or overwrought. I'm just mad."

Redford glared at Viv, his face turning bright red. Then he scowled.

Viv knew her speech was as much for her as it was for him. But she prided herself on her good manners and knew this wasn't the time to appear superior. Not if she wanted answers.

So she kept calm, making her face appear pleasant instead of vitriolic. She'd learned to do this over the years, every time she had to put a man in his place.

Then to her surprise, as her adversary squirmed, she felt better and better. This sense of confidence gave rise to an odd thought. She'd be the first to admit Laurence was an excellent provider. It took her years to realize that he was also an emotional abuser. Oh sure, she'd stood up to him the best she could, but the constant defensiveness had taken its toll, distancing her from her own feelings.

It had just been lately, after her doula agency went belly-up, that she was able to realize how the emotional barriers she'd built in her marriage had impacted her other relationships, including the one with herself.

Redford glanced over her head toward the door. Then his gaze came back to meet hers. "I see I can't persuade you to let this go. So okay. I'll admit it. You saw a man fall off the elliptical in the gym. Happy now?"

32

REX REDONDO

Rex awoke feeling hands on his body. He felt himself being turned over in his bed. A gravelly voiced man issued instructions. "Prop his head. Lift the sheet higher." Rex tugged to release his arm, but two hands held him with a firm grasp. *Too bad I can't open my eyes.* He felt himself drifting back to sleep, then awoke with a start.

I'm really thirsty.

He wasn't sure he'd spoken aloud, so he tried to shout, but the words got caught in his throat.

"Settle down, buddy. We're taking you to sick bay. Looks like you're dehydrated. Good thing your steward popped in when she did."

"I'm fine," his voice slurred.

"You're obviously not fine," came a tart reply.

I know who that is. Just give me a minute.

Cricket's voice continued, a softer tone this time. "Don't worry about a thing, Rexie. A couple of days in sick bay and the doc will fix you right up. Just lie back. We'll make the transfer to the gurney and off we'll go."

Rex shuddered. *Rexie. Really? This feels like one of*

those creepy hospital movies. What was that one with Big Nurse? One Flew Over the Cuckoo's Nest. *The next thing you know they'll whip out the straitjacket and shove pills down my throat.* He tried to roll away from the man with the strong arms.

To his disappointment, expert hands rolled his body right onto the waiting gurney. "Thanks for helping," the rough-voiced man said.

Wheels bumped against the carpet in the corridor. By the time the elevator door swished open, Rex was unconscious.

He awoke to a tingling on his arm. *Where am I?*

Patting the bed next to him, he winced. He turned his head and opened his eyes. An intravenous needle had been inserted into a vein on the back of his hand. He glanced farther. *Another bed with someone in it,* he thought. "Hey buddy," he called out.

No one answered.

Rex blinked, realizing the body had not moved. *Maybe he didn't hear me...* The face had been covered with an oxygen mask. The body had an IV in one arm.

Feeling weak, Rex's head fell back into the pillow. He closed his eyes. *That's pretty nice. Quite soothing. Maybe I'll take a nap.*

Drifting in and out of consciousness, Rex attempted to open his eyes again. *Too much trouble,* he decided, closing them. He felt someone touch the needle on his hand. They adjusted something and then quietly left. *Open your eyes, Rex old buddy,* he coached himself. But then he fell back to sleep.

Finally he coughed at the back of his throat. *I'm thirsty,* he remembered. But even the thought of calling for water made him exhausted.

The next time he awakened, he saw man adjusting the IV apparatus through half closed eyes.

They're trying to hydrate me, he thought. *That's okay.*

The man moved to the other side of the bed. He took Rex's wrist to check his pulse. Then he left the room, without speaking.

Rex yawned and closed his eyes.

The next time the door creaked open, Rex reconsidered. *I don't know where I am or if I'm being held against my will.* He deliberately kept his eyes shut, conserving his energy to listen instead.

Two people stood in the room, both at the foot of the other person's bed. "Still on a respirator," came the comment.

"We can keep him until we reach Pearl Harbor. Then do what's necessary." The doc had a distinct tone to his voice that Rex recognized.

"At least he'll be off our hands then," Robert Redford replied.

Rex inhaled deeply as the two men walked past his bed toward the door.

Feeling more alert, he considered his options. *I think they're mostly worried about the person in the other bed. But "do what's necessary..." That has an ominous ring.*

The pump squished in, then out as the person in the other bed lay quietly. Rex closed his eyes. But this time he didn't fall back to sleep.

I think someone said I'm dehydrated. The IV is helping. It all started with a cold. Maybe the flu. Possibly norovirus. Depending on how long I've been asleep, I should feel much better in a bit.

Rex felt a shudder, wondering about his roommate. He slid his arm out from under the sheet and wiggled his fingers. *I am getting some strength back,* he thought. *But can I get out of bed on my own?*

Nah. Not yet. Have a nap and figure this out later. His eyes closed.

Rex woke with his head pounding. Rolling to his side to check on his roommate, he blinked. The body was gone and the respirator had been removed. The bed, stripped of sheets and the spread, revealed a mattress with a white quilted cover.

The door opened as he quickly closed his eyes, pretending to be asleep.

"Okay, one down and one to go," came the voice of the doc.

"At least we got the one guy to the lifeboat," Redford added.

Rex felt confused. Why would they be transferring a sick guy to a lifeboat?

Wait a minute. Lifeboats are for emergencies—if the ship is taking on water, for example. Everyone musters on the promenade deck. That doesn't make sense.

He waited for the men to talk about him. When they didn't, he felt relief. Then the door closed, leaving him alone.

Tucking his arm under his torso, he rolled to one side. After dropping his feet to the floor, he used one hand against the mattress for leverage.

He felt a tug on the IV. Looking up, he saw that the bag was nearly empty.

Rex tried to stand up. Balancing with both hands on the

mattress, he rose to both feet. He wobbled but managed to keep his balance.

The needle in his arm pulled against his skin. He reached for the pole to bring it closer. *I have to get out of here and find Viv. Who knows what these people are up to. I trust her. She'll make sense of what's happening...*

Rex gripped the table next to his bed for support. He closed his eyes to make the room stop spinning. *I have to get this needle out of my hand.* After a moment he inched his fingers to the needle to gently grasp it. Then he tugged. *Gently now*, he reminded himself.

The needle came easily, some blood oozing from the vein. He dabbed it with his hospital gown sleeve. Once the blood stopped seeping, he'd come up with a plan.

Rex took tentative steps toward the door. His feet were bare and there was a draft from the open gown, which flapped around his naked body. He reached behind to close the gap. With his free hand, he touched the doorknob. *At least I'm not locked in.* He stuck his head outside. *No one coming*, he concluded.

He stepped into the corridor, realizing, *This isn't in staff territory. I'm on the passenger side.* His plan fell apart. Forcing his backside against the wall, he closed his eyes to ward off dizziness.

A minute later he scanned the corridor. *Toilet. That's my next stop.* Rex clutched his gown in the back with one hand. He shuffled his feet across the thin carpet, edging his way toward forward. *Unoccupied. That's good.* He pushed the door open and stepped inside.

The door closed from behind. He jiggled the door handle to make sure it was locked. Rex reached to steady himself, one hand on the counter. His knees began to tremble as he collapsed to the floor. "So cold," he murmured aloud.

Sure could use a pair of pants right now.

Minutes later he was ready to make a personal assessment.

Rex old boy, you're obviously not well. And you get dizzy when you hurry. And you've locked yourself in a toilet. Oh, and you've gone Winnie the Pooh with no pants.

And in case you haven't noticed...

He opened his eyes.

You're not wearing any shoes.

33

REX REDONDO

A pounding on the toilet door brought his head up. He leaned back on the wall to shove himself to standing position. "Occupied," he called out. The pounding stopped.

Rex glanced toward the pristine countertop. Next to the sink were two soap dispensers and a basket of freshly laundered hand towels. He braced himself against the wall to stand.

With each hand on either side of the sink, he stared. The reflection in the mirror gave him a start. *You look awful,* was his first thought. And then, when he was able to look past his own face, he felt a surge of hope. *There are two doors in this bathroom. The one's covered with wallpaper, but it could be an exit. Maybe a hidden corridor. Look at that handle. That's has to be my way out of here. Can't hurt to try.*

Rex opened the door slowly. He could hear the sound of a hair dryer whooshing in the background. There was also a low mumbling of people conversing. He sniffed. Nail lacquer. *Maybe this is the restroom for the spa and salon.*

With one hand behind his back, he held his gown together, stepping farther into the hallway. *I'm alone so far.*

He followed the corridor and suddenly stopped at the sound of voices.

Leaning his back against the wall, he nodded as two women walked past. Both wore white aprons with a spa logo and identification badges. Instead of hunching over, Rex stood tall. He drew back his shoulders and offered the two women a huge smile. "Ladies," he said with confidence.

It wasn't until they rounded the corner that one called out, "The massage robes are available in the men's dressing room."

That was a close one. He grabbed the back of his gown.

Once inside the men's dressing room he heaved a sigh of relief. Two other men stood in front of the bank of lockers, removing their clothing and shoes. Spa bathrobes hung on hooks nearby. When the men didn't look up, Rex breathed a sigh of relief.

He turned to look for another bathrobe. Several had been folded and left in a stack on the counter. He grabbed the one on top just as the two men headed toward the sauna.

Dropping his gown to the floor, Rex slid on the robe and cinched the waist. *Now that's much better. A man in a spa shouldn't draw any attention. Just a guy waiting for a massage or a shower or a pedicure.*

He bent and picked up his gown and deposited it in a nearby hamper.

Rex turned his back as an employee entered the locker room.

Before the man could ask any questions, he announced, "No slippers."

"Sometimes they forget to put them inside the lockers. Let me get you a pair."

A minute later he handed over the slippers to Rex. "Put

them on. Then when you're finished with your appointment, you can leave them here or take them to your room." He pointed to a wicker basket and then asked, "Do you need me to check on your massage therapist? What's your name?" He held up his tablet, waiting for Rex to reply.

"I'm early. Going to take a sauna first. But thanks." Feet nestled into the slippers he walked quickly away. Exiting the locker room he flung his shoulders back. *Okay, I'm wearing a bathrobe and slippers. Just pretend you're the emperor, Rex. Own it.*

He held his chin at an angle and slapped a smile on his face, exiting the spa to circle the pool and make a beeline into the gym.

Eyes fixed on the coffee bar, he lengthened his stride, hoping to look more confident than he felt.

Several people stopped talking to stare. And then a rule-following woman called out, "You need to change before you leave the spa."

Don't stop, he told himself, heading straight toward Tonya, who was trying not to laugh.

"I'm such an ass," he said, sitting on an empty stool. Leaning forward, he added in his most confiding voice, "I left my key somewhere and my clothes are still in my locker. I don't suppose there's any chance you could whip me up a double latte. I'll be very quiet pretending to be a passenger until I sort this out."

"I can do that," Tonya assured him, clearly in a better mood today. "By the way, you wouldn't be the first guy to make this mistake. I turn at least three men a day back to the locker room. A double, you say?"

She made the coffee, then slid it toward him. "Watch out, it's hot." She watched as he took a sip. "I have an idea," Tonya said. "Why don't you call downstairs? Menswear will bring whatever you want. They won't be able to free your clothes until later. Plus you won't need to look so awkward on the way back to your room."

Rex frowned. "I don't have my cell or my wallet."

"Oh, no problem. You can use the bar phone. And give them your room number. That should work."

"Do I get an employee discount?" Rex teased.

"Not unless you have a coupon." Tonya smiled.

"Hand over the phone," he told her. "You make a fantastic latte and you're helping out a man in need."

She handed the receiver to Rex and hit a few buttons on the phone.

"Anchors Away Gift Shop. May I help you?" came the voice on the other end.

"I want a pair of black athleisure pants, the most expensive you've got. And one of those Aloha shirts, not too gaudy, size large. Then throw in a pair of size ten flip-flops. Right. Money is no object. You can put those on my bill. Room 561. That's right. Vivienne Rose. Her credit card."

As Tonya walked to the other end of the counter to serve another customer, Rex realized, *I'm feeling a bit better. Not dizzy and not itchy.* He ran his hand over his forearm. *At least not as itchy...*

And then a woman with a square face and sizable arm muscles made her way toward him. She was dressed in the all-white uniform of the spa. "Mr. Abernathy. We have an opening a bit early for that massage. Come this way." She looked Rex up and down as he stood.

"He's not Mr. Abernathy," Tonya began to explain.

Rex held up his hand. "No, no. Don't worry. I've got this. Would you have them bring my new clothes to the spa? I didn't give them my name, but you can leave them in room..." He glanced at the woman still waiting.

"You'll be in room ten with Ginger," she replied in an efficient tone.

Rex winked at Tonya. "I can't keep Ginger waiting. Thanks for your help."

He walked alongside the other woman without glancing back.

34

VIVIENNE ROSE

Still seated, Viv fumed at Redford. *He thinks any of this has made me happy...*

"Not quite," she tartly responded. "Besides observing the man falling and then magically disappearing, I also want to speak to Rex Redondo. The Wi-Fi excuse has gone far enough."

"You only have another day," Redford muttered. "Then you can both resume your holiday in Waikiki. We'll comp you a night at the Hilton Resort."

"You'll comp us more than that," Viv retorted. "You'll give me answers right now."

"You ladies take things way too personally. And you're overly sensitive. We really do keep passengers and staff separate," Redford said. "It's a very firm policy of Aloha Cruises. So if you can just wait one more day..."

Too sensitive... I've heard that before.

"Tell me about the body." Viv realized if she got triggered by Redford, albeit for a good reason, she'd only play into his excuses. And then the ship would dock and she'd never find out what happened.

She waited, and finally Redford broke the silence.

"Why don't we do it this way." Redford had shifted to a lofty I'm-the-boss tone. "I'll get the captain's approval first. He needs to sign off before I share any information with a passenger about another passenger. It's company policy."

Viv's jaw tightened.

Having failed to appeased her, he doubled down. "I don't have to explain anything more to you. Isn't it enough that I admit what you saw and to say we're handling it? Why do you need to know more?"

She used a measured voice to explain. "I care because you dismissed me and then covered up what happened. That made me suspicious that you're trying to hide something. At the very least a police report must be filed." Viv stood.

"It happened on the high seas," Redford objected. "We handled the situation according to protocol. A report has been filed."

This time Viv pretended she wasn't listening. Door open, she turned. "I expect you to let me know about the man as soon as you talk to the captain. In the meanwhile, I'm going back to my stateroom to compose a scathing review of Aloha Cruise Lines. To be posted as soon as my pink manicured toes hit the sands of Waikiki."

She made her exit without further explanation. In the corridor she heard voices from around the corner. She stopped in her tracks.

"Did you get the body bag?" A man asked.

"Yes, sir. And what was left in his room. Everything's together."

"We'll do it tonight then. Heave ho. That's an order."

Viv blinked. The words body bag stuck in her head.

Could Bertha be right? Are they pitching someone overboard to get rid of evidence? Is that the man I saw and is he dead?

Viv hurried around the corner, hoping to catch sight of the two people she'd heard. The sound of a door closing at the far end of the hall made her frown. A tingle of nerves traveled up her spine. *I need to get back to my stateroom. If I'm caught eavesdropping, who knows what they'll do to keep me quiet.*

For the first time she realized, *I might be in real trouble. Especially if they have a body bag in my size...*

Viv opened the door to her room. She'd found her way onto the crowded elevator, keeping her nerves under wraps. And now the sight of her freshly made bed and an elephant made out of towels made her smile.

So cute.

Inspecting the elephant more closely, Viv looked up when a knock came to the door. "Yes?"

A steward poked her head inside. "Anything I can get you?"

"A pot of tea would be nice," Viv said. "I'll be out on the balcony. Just let yourself back in. And thank you for the elephant!" She smiled as the young woman nodded before she shut the door.

Half an hour later the employee arrived with a tray. She poured a cup of tea for Viv and then unfolded a cloth napkin to place on her lap.

"That's not necessary." Viv grabbed the napkin midair. "And thank you again."

The steward looked nervously away before asking, "You're the mentalist's lady companion, right?"

Viv settled the napkin on her lap before responding.

"Yes, I am. He was supposed to be staying over there." She pointed to the veranda next door. "But he took the job because your staff mentalist didn't show up for work."

The young woman cleared her throat. "I thought you might like to know that your friend has been taken to sick bay. He's been feeling poorly, and then I found him nearly unconscious in his stateroom."

Viv put her cup down with a clatter.

"What's wrong with him, Cricket?" She used the name displayed on the woman's badge. "What happened to Rex? He never gets sick."

"He's been dizzy and congested mostly. Off his food. Then he got dehydrated. Mr. Redford took him to see the doctor on board."

Viv's stomach churned. What she'd overheard about the body bag seemed even more ominous now.

Cricket kept talking. "But I can take you to him. I'm sure he'd feel better if he saw you."

Viv didn't hesitate. Her napkin dropped to the deck as she stood. "I would really appreciate that."

"Why don't you put on some other clothes so you won't look out of place," Cricket said.

Once Viv had changed into her black jeans and shirt, she picked up her purse and followed Cricket into the hallway.

Waiting for the elevator, Cricket turned to face Viv. "Take the passenger elevator to the lido deck. I'll meet you in front of the gym. Then we'll go from there." Cricket disappeared around the corner before Viv could ask any more questions.

She stepped inside the elevator, her nerves tingling with excitement.

Glancing at the woman standing next to her, Viv

noticed she held a bundle of neatly stacked clothing in one hand. A pair of flip-flops with a tag made Viv's eyes grow round. She recognized the brand. *Size ten and a whopping three hundred dollars. Someone has expensive taste.*

"Do you deliver from the shops?" she asked.

"On the last day, we take orders on the phone and deliver. Some fancy guy. He wants them dropped off at the gym." She clutched the stack to her chest.

When the elevator opened, Viv walked out first. Steam from the indoor pool hit her face. The disinfectant mingled with the distinctive spa scent, giving rise to a sneeze.

A few people had gathered at the small round tables holding cocktail glasses. But no sign of Cricket.

Viv moved closer to the bar, leaning on the side as she continued to scan the room. She felt a tap on her shoulder from behind.

"Good, you're here. Come this way." Cricket gestured with her head.

The gym was alive with activity, all of the machines in use. They made it past the coffee bar, and then Cricket took a quick turn down a corridor. To Viv's surprise they didn't get on the staff elevator. They stopped outside stateroom 717, still on the passenger side.

Slapping her key card on the pad, she explained, "He's in here."

They entered, and Viv heard the door close behind her as Cricket flicked on the overhead lights.

Two beds stood side by side. One had been stripped, only a mattress pad remaining. The sheets on the other bed were wadded into a bundle. Viv shuddered when she saw drips of blood along the floor, next to an IV pole.

"He's supposed to be here," Cricket said. "I left him only a bit ago."

Viv felt lightheaded. She reached with her hand to steady herself against the wall. "So where have they taken him?" She glared at Cricket.

"I have no idea where Rexie has gone. I thought he was doing better, but now..."

Viv dropped her hand. "He's obviously been taken somewhere."

"We could check the morgue," Cricket suggested in a quiet voice.

Viv's eyes blazed. "If you've hurt one hair on that man's head, you will pay."

"I-I just work here," Cricket stammered, holding up her hands in protest.

"I want to see the morgue," Viv demanded.

Standing back in the corridor, Cricket spoke under her breath. "I'm not supposed to talk about it. But people die on cruises. More often than you'd think. Especially if there's a virus going around. It's not our fault!" she added loudly. "Passengers usually bring the viruses on themselves and then pass it around despite our hygiene checks and measures."

Fear clutched at her heart. Viv didn't want to hear any more excuses.

Cricket continued, "The company keeps all the bodies nice and cold until we get into port. Then authorities come aboard and take over, contact relatives, stuff like that."

"Take me to the morgue," Viv said. "I want to see if Rex is there."

Cricket pointed to the right. "The morgue is on staff side. Next to the kitchen. They use the same refrigerator installation. I could get into real trouble." She paused. "But if we go that way," she pointed in the opposite direction, "we might not be seen."

Viv followed, her mind filled with worry. "He better not be dead. Sutton will never forgive me."

It wasn't until they stepped onto the elevator that Viv realized, *Neither will Kevin.*

35

VIVIENNE ROSE

Viv ducked her head as Cricket maneuvered her way along the corridors.

The distinct navy-blue floor covering with the wave logo had shifted to a faded and thin gold carpet. There were gaps between the carpet squares; some had been unevenly stitched back together. *Have we made it to the staff area?*

Loud laughter met Viv's ears.

Cricket pulled her to the side. "Come this way." She ducked behind a food service counter. Lifting a company blue apron off a peg rack, she held it out. "Put on the apron and you'll look like you work here."

Viv objected. "But I'm in black and staff wears navy blue. It won't work."

"Trust me, they're too busy to see the difference. So long as you don't look like a passenger, everything will be fine."

Viv wanted to disagree. But then she knew Cricket was her only chance to look inside the morgue.

Cricket reached for a hairnet from a box as Viv slipped on the apron. "Put this over your hair," Cricket instructed.

"The morgue shares a wall with the kitchen. That's our next stop."

"Let's walk side by side," Cricket hissed. Make conversation and avert your face."

As they weaved their way in and out of the crowded dining room Viv asked, "Why are you doing this anyway, helping me find Rex?"

"I knew the other mentalist, the one Rex is replacing." Cricket's voice was barely audible. Viv leaned closer as she continued. "Jon Jon was a nice guy too. We got along and worked...closely together. When he didn't show up for work, I was devastated. So I've been keeping an eye out for Rex." Her voice dropped to a hush. "I didn't know he was attached to a passenger," she explained apologetically.

Viv felt confused. "Do you mean you got along with Jon Jon as in sleeping with him?"

Cricket flushed. "We were an item on the previous cruise. I was worried, you know, when he didn't show up on this one because he'd already texted me his room number and I thought I'd be his girlfriend."

"His girlfriend?"

"Just for the week. It happens all the time. Employees and staff. We hook up with someone and have a fling and then it's over. Off we go to the next cruise. But the San Diego to Honolulu route is different than the others. The ship is at sea and doesn't make any port stops until we get to Pearl Harbor. Not everyone likes that. So a lot of the same staff get recruited again and again."

"Move aside," a man in front called out. "We've got an event and we're late." He rolled a wheeled cart with various serving utensils and burners past Viv, who kept her face averted. He was followed by two more employees with small carts that carried plates and piles of utensils wrapped in napkins.

"Where are they going in such a hurry?" Viv asked.

"Oh, it's the memorial for that crazy woman. The one who carries around her father's ashes. She kept inviting more people. Cremains. That's what they call them."

Viv gave her a sideways glance.

Cricket continued, "After they release the cremains, they'll have a reception with a ton of food."

"I told Sandi I'd be there," Viv muttered. "And I think I should honor that commitment. Even if it is a cruise, one doesn't forget to pay their respects."

"Here's the kitchen." Cricket nodded. "I'll go first. We'll walk through to the far side and then meet up in the hallway. Ready?"

She ducked through the swinging door before Viv could answer.

The clang of pots and pans combined with voices shouting and water rushing into the sink gave Viv confidence. She felt certain she'd not be recognized because everyone was so intent on their job.

She looked over as Cricket disappeared out the exit. Viv followed, relieved when the door closed behind her. "That's loud in there," she told Cricket.

"Kitchens aren't peaceful on a ship," she explained. "We're heading over there."

Cricket took a key card from her pocket. She tapped the pad and opened the door. "You go first," she offered.

Viv stepped inside. She turned to speak to Cricket but she'd disappeared. She tried the door handle, but it didn't budge. Then voices from the hallway could be heard.

"Plans have changed. We're going to do the dump sooner than we thought." The man sounded impatient.

"I want no part of..." Cricket whined.

"Be quiet. She can hear us. Come on. We can talk somewhere else."

Viv tried the door handle again, then she gave it a yank. Releasing she stared at her red fingers. Raising her foot she gave the door a kick.

Finally she wrapped both hands around the handle, leaning backward. When the door didn't budge her situation became clear. *I need a key card to get out. Cricket took it with her.*

With a groan, Viv let her hands go.

Turning to face the room, her eyes stopped on a blue tarpaulin bag stretched over a stainless-steel table. "Oh no," she groaned. There was a zipper down one side.

Viv shuddered. *Is that what I think it is?*

She inhaled deeply to calm her nerves. Stepping closer, she realized the bag was not empty. Something or someone had been stuffed inside.

Viv turned away to compose herself.

He can't be dead. That would be so unfair.

It took several minutes for her to gather the courage to approach the table and inspect the bag further. *It's better to know the truth than to back away*, she told herself. *If Rex is in that bag, I need to know now.*

She ran her hands over the outside. To her relief it didn't feel like a body. She tugged at the zipper to peel back the top. The flowery scent of dryer sheets hit her nostrils. She looked inside and concluded that this was somebody's laundry bag.

First thing out of the bag was a rumpled sports coat. Viv held it in front of her with a good shake. *Rex wouldn't be caught dead in one of these.* She felt a nervous giggle in the back of her throat.

Caught dead. Very funny. Holding her hand over her mouth, she realized she was at the point of hysteria. *Stop giggling. You're acting really stupid right now. There's nothing funny about a bunch of clean laundry in a body bag.* Laughter erupted, coming out in big guffaws, as tears ran down her cheeks.

Get ahold of yourself, Viv! Her fingers began to examine the jacket. *So many pockets*, she thought. Four on the outside and another four on the inside.

I've seen these in catalogues and on TV. "For the discerning traveler," she mimicked the voice from the advertisement in her head. Shoving her hand inside the first front pocket, she held up a clip-on bow tie.

Not Rex's style. Her lips began to quiver again as anxious laughter threatened. *I can't imagine him wearing anything like this.*

She removed a white handkerchief from another pocket. It had been folded neatly into a square. She set it on the table next to the bow tie and then patted the other outside pockets. *Nothing in those*, she concluded.

Finally she turned over the button side of the jacket to check the inside pocket. She reached in and held up her find. Extending one finger, a pair of delicate women's panties unfolded in front of her eyes.

She held them in her fingers feeling the silk against her skin. *You'd have to hand-wash these; I bet they cost a fortune.*

Viv took a closer look at the lace construction. She ran her finger along the delicate fabric. *Liquid gold. So luxurious.*

Her cheeks grew hot. *I'm standing here in the morgue, playing with someone else's underpants. If Cricket were to return right now, how would I explain?*

Viv dropped the panties on the table.

Do they even belong to a woman? she pondered. *Maybe the person who wore that jacket liked to wear lacy things themselves.*

Viv knew there were men who liked dressing in women's undergarments. She really had no opinion about that one way or another. She picked up the panties again to run her finger over the waistband. She turned the elastic over. On the back, she saw embroidery.

"Sunday," she read aloud. *A day of the week. Very odd.* She released the panties onto the metal table again to keep rummaging in the bag, pulling out more small items.

Observing her collection, she counted. Five white handkerchiefs and six pairs of men's underwear, three blue and three bright green. The kind made out of recycled water bottles with a special sling-like pocket in the front.

For his... Viv blushed. What ever happened to the old-fashioned white cotton undies or boxer shorts?

Why would someone put clothing in a body bag?

A series of raps on the door from behind startled her. Viv turned to look toward the door.

She called out. "Cricket, is that you?"

The door handle twisted. Noone entered.

"You have a lot of nerve, trapping me," she called loudly.

Then she heard the keypad beep. When the door opened, she gasped.

A familiar man stepped inside and shoved the door closed behind him.

"What arc you doing here?" Viv demanded.

He stepped closer and raised his hand, clamping it over her mouth.

36

REX REDONDO

Lying on his belly with his face in the massage pillow, Rex listened to the steady down-tempo of the piped in New Age music. *Reminds me of the '70s.* He felt his shoulders relax. The light sheet draped over his back kept him just warm enough, and the smell of the warm floral blend, lemon, lavender, and honey, reminded him of more pleasant times.

That same scent is everywhere on the ship, he thought. *In the lobby and elevators. And coming from open stateroom doors above deck. Maybe I can buy a bottle to take home. I could have added one to my recent clothes order...*

He felt his lips stretch into a smile. *Just wait until Viv gets the bill.*

He stared at the navy-blue carpet underneath the massage table. His mind felt freer, leading him to think he was feeling better. He closed his eyes. The familiar spin of images began.

They're back! With a quick inhale, he waited. But then there was only spinning. Nothing that made any sense.

He took an involuntary deep sigh.

Strong hands pushed into his tight shoulder muscles.

The fingers dug into his neck and then traveled down his spine. Massaging at his lower back, the fingers inched their way up to knead his shoulders again.

I guess we're starting, he thought to himself.

"Mr. Abernathy," came a calm voice over his head.

Rex froze. But not for long. "I am Abernathy." He put his face back into the pillow as the therapist continued to speak.

"You paid for the premium massage—that includes hot rocks. May I interest you in a special foot package as well?"

"I'm good," he told her.

She dug her thumbs into his left shoulder, causing him to wince.

That's not therapeutic. More like retaliation.

Ginger lifted the sheet from his back as Rex explained. "Sorry, I forgot my underwear."

"Most of my clients leave their underwear in the locker," she replied tartly. "I'll hold the sheet over your body for privacy so that you can roll onto your back.

"Just relax," Ginger assured him. "I'll take care of everything. You can sleep if you'd like. Let your cares drift away."

Rex wasn't fooled by her soothing voice and suggestions. He used the same technique when he wanted to mesmerize someone on stage in a performance. Now that he'd turned down her upsell, he wasn't sure she could be trusted.

As her hands smoothed his calf, he had to admit he was feeling better. *Maybe the hydration helped.*

The cylinder in his head began its familiar spin. It spun faster as Rex focused on the images. Finally it slowed down to reveal him lying in the bed in the ship's infirmary. *Okay, so what does this mean?*

The image disappeared as pan flute music played in the background. Ginger massaged his belly. Rex felt his arms tense as her fingers moved lower. He pictured the IV again to avoid feeling aroused.

I might be shaking that virus. I'm definitely feeling better. Rex suppressed a chuckle. He willed his inner vision into one more spin. The images went round and round, revealing a room. Everyone in military gear. Men and women leaning over their food.

His palms became moist; his heart rate increased. His tongue searched inside his mouth and then recoiled at the tang of burning and metal.

That putrid metallic stench.

His body grew rigid, forcing him to remember.

When he served in Afghanistan. How Marines sat at tables in the mess hall. They told stories about the burn pits. And how the stench was so strong, even a mask didn't help.

Ginger dug her fingers. He winced as a sticky mass of helplessness settled over him.

His job was intelligence. He worked away from the burning. But he still felt responsible while the others did the dirty jobs.

Rex coughed. And then he sneezed. Once, twice, after the third sneeze Ginger spoke. "Do you require a tissue?"

She placed one in his hand. He dabbed at his nose, aware that tears formed in his eyes.

She held a plastic bin next to him, and he dropped the tissue.

Rex closed his eyes to ward off his tears. To his relief, the black images and the smell were gone. Of all his military service, those particular memories were the worst. He didn't want to acknowledge, let alone talk about his feelings.

Ginger stood behind him, pulling with both hands to stretch his neck. The mantra began quietly. The one that had worked for years.

I don't want to remember any of that. I don't want to remember. I don't want to. "Harder," he croaked to Ginger.

She obliged by digging her fingers in deeper.

Using the pain to keep his memory at bay, he groaned.

"Too strong?" Ginger asked.

"Not at all," he growled. "I can handle it."

Finally Ginger lifted the sheet to cover his body. She left the room and then returned with a bowl of hot rocks. "Turn over again," she commanded.

The stones burned against his skin, making him wince. She lay another and another down his spine. Finally she began to move them up and down, back and forth.

He felt the ache through his body as the rocks clicked against each other.

"Harder," he groaned, willing the lingering metallic taste in his mouth to go away.

After removing the price tags, Rex slipped into his new clothes. Underneath the bright overhead light, the massage room looked rather ordinary.

He had to admit Ginger knew her business. He'd released a lot of stress during that massage, as well as some memories he preferred to keep in the past.

Rex opened the door to the hallway and looked in both directions. Instead of stopping by the reception desk, he headed toward the sign that read Poolside.

He'd planned to make a quick exit, before anyone found out that he'd taken another person's appointment.

As soon as they realize I'm not Abernathy, they might stick me back in the infirmary.

On the pool level, Rex gratefully inhaled the clean smell of disinfectants. He ducked his head to go unnoticed.

If I circle to the other side, I can walk through the entrance to the gym and then ask Tonya for help. Maybe she knows a way I can get back inside my stateroom.

He was greeted by Tonya. After explaining the situation, she replied, "Of course, you can always stay with me..."

He realized immediately that she had other ideas. That she was interested. Unfortunately he had no one else to turn to. Without Sutton or Viv he was left to his own devices.

"I'm happy you made your way back here from the massage." Tonya pushed an imaginary strand of hair behind her ear. "How was it, by the way? Did Ginger do a good job?" Her voice, filled with innuendo, made Rex swallow hard.

"She was great. I'm feeling better. Like I was saying, since I don't have my room key or phone, I'd appreciate hiding out with you, just until I can get access."

He hoped she'd hear the seriousness of his situation as just that. Not a pickup line. When she patted his arm in a familiar way and winked, he let out a deep sigh. *She misunderstands. That's obvious.*

"I'm still not well," he explained. "Not up to par..." He hoped that might take any sting out of his disinterest in a more intimate exploration.

"Oh, I can fix that," Tonya purred. "Just you wait and see."

Rex had to go along with Tonya's assumption. He needed a place to hide if nothing else. Otherwise he'd be a no-show for his last performance.

Up until now, Rex Redondo had never canceled an act. He wasn't going to let Aloha Cruise Lines be an exception to his stellar record.

"When is your shift over?" he asked.

"Five o'clock. Then I get a break until after dinner. Plenty of time." She lifted her eyebrows.

"I'll need a nap." He pretended to yawn.

"Oh, me too," she giggled.

Rex looked away. Fortunately, Tonya moved down the counter to help another customer, giving him time to think.

I can't keep up this chitchat very long without telling her I'm not interested. But I do need a space to get my head together. Not a public one either. If Tonya thinks I'm her next best fling, well then I'll use that to my advantage. But the last thing on my mind is...

He looked over his right shoulder. The Old Lady of the Sea stared back, contempt written on her face.

What's her problem? he thought.

Tonya, finished with her customer, returned. "I've got half an hour until my break. Then we can take the staff elevator to my stateroom."

"What about my key card?" he insisted.

"We'll figure that out later. Maybe after our nap." A small smile came to the corner of her mouth.

Rex stood from his seat. "I'll meet you around the corner when you're done."

37

REX REDONDO

When Tonya's back was turned, Rex looked around. Her room appeared to be even more cramped than his with barely space to turn around. He knew he was sensitive to spaces. The bigger the space, the less he had to deal with the smells and accompanying claustrophobia.

For years Navy ships had been his main mode of transportation. He usually had his own stateroom as an intel officer. And then when he retired and started taking cruise ship gigs, he'd be assigned a berth with eight to ten others. After the second time, he wrote a private stateroom into his mentalist contract.

But cramped quarters and small storage were a given on any ship.

"You can sit over here." Tonya perched on the edge of the bed and patted next to her. "I'll put on the TV. I need to get out of this work uniform and take a shower. Then we can do whatever you want."

On her way to the bathroom, she stripped off her top and wiggled out of her bra. Rex averted his eyes. Aware that she'd most likely look back to see if he was watching, he picked up the remote and turned to a news station to act busy.

Once she'd disappeared, he saw that she'd left her clothing strewn on the carpet, like breadcrumbs leading to the partially open bathroom door. He took a quick breath. Something familiar caught his eye.

Bending over the clothing she'd left behind, he extended one finger to lift a pair of silky panties. He recognized them instantly.

Like the ones I found in the safe. Same ecru color. Same silky feel. Same lace. And same... He twisted his finger ... *embroidery.* "Monday," he said aloud. *Tonya's wearing the Monday pair. Even though it's not Monday.*

Rex lowered his finger, watching the panties float to the floor.

He'd lost his sense of time since his ordeal of being taken to that hospital-like room...maybe even before then. *We got here on a Saturday. We've been at sea for...* He counted on his fingers. *That would make today Wednesday. I don't know how long I was in that bed with the IV in my arm, but if I'm right, we'll dock in Pearl Harbor tomorrow after lunch. That will be Thursday.*

No matter how hard he tried, Rex found it very difficult to make sense of the panty situation. He scratched his head. The shower went off inside the bathroom. He made his way back to the bed to sit down again, wondering what to do with this newfound information.

Tonya emerged with her hair pulled up in a towel, another one wrapped around her thin frame. She walked over her clothing, straight toward Rex. He took a deep breath.

Oh no. She smells nice too.

But Rex knew this wasn't for him. What he wanted to

do, more than anything, was to rush past her, open the door, and call, "Help!"

To his amazement someone came to his rescue; someone was knocking from the hallway. *Maybe I won't have to hurt Tonya's feelings after all.*

Rex looked up to the ceiling, feeling immensely grateful. *God, or almighty presence, or she who must be obeyed...* He tried to think of another inclusive way to say thank you. Then he stopped and muttered, "Thank you," under his breath.

"I'd better get the door," he said, pushing past a pouting Tonya.

"Just leave it," she called.

He pretended not to hear as he pulled the door open.

Cricket Hicks stood on the other side. "We need to talk," she said firmly.

Rex stepped into the corridor, letting the door close behind him.

"What are you doing in Tonya's room?" Cricket's eyes narrowed.

"Have you forgotten? I was taken out of my own room without a key to get back inside."

"You were dehydrated. Probably hallucinating. No one was deliberately trapping you." Cricket glanced over his shoulder toward the closed door. "I'll take you back to your room right now. Will that help?"

He nodded. "It would."

On the way down the corridor he asked, "How did you know I'd be in her room?"

"I didn't know," Cricket admitted. "Tonya and I are friends. Cruise friends. We've had our ups and downs. I asked Redford if he'd seen her. He was the one who mentioned that you were with her. I decided to interrupt."

Rex's first thought was, "How did Redford know that Tonya and I were going to her room?" And then his very next thought was more of a vision. Two naked women and himself. He brushed that aside. "So you're friends?"

"Not our first cruise together. On this particular route you often run into familiar work friends. We know each other fairly well."

Finally they arrived in front of his room. "Here we are. You have the master key, right?"

"I do." She held up her phone to the electronic pad, which beeped.

"You'll find the place clean, and all of your belongings have been put away." She opened the door. "I'll stay around until you check, just to make sure."

If it were up to him, he'd have left Cricket in the hallway. All he wanted was to be left alone. But he took a quick glance around the room, adding hastily, "Things look okay. You don't have to stay."

She closed the door behind her.

"Check it out more closely. Look around a bit more. Your wallet is right there. With your phone." She pointed to the desk. "And see, Rexie? I left you a towel elephant." She took his elbow and turned him toward the bed.

"Don't call me Rexie," he muttered. But he had to admit the elephant was pretty cute.

Rex picked up his wallet to check inside. "Everything's here."

"And your phone, over there." She pointed to the counter.

"Yep. I see it," he said.

"Good. I'll give you a chance to rest up before dinner. Then you have the final show."

In all the turmoil, Rex forgot that he had one more show.

"Glad I could help." Cricket's voice assumed a professional tone.

When the door closed, Rex put the cabin lock in place. He didn't want to be disturbed. *I have one more thing to check.* Turning to his left, he slid open the closet door. A quick turn of the dial and the lock clicked.

He removed the fortune globe and held it in both hands. *It feels heavier.* "Reunited and it feels so good," he mumbled. "I'll need your help tonight."

He reached inside the safe one more time. His fingers probed the back corners. *That's odd.* His jaw tightened. *Someone removed the panties.*

Rex left the door of the safe open to sit on his bed and think. *Maybe it was Cricket. The elephant, don't forget.*

Maybe that's why she made such a big deal about me looking at my wallet and phone, to distract me from looking into the safe.

All that redirection to keep me from noticing that the panties are missing...

38

VIVIENNE ROSE

Fernando Gutierrez kept his hand over Viv's mouth. "Keep it down," he warned her.

Viv, eyes wide with fear, did as she was told. As soon as he removed his hand she asked, "What are you doing here?"

He held his finger in front of his lips.

"I said keep it down," he warned. "I can tell you later. But first I need to get you out of here and back to your room."

Viv felt annoyed and at the same time relieved to see the bodyguard. Maybe he could tell her later, but she was about to burst. "I asked Cricket Hicks for help in finding Rex. We were looking for him in the infirmary. That's how I ended up locked in the morgue."

Fernando nodded. "Like I said, let's get you out of here before she comes back. Then you can fill me in on all the details." He glanced to the table toward the body bag. "That's not Rex, by the way."

"I know." Viv's voice faltered, as her eyes filled with tears. "I already looked in the bag. Just a bunch of clothes.

But who knows what's behind that door." She pointed across the room.

"The cold lockers. For bodies," Fernando explained. "I've been in there. Take my word for it, Rex isn't being stored on ice. There's a body in storage, but it's not his."

"So where is Rex? My phone—"

"Like I said, I'm getting you out of here and back to your room. Then I'll tell you what I know right after I check in with Sutton. She's more worried about you than Rex."

That came as a surprise to Viv. She knew how Sutton and Rex were close since their military years together, but she never imagined that Sutton cared about her.

Fernando smirked. "I think Sutton's also tired of cat sitting. Not her exact words, but you get the drift. My instructions are to tell her as soon as you and Rex reach Pearl Harbor."

Viv sighed. "I get that. Miss Kitty can be a handful." Just the sound of her cat's name made her feel better. She glanced to the exit door. "How did you get in here? The door's locked from both sides."

"It took some doing," he explained. "But I wanted to have access, so the first night, I chatted up that Allison Thompson woman. We had a late-night drink in the bar. To my great fortune, I didn't have to work very hard.

"She left her phone on the table to use the restroom. I cloned her key. And for the rest of the week I had access to all the staterooms and offices."

"That's terrible security," Viv mumbled.

"You're right. But we can talk about that later as well."

"Do you have a plan for getting us out of here?" Viv asked.

"Do I have a plan?" He scoffed. "I've got plans for my plans.

But in this case I only need to open the door and escort you back to your room." Fernando tapped a code into the keypad and the door clicked open. He gave Viv a slight shove. "Ladies first," he mumbled before following her down the corridor.

Standing in front of cabin 561, Fernando waited as Viv used her key card. "Are you coming inside?" she asked.

"Actually, I'm right next door." He pointed to room 563. I'll meet you on the veranda in a couple of minutes. Right after I make a phone call."

Viv sat next to her towel elephant. She nearly teared up with relief.

I've been so occupied with the cruise it never occurred to me that Fernando was in Rex's room. He must have been watching me all along. "You stay here," she said, patting the elephant's head. One ear had drooped, making him look like a discombobulated dog.

Viv pushed aside the heavy glass door to the veranda. The sound of the ship's horn met her ears. A familiar voice called over the noise.

"May I come over?" Fernando stood on the veranda next door. He'd moved the barrier and waited.

Viv nodded, gesturing toward a chair.

"I promised you the explanation," he began, sitting down. "And then you owe me yours."

"I think I put it together myself," Viv said. "You're still my bodyguard. I thought Rex dismissed you, but apparently not."

"I have a contract. Even if that meant you were taking a cruise. I thought you understood." He glared at her.

"And I thought you agreed to let Rex take care of me.

This cruise was unexpected, you know." Viv smiled. "This was all Rex's idea."

"And then he screwed up my plan and his by taking that last-minute mentalist job," Fernando said. "By that time I'd already booked a cheap inside cabin on a lower deck. But once Rex knew he'd be sleeping in staff quarters, he told me to take his room right next door."

"I never imagined my neighbor was you," Viv admitted. "You kept very quiet."

"It's my job," he said with a frown. "And I'm good at it, don't forget."

She leaned back into her chair, appreciating the breeze on her face. *This feels more like it. Getting to know Fernando. Having a meaningful conversation. I was depending on Rex for this, but now...*

She glanced at her bodyguard with renewed interest. It was just over two weeks ago when they'd first met. But with Rex busy, she had time to assess him more thoroughly.

Dark hair, cut short, brushed back from the brown skin of his face. The slight wrinkles around his mouth put him in his early fifties.

What she found most attractive was that he didn't flinch as she looked him in the eye. Fernando wasn't inviting more questions, but he wasn't evading her look either. Suddenly all of her problems with the cruise and finding Rex were put on the back burner.

"Tell me, how did you get into bodyguarding?" She watched his face move into an easy smile.

"People ask me that all the time. I'm a fourth generation Latino from Colombia, and believe it or not, I fell into body-guarding because of a movie I saw on TV. Whitney Houston and Kevin Costner.

"Of course, my family was against me doing anything

that ridiculous. They consulted with my grandparents and proposed a different plan for my future. My grandparents own acres in Northern California, where they run a very successful artichoke ranch, so the idea was for me to work with them.

"When I resisted, telling them how much I loved working out and how good I am with weapons, they listened. And then made me wait while they considered. And then they called me in with a proposal.

"Get my college education first. And a master's degree." He shrugged. "I could pick anything I wanted to major in. And since they were paying, I thought that was pretty generous. So I graduated from Cal Poly Pomona, with an undergraduate degree in psychology and then a master's in business."

He smiled. "This bodyguard gig is something I do until I get back to the farm. I want my wife to get through law school and we need the extra cash. After she's set, we'll move back up north, and then I'll learn about the business of raising artichokes, from the ground up."

Viv liked hearing his story. "I expected you were going to bust out of your family ties and go rogue on your parents. But you didn't. You found a middle way. They must be proud of you, Fernando."

"I'm proud of them," he admitted. "Our roots are strong in California, built on hard work and amazing luck. I don't take that for granted."

"You remind me of my son, Lucas. He's a professor at Cal Berkeley. People thought he got the job because he knew somebody who put in a good word. But he was hired on his own merit, and he applied because he wanted it, not because it was easy. Like you returning to your family business because you want to.

"Most people think I'm an immigrant. Here on a visa. That kind of thing. I appreciate your interest."

A hiss from the loudspeaker interrupted. Viv looked up, feeling annoyed.

"This is an announcement from the captain. For those attending the memorial for Farley Hughes, the ceremony has been postponed. I repeat, postponed. Not canceled. We will meet tomorrow. Same time, same place. Over and out."

"Enough about me," Fernando said. "Tell me what's going on with you."

Viv explained. "I have two problems really. First I saw a man in the gym hit his head and fall to the floor, and I reported the incident within minutes. But the body had been removed and no one believes me. Although the customer service coordinator did finally admit it, but only to me.

"And then my phone isn't working, so I can't connect with Rex. Now that I know you're on board, please understand that I can't text or call you either."

Fernando's jaw tightened. "You don't say. Tell me every detail from the beginning."

"And there you have it," Viv said. Telling Fernando the story, having him listen attentively, didn't change the situation any, but it did make her feel so much calmer.

"Sutton filled me in on much of what you told me. There are a couple of details I didn't catch though. The one thing I didn't hear before is that the guy might have hit his head on the machine next to him?"

"That's what I saw." Viv took a minute to think back. "He lost his balance and fell over. His head bounced against the arm of the nearby elliptical."

"That sounds like it might have been deadly. I wonder if he regained consciousness..."

"I wonder too. Plus they covered up the incident. That couldn't be good. Robert Redford was, what can I call it..." Viv's jaw tightened. "He was demeaning and surly when I last spoke to him. After I threatened to write a scathing review he finally admitted there was a man. I left without another comment. I do realize that time is on his side. We'll be ushered off the ship tomorrow, and I'm convinced he thinks putting me off will solve his problem."

Fernando smirked. "He doesn't know you very well, now does he..."

"I appreciate that," Viv told him. "And it's true. I've been known to hang on to a topic too long, Just ask my ex."

She pushed her chair backward. "Now that Sandi's memorial is postponed, I'd like to catch a nap before dinner. Rex has his last show tonight. I want to be there. And then it's time to pack up."

Fernando took her lead and stood. "You're sounding better. And pretty resilient, considering."

"You mean considering that I'm an old woman?" Viv teased.

"You're not that old," he said. "But kind of. I know my grandma wouldn't be nearly as flexible. I mean, if grandpa changed his mind and abandoned her on a cruise, she wouldn't be as pleasant."

"I've always preferred my own company. I guess it doesn't change with age."

Fernando looked thoughtful. "Or maybe you appreciated the diversion from hanging out with Rex the whole time. He has a big personality, especially in such close quarters."

Viv reached for the veranda door. Her cheeks felt hot.

Fernando had touched on a bit of truth, one she'd not been able to think about in all of the turmoil.

Maybe Rex was pushing a bit too fast. Booking the cruise and coaxing her to come. She knew that he was pushing the intimate aspects of their relationship to the next level. And maybe she'd not objected when he changed plans to work for the cruise because she wasn't quite ready.

She'd freed Rex to do what he loved. That's all she'd considered when he'd brought it up.

Fernando's phone buzzed. He held it to his ear. "He's safe," he spoke into the phone. "Didn't get eyes on him, but something tells me he's back in his cabin. I can check later."

He looked over at Viv and kept talking. "Yeah, I've got her. Nope. Let me repeat, I haven't exactly set eyes on him. Like I said—" He paused to listen. Then answered, "Will do." He clicked the phone off.

"That was Sutton. She's worried. She hasn't heard from Rex. But she did say he'd turned his cell back on just a few minutes ago, according to her tracker. So she'll try to call him again."

"Are you sure that was Rex? Maybe someone else has turned on his phone," Viv suggested.

"That may be. But we'll know for certain by tonight. He's scheduled for his last show. If he's on stage, then he's okay. Can you wait that long?"

"I need to get a bit of rest," she told him. "I don't remember eating lunch. Maybe I'll call for room service and have a nap. I suppose I can wait until the show to find out about Rex. Especially now that I know you're on the job."

"I'll be right next door. And while you're busy, I'm going to check on the ship's Wi-Fi. It may be your server, but the disconnect may also be to keep you from contacting anyone with your legitimate complaints. You can come and knock on my door when you're ready for dinner."

After a warm shower, Viv slipped into her bathrobe and lay down on the bed. She stretched out her body, appreciating the clean smell of the sheets and the coziness of the comforter.

Fernando's presence made her feel less isolated. But now her mind raced again. Was Rex really safe?

What about the body bag full of clothes? And the panties...

At least they don't belong to Rex, she reassured herself.

Viv closed her eyes. She reached her hand toward the towel elephant to scratch behind his towel ear.

Not Miss Kitty, she reminded herself. *I'm ready to get away from this floating hotel.*

39

VIVIENNE ROSE

That evening, Fernando and Viv sat across from each other. This time near an expanse of windows in the formal dining room.

Viv felt proud to be seen with him. Fernando looked splendid in his light blue shirt with a tie. She'd noted his pressed slacks and slim waist as they were shown their table. *He's so confident.*

Viv felt as if they were on a date. She realized he wasn't that much younger and that it wouldn't be so impossible. Viv sighed deeply, feeling slightly confused.

Fernando reached for his wine glass. Holding it up, he offered a toast. "To the best laid plans."

Viv laughed. "Plans do crumble. I can attest to that." She clinked his glass.

By the time the waiter brought their entree, Viv was aware that other diners looked their way. She leaned across the table. "We're attracting attention," she told him.

"Good," he insisted. "I've done my research. Assaults on cruise ships are the most frequently reported crimes. Especially with the ready availability of liquor. As you know from experience, staterooms can be safe but also a trap. Better the other passengers think we're an item, than to think you are vulnerable."

Viv hid her smile and patted his hand. *I believe he just lectured me for my own good. Definitely reminds me of my son*

The waiter arrived with a bottle of champagne and a bucket. Placing the bucket on a stand, he twisted the bottle to the sound of crunching ice. "Compliments of Bertha Alcott." He set two flutes on their table and then nodded toward the corner.

Bertha's bright eyes stared at Viv. *She looks like a ferret,* Viv thought, adding a slight wave of hello.

A gentle pop from the cork brought her eyes back to the waiter. He wrapped a white towel around the bottle. Filling both their glasses, he returned the bottle to the silver bucket, standing tall as if waiting for instructions. "Is there anything else?" He turned to Fernando.

"Please thank Ms. Alcott," Fernando said politely.

Once the waiter left, Viv raised her flute. "I've been feeling a bit adrift since day one on this cruise, and now I want to thank you for being my anchor, making things better."

He touched the rim of her glass to his, warm brown eyes smiling their appreciation.

Later that evening, Viv waited in the audience as Rex walked on stage. *He's made a good impression,* she thought, hearing the solid round of applause.

Rex's opening banter sounded familiar, giving Viv a minute to assess her situation. Fernando's appearance had changed her mood. Though she relished her alone time, she did appreciate a good conversation. Then a quote she'd heard from a doula friend of hers came to mind: "A man's not a plan, he's a companion."

Once Fernando had arrived, she felt able to relax and even take a nap. No longer as critical of the other passengers, she'd looked forward to dressing up and then sharing dinner and a show.

After her nap, she folded her jeans and shirt neatly in a drawer. Viv dressed in her flowing black slacks and slim-fitting top. When she turned in the mirror, the hem of the slacks skimmed the floor just past her heeled black sandals.

She'd pulled her hair into a messy bun, lifting it to the top of her head. Instead of the usual scrunchy, she tucked in a pearl hair clip close to her scalp, one she'd purchased earlier that year from a street vendor.

Not bad. Viv leaned forward to get a closer look at her lipstick in the mirror. *I may be old, but I won't embarrass my bodyguard.* The very thought of needing a bodyguard made her blush.

And now she sat next to Fernando, who applauded at the end of Rex's opening dialogue. He seemed comfortable and to be enjoying himself. Viv turned her focus toward the stage. A spotlight formed a circle of light around Rex's body.

He stepped to the end of the stage. "Normally I don't give away any of my secrets," he confided to the audience. "But tonight I'm feeling different." He took in the crowd, glancing slowly from side to side. "Maybe it's because we're friends. Traveling together for the past several nights. You've come to my show and I've gotten to know you better."

He reached into his pocket. Holding the fortune globe covered by a white cloth, he explained, "Last time we had some luck with the fortune globe." He looked out to the audience, taking his time, waiting for them to focus on what he held.

"I hope you've stayed away from ellipticals after my warning." He grinned as the audience bubbled with laughter.

"No one ignored the fortune globe and used the elliptical, did they?" His grin widened as he doubled down on the joke, the playful accusation bringing even more laughter.

Rex kept his momentum with his next comment, timing it perfectly. His voice grew warm and friendly. "I know. We've all eaten our share this week. I've put on a few pounds too." He patted his waist, which was thinner, if anything. "But we can get rid the extra baggage when we get home, right? That's the time for working out."

Now the audience guffawed. Rex waited, and just as the noise died down, he lifted the ball to be level with his head. The audience gasped. Rex removed the white cloth in a single flourish as the light went out.

Slowly but steadily, the spotlight rose to illuminate the fortune globe. Rex lifted the globe to his forehead. Viv blinked, dimly aware of the outline of his face reflected in the glass. The liquid inside the globe began to swirl. Mesmerized, she watched as it turned from clear to a milky white. Viv inhaled quickly.

The liquid inside the globe began to swirl faster and faster. The color turned from milky white to black right as Rex held the ball higher, over his head this time. "Help me," he said to the audience. "Call the magic forth. Repeat with me: fortune globe, fortune globe, shining and spinning. Probe beyond the veil and give us a vision."

He repeated the incantation again, making the hair on Viv's neck stand up.

No more prompting was necessary, as the audience kept

repeating the incantation. Viv felt a shift in the atmosphere, a highly electric energy swirl that made her skin tingle.

"Silence," Rex demanded, his voice thunderous and all-powerful.

The audience stopped chanting as the lights went to dark.

Viv stared at the stage, reaching for Fernando's hand.

40

REX REDONDO

Lowering the fortune globe with both hands, Rex held it in front of his waist. The spotlight focused on the ball and the black liquid within. Suddenly more lights came up to illuminate the stage. Sparks reflected off the globe, bouncing like lasers in and around the audience.

Rex widened his vision by focusing on the peripheral lights. Seconds later, the liquid inside the globe released a precise image. A navy-blue body bag. Rex's hands tightened on the globe.

He knew he was closest to the image and that he could confirm to the audience what they thought they may be seeing. Due to the overhead lighting and his distance from the stage, even the first row of people couldn't see clearly what he saw.

He took advantage of their attention and the silence to consider what he'd say. The zipper on the body bag came away, revealing an indistinguishable face. Rex held his breath. The zipper inched downward one link at a time.

The face came into closer view, but Rex didn't recognize him. *He's got something in his hand*, Rex realized.

Bringing the ball closer to his eyes, he nearly smirked. *What, again?*

An ecru-colored ball of fabric was clutched in the lifeless hand. Rex blinked right as the image began to fade. His mind raced. *More panties. How is this possible? And how am I going to explain to the audience that's what I've seen in the fortune globe?*

At his signal, the lights came up slowly, revealing Rex with head bowed. He made an effort to look thoughtful to give himself some time.

"Ladies and gentlemen," Rex began in a slow deep voice. He draped the fortune globe with his handkerchief, sliding it back into his pocket. Brushing his hands together, he raised one finger to his temple.

"Frankly, I'm a bit embarrassed about what I saw tonight. You may even say my vision was rather personal and a bit risqué."

A high-pitched titter came from the front row. Rex looked down at the woman. He searched her face.

"Would you like to join me on stage. I think I may have seen something that you think you've lost. In your stateroom perhaps..."

The audience inhaled collectively.

"I saw your panties in my vision."

Now the audience burst into laughter. *This was not what they expected, but it doesn't defy their credulity. Everyone knows how articles of clothing get lost in staterooms.*

To Rex's delight, the young woman blushed. No one wondered if it were even true, the bit about the panties. They just wanted to watch her.

Rex turned his attention to the man sitting next to her. *Come on, buddy. You know you want the last word.*

The young man shouted, his face alight with all the attention. "I'm pretty sure she won't need any panties tonight."

Ripples of laughter followed his remark as the young woman shielded her red face.

Rex stepped backward as the laughter continued. He felt slightly embarrassed because he'd gotten out of a tight place at the woman's expense. But now she'd dropped her hands and laughed with the man sitting next to her.

He felt a bit better but knew in his heart that he'd taken a cheap shot.

After the show, in his dressing room he found the Old Lady of the Sea.

"Ms. Alcott, what a pleasant surprise," Rex lied, going about his business and slathering cold cream on his face.

"Bertha," she corrected him.

He raised his eyebrows but didn't acknowledge her first name. Instead, he said, "I was a bit nervous tonight, but I pulled it off."

"Do you mean that bit with the panties?" she said slyly.

"Everybody knows what happens at night on a cruise ship. I only had to improvise."

"But panties." Bertha scoffed. She sat in the middle of the sofa, making herself at home. He continued to remove his stage makeup. "Surely you didn't really see panties in the fortune globe," Bertha said.

Rex wiped the cold cream from his nose. *I can tell her about the guy in the body bag, which was probably the important message.*

He glanced at Bertha in the reflection of the mirror. *I don't trust her. Just because she's older it doesn't mean she's safe. Or remotely kind, based on our last interaction. I think people forget that just because you've beaten the odds and managed to age, that doesn't mean you're a good person.*

"I've seen my share of women's undergarments." He winked at Bertha in the mirror.

"Oh, I'm sure you have." She crossed one knee over the other. "Your last show. Not very remarkable, was it? That poor young woman. Most likely on her honeymoon. You embarrassed her while the husband got the laughs.

"But enough of that. Tomorrow's the final day of the cruise. We'll be across the ocean and into Honolulu before you know it. Will you and your lady friend—what's her name again?—be reuniting then?"

Rex ignored her dig about his performance. "Her name is Vivienne Rose," he said. "You know that. I've told you before. Why do you keep forgetting?"

"I only have eyes for you," she said, pursing her lips.

Rex screwed the top on the cold cream with a swift twist of his wrist. The woman was getting on his nerves. She'd deliberately mentioned Viv. Plus he didn't like being manipulated and criticized. *What does she know about mentalist performances? It's an art. Some shows go better than others*, he fumed to himself.

The thing that puzzled him, that made him really angry, was Bertha Alcott herself. The way she had dropped into his dressing room for a second time, as if she owned the place, and then inserted herself into his professional and personal life.

What did it matter to her who he spent his time with and how he came up with the panty image? He shoved the cold cream jar aside. Then he felt guilty for being mean to an older woman.

Be patient, he told himself. *She's the Old Lady of the*

Sea. Maybe this is how she keeps herself from getting bored; by showing up in peculiar ways and chatting to strangers about their personal lives.

He stood to his feet. "How about I take you out for a nightcap?" he offered. "We can stroll along the promenade afterward. That would be a good opportunity for me to unwind after the performance. What do you say?"

He offered her a hand as she rose. "That's very gallant of you," Bertha said. "But I have other plans this evening. Maybe another time."

Relieved that she no longer demanded his company, Rex opened the dressing room door for her to leave. When he closed it again, it was with a sigh. *Here I was trying to be polite and she had other plans. And I thought my company would thrill her to pieces, and I was dead wrong.*

Sitting back in his chair, he contemplated the rest of the evening. Then he remembered something from earlier. On his way to dress for the performance, he'd stopped by the formal dining room. Worrying about Viv eating alone, he wanted to see if he could catch her eye.

He turned the corner of the main hall, and was rudely awakened. He heard the sound of her sparkling laughter over the din of other voices. Once he stepped inside the dining room to have a closer look, he saw that she wasn't alone. Not at all. She was sitting with Fernando the body-guard. *What the devil...*

Ducking behind a plant, he was able to observe them without being seen. Viv laid her hand on Fernando's with a friendly pat. And then the waiter brought them a bottle of champagne.

Looking beautiful in her black sequined top, Viv's skin glowed in the flicker of candlelight. And Fernando was discussing something that held her interest. Rex could tell by the way she leaned in that she cared about Fernando's conversation. He felt a tug in his gut. *She's beautiful. How she cares about people and actually listens. Why wouldn't Fernando be having a great time? He's figured out what I have: Viv Rose is a seductive goddess.*

Then he felt his temper rise to an indignant conclusion. *Why are those two so friendly all of a sudden? He's too young for her.*

Rex turned away, fuming as he walked toward a mirror in the hall. He stopped to look at himself. *You've still got it.* He patted underneath his chin. But then the memory of Viv's laughter, bubbly and happy, overrode his pep talk. *You may have some of your looks, but that doesn't mean that you have her.*

He wasn't used to feeling insecure. *I told Fernando to take my room to protect her, not to take her to dinner.* He turned away.

I brought all of this on myself. I ruined a perfectly good opportunity with Viv on a cruise because I didn't stop to think. Fernando is younger than me. And really handsome. I knew they had a connection even before the cruise. What was I thinking...

He stretched his chin to take another look in the mirror. *Folds on my neck. I'll get an appointment with my dermatologist when I get back. I've been avoiding surgery, but maybe it's time.*

Rex lowered his chin to stare at himself one last time. *You're a fool, Redondo.*

41

REX REDONDO

Rex didn't want to be alone in his stateroom. Still angry, he didn't appreciate how his privacy had been invaded for one. No matter how well-meaning the transfer to the infirmary might have been. His skepticism had been aroused at the entire situation, considering he'd been locked in a room with another man who couldn't speak for himself. And had to escape with his you-know-what hanging out.

Plus there was Viv. Obviously she'd decided to stop talking to him or she couldn't communicate for some reason. Either way he felt detached. And a bit adrift. Without Viv he wasn't sure what his purpose was, other than to entertain a few bored and buzzed people with his mentalist show.

And then the show wasn't that easy, since his images had taken a hike. He tried to interrupt the flow of discouraging thoughts by pushing back.*Wait a minute. I may not be psychic, but I have certain gifts.* This particular turn of events had left him feeling physically and emotionally spent.

Rex decided the unfamiliar feeling was nothing more

than a little discouragement. "I better fix that," he muttered. So he made his way to the staff bar.

"Whatever you have on tap," he told the bartender.

He found an empty table near the window where he sat with a huge sigh. *That's what old men do, make noises when they sit down*, he admonished himself.

From his seat near the window, he felt the hum of the ship's engine. One look outside toward the dark sky only made him feel more alone.

This would be a good night to loiter on the smoking deck, he thought. *The stars look close enough to touch.* Just the idea of the smoking deck brought up memories.

The USS *Nimitz*, a Navy aircraft carrier, had transported him and a battalion of Marines across the ocean. Afghanistan was their final destination. Despite his top-secret job, Rex knew what to expect and that someone always had his back. *Unlike on this crazy cruise*, he muttered to himself. Rex inhaled, remembering when he used to smoke.

He'd stopped after retiring from the military. But this week, feeling ill, reminded him of how short his breath was before he quit. It had taken months, even a year, to regain his lung capacity.

"Mr. Redondo," came a voice. He turned to discover Bertha Alcott. "Would it be all right if I join you?" She leaned her cane against the table, anticipating a yes.

Rex pulled out her chair. "I'm tired of my own company, as a matter of fact. But I thought you had other plans this evening."

"I did, but now I don't," Bertha said. "Order me a sherry, would you? The bartender knows my label."

Standing, he groaned.

"You're too young to be making a fuss every time you stand up," Bertha scolded.

"I've got some aches and pains," he admitted. "So I must be old enough. Be right back."

Returning with the sherry, he leaned slightly forward to place the drink in front of Bertha. Then his knee gave out. The sherry went flying, spraying the amber liquid on the tablecloth and the floor. He managed to grip the table to stop from falling. The glass rolled under the floor length cloth.

"I'm so sorry. I'm not usually that clumsy." He adjusted his knee and then made a smart turn back toward the bar.

"Clean up over there," he told the bartender. "And I need another sherry for the Old Lady of the Sea."

This time a server came to Rex with a tray carrying the drink. Bertha sat demurely looking at him, a slight smirk on her face. "Not too stable, are we?" She used the plural, drawing a quick comparison to herself and Rex.

He pointed to her cane as he sat down. "I'll be needing one of those pretty soon. Then you'll have to get a younger man to do your bidding."

This time he made a deliberately loud groan. "See, I'm getting worse. Dropping things. Making old man noises. Falling over for no reason. Right after I get a cane like yours, I'll be forgetting my own name. Just you wait."

Bertha frowned. "It does come in handy." She nodded to her cane.

Rex kept a pleasant expression, already tired of the conversation.

To his surprise, Bertha took two long gulps of her sherry and then pushed her chair back. "I'll be saying goodnight now," she told him sharply. "And I suggest that you get some sleep. That last show wasn't your best."

She said that earlier.

Before he could defend his performance, she continued, "Stay away from the ladies too. I suspect you'll have them lined up at the door for a last night rendezvous before the ship docks. Not good for your rheumatism, all that cavorting."

"I have no idea what you're talking about," Rex mumbled. "See you tomorrow," he added politely.

Once she was gone, he turned his head back to the window. *Bertha's really good at poking people. I suppose I feel better. Grumpy is better than depressed. I know that show wasn't my best work, but did she have to keep bringing it up? And now she's telling me how to conduct my personal life.*

Watching Bertha and her cane making their way across the room, Rex felt immediately guilty. *Stop picking on an old lady,* he chastised himself. *She's just feeling her age. There's no need for you to take what she says personally.*

Rex to a moment to read the room with his senses. Two servers wandered past, holding drinks on trays. The sound of laughter burbled from the bar. He smelled the distinct odor of flowers and fruit that he associated with the ship.

It's not just the passengers who party on the last night, he surmised. *An open bar and plenty of food. The entire ship will be hungover tomorrow.*

Unlike the passengers who anticipated the beauty of the beach on Waikiki, the staff had to work even harder. Then the ship's changeover would begin. Staterooms required a deep sanitization. Linens needed to be stripped away for the laundry.

As passengers dragged luggage off the ship, fresh food

would be brought on board. Each deck would be inspected for stragglers and forgotten belongings. All of that needed to be arranged before the ship could make the turnaround back across the seas to San Diego.

Rex stared into the dark. His gaze followed two shadows with something large connecting them. Two men walked outside on the deck. One of the men walked backward.

Rex narrowed his eyes. *They're holding a bag.* Standing quickly, he made his way toward an exit door. "Excuse me," he mumbled, pushing past a woman who blocked in his way.

"Mr. Redondo. Just the man I want to talk to." Allison Thompson's voice was muffled in the overcrowded bar noise.

Rex kept walking, pretending not to hear.

He pushed open the door. Outside, the wind brushed past his cheeks. He shivered. No sign of the men or the bag.

Then he remembered, *the promenade deck circles back on itself.* He broke into a slow jog, keeping close to the rail.

Take that, Bertha. I've still got the moves.

His breath came heavier as he continued to jog. *Still no sight of them.* Turning a corner, he stopped.

The two men held a sagging bag at each end. *That's a body bag.* He stood in the shadows to watch as they edged the bag closer to the railing.

"Come on, lift," growled one of the men.

"Just give me a minute. My phone is buzzing."

"Forget the phone. We've got a job to finish."

"I'll count to three. Then hoist," the taller man instructed.

"Stop telling me what to do. I can lift this thing by myself, even if it is dead weight."

"Dead weight," the man scoffed. "Now that's funny."

Rex felt his gut clench.

The man dropped his end of the bag. "Just try it yourself then, if you're so strong."

"Ah come on, Charley. Give me a break. Just get this thing done. Then we can go have a drink."

His companion bent to pick up the other end of the bag. "One, two, three," he called out.

And on three, both men heaved the bag, which disappeared overboard.

Rex heard the splash.

He waited for them to walk away before stepping closer. Leaning over the railing, he watched the water rush past, careening off the hull. The bag had disappeared. Sight unseen.

Did I just see two guys toss a body overboard?

Nah, that couldn't be. Am I hallucinating?

A sliver of guilt crept in, followed by the memory he dreaded most.

I was an observer of a potentially criminal act and I did nothing. Only stood there and watched. Just like before...

His body started to uncontrollably shake. Rex felt his head buzz. His chest felt tight, and tears came to his eyes.

After several deep breaths, he was able to stop shaking. He looked up toward the night sky. *I think that's the Milky Way Galaxy.*

Then he gulped.

I'm just a mess. I wish Viv were here.

The first person Rex ran into by the elevator was Allison Thompson.

"There you are. You didn't hear me back in the bar. Everyone's saying your final show went well."

"Not what I heard," he mumbled. "Did you have something more you wanted to say?" He glanced at the elevator lights above the door.

"I do have some final business to discuss. Since we're docking tomorrow."

"Okay then, now's a good time," Rex said.

"Not here. Let's talk somewhere private; on deck three. The chapel. They've set up for the memorial, but no one is there now. How about in an hour..."

"See you then," he agreed.

Rex held his arms stiffly to his sides as the elevator door closed. He pushed back his memory of what he'd observed on the promenade deck. *I don't want to start shaking again. I have an hour. I'm going to start packing.*

In his stateroom, he began tossing his toiletries into a bag. Then he checked each drawer for anything he'd missed. That done, he took an armful of his clothes out of the closet, removing the hangers to shove each item into his suitcase.

He opened the safe and found the fortune globe. Rolling it up inside a sweater, he placed it in the center of his suitcase. Before he could zip his bag shut, his phone began to ring.

"Sutton. Yep. Checking up on me... I know I've been out of touch. Can't talk now. I'll call you later. I was hauled to sick bay if you can believe it. Okay, I'm feeling a bit off.

"Stop fussing over me. And tell Kevin to stop barking. I'll bring him something from Oahu. One of those fancy collars they sell in gift shops." Rex listened for a moment and then said goodbye, slipping the phone into his pants pocket.

By the time he made it to the chapel for his meeting with Allison, he felt much better. Waiting for Allison, he did his usual inventory. Chairs had been arranged in rows. The table in front, draped in a white cloth, held a wooden cross and some leaflets.

"Have you ever attended a burial at sea?" Allison spoke from the doorway.

Rex turned. "Actually, I have. Several. The chaplains would do services on board Navy ships for Marines and sailors. They'd record the ceremony and send it to loved ones if they couldn't attend. Intel officers are assigned interesting collateral duties.

"I grew to appreciate the memorials. It's easy to take life for granted. Showing up for the dead helps me appreciate my life more. But enough of that." Rex didn't care about Allison or why she'd called this meeting. He'd decided in that instant to take a chance and correct his course.

"I was very disturbed this evening. When I saw two guys with a body bag. I watched as they dumped it over the side of the promenade deck."

Allison's expression turned from shock to stony-faced. "You must have been imagining things. I know you haven't been well for this cruise. Maybe the doc can check you out. I can call him." She reached for her cell phone.

"I don't require a doctor," projected Rex's firm voice. "You're not going to trap me in the infirmary again. And I know better. I saw what I saw."

Phone suspended in midair, Allison's voice coaxed, "It's really dark outside. You must be exhausted after the last show. I saw you having a drink at the bar with Bertha. A figment of your imagination got the better of you."

"I saw what I saw," he insisted again.

No wonder Viv was so upset. This is frustrating, to be treated like you're stupid or sick or crazy or old. Or all of the above.

"Okay, I'm done here," he told Allison. "You are obviously covering up something." He made his way toward the door without a backward glance.

"No. Wait," she called after him.

He went through the doorway without turning back.

Instead of looking down to avoid being seen, he raised his chin with a wide grin. *No more hiding for me.*

"Aren't you that mentalist?" a woman stopped to ask.

"Yes, I am." He sounded confident. "Hope you enjoyed the show."

Rex walked quickly, arriving at the closed door of his previous stateroom. He tapped as the door opened slowly. Fernando rubbed his thick hair back with one hand. "Hey, Redondo. What can I do for ya? It's two in the morning."

"You might want to step back before I punch you," Rex suggested in a dry voice.

Fernando gave him a puzzled look. "What's that again?"

"Don't act innocent with me. I saw you with Viv at dinner. You ordered champagne. I know what that means." Rex gave him a shove with both hands.

"Come on, man. I didn't order the champagne," Fernando protested. "That Alcott woman sent it to our table. This is a job for me, remember?"

"Sharing my room to keep Viv safe is one thing. That doesn't mean you get to ply her with bubbly and pretend you're on a pleasure cruise," Rex said. "Unless she's agreeable, that is. And if that's what Viv wants, I guess I'll have to step aside. Until I can convince her otherwise. Which I will, given half a chance."

"You left Viv alone. That was your decision," Fernando stated flatly. "And I'm not a relationship counselor. Just a bodyguard hired by the Palm Desert Police to keep her safe. And that's only because she's a protected witness."

Rex followed Fernando inside and took a look around his old room. "Sure is nicer than my berth on deck three," Rex muttered.

"Want it back? I can get out of here in ten minutes. I am happy to return to the cheap inner cabin without a veranda." Fernando looked slightly amused.

Rex realized he'd made a fool of himself. He brushed his hair back with his hand. "So tell me, bodyguard. Has Viv gotten into any trouble on your watch?"

"I found her trapped in the morgue," Fernando said. "I consider that trouble."

What are the chances both of us would be trapped somewhere on a cruise ship? Rex wondered. *Coincidence? Probably not.*

He glared at Fernando. "Was she okay when you found her? I assume you were the guy to rescue the damsel." He lifted an eyebrow.

When Fernando only chuckled, Rex felt better.

"Get out of here, would you? I want my room back."

"It's two in the morning," Fernando protested. "I didn't think you'd take me up on it at this hour."

Rex quirked his eyebrow again and then made his way toward the glass door. "Don't care what time it is." He stepped onto the veranda.

He easily walked the few steps closer and stopped at the sight of Vuv's pulled curtain.

There's a good chance she'll be furious. And I don't blame her. But I won't know until I try.

He pulled a chair from the table, making a deliberate racket. Then he sat down to wait, his back facing her door. *She must have heard me.* Finally a light came on from inside the room. When the door opened behind him, he held his breath.

"Fancy finding you here," came Viv's calm voice.

"Job is done." He didn't turn his head right away, appreciating the smell of hybiscus and roses, her familiar scent. When she didn't say anything more, he gathered his courage to turn his head and glance her way.

She wore the fluffy white Aloha Cruise bathrobe cinched tightly at her waist and a slight smile on her lips.

"So I told myself," she began. "I said to myself, Viv, you can be mad that he abandoned you. Maybe it's your perfect right to pout for the rest of the trip in self-righteous indignation.

"Or, Viv, you can live in the moment. You can just pick up where you left off and enjoy his company once he shows up. If he shows up, that is. And really wants to join you."

He caught a glimpse of her hopeful expression. His heart quickened.

Rex felt a lump rising in his throat. *She's not mad. Just look at her face.*

He stood and asked hopefully, "So there's no hard feelings for the stupidest decision I've ever made?"

And then, because he was so relieved, he started to talk faster. "I guess there was the time I nearly married a woman from Brazil. Now that was stupid. It was thirty years ago now. Oh, and the time I told Sutton she had to wear a flowered dress. I paid for that dearly. Both nearly as stupid as taking this job."

Viv stepped closer. She reached to touch his arm. "No hard feelings. Absence made my heart grow fonder. How's your heart, by the way?"

He couldn't wait another minute. He wrapped his arms around her body, pulling her close. Bending his head, he whispered, "My heart is more than fond. I think this is love. The kind that lasts."

She leaned away from his grasp to look into his face. "I see," she said. "I suppose there's only one thing to do in that case." She took his hand and opened the door to her stateroom.

"I'd like to eat breakfast and watch the sunrise with you. But that means we only have a couple of hours. No time to lose." Viv made her way to the bed.

Rex's heart skipped a beat as he pulled the curtain closed, right as she dropped her robe and slipped under the sheet.

He turned off the light.

42

REX REDONDO

Rex felt more peaceful than he had for weeks. Sitting next to Viv, he knew he'd done the right thing, telling her about his feelings. The sky began to gradually lighten as the sun rose in the horizon.

Viv, who sat only inches away, sighed. He reached for her hand.

"I had very little sleep last night," she commented. "I'm surprised I feel this chipper."

He gave her hand a squeeze. "I have that effect on women," he assured her.

"I've seen your effect," she responded dryly. "How about I order our breakfast right now? I've certainly enjoyed being pampered these past few days. I'm ready for a plate of scrambled eggs."

"And buttered toast," he added. "I feel much better now."

"And a giant pot of coffee," Viv agreed. "Remind me. Did you apologize last night? For being a dumbass. I think I heard you say that, in so many words."

"I did," he nodded. "And it worked." He smiled from ear

to ear. "Make that two pots of coffee. We have some work to do."

Once she'd ordered, he turned to her. "If you're up for it, I'd like to talk about a few things. The first being we were both locked into a room and left there."

"Fernando told you," she said.

"Yes, he did. Right before I booted him out of my stateroom," Rex growled.

Viv smiled. "I have plenty to share with you since we last spoke. A lot of unfinished business with Aloha Cruises. I'm concerned that will all be swept aside once we come into port."

"There is a time frame here. I'm beginning to understand all of that myself." He pulled out his cell phone. "But first I'm going to have my luggage delivered. Then I'll tell you about the two guys I saw tossing a body bag overboard."

He could tell he'd piqued her interest. The way she gazed at him with wide eyes. "When was that?"

"Right before I came upstairs to find you," he replied.

"Did you report the incident?"

"Just like you did when you saw that guy fall. And guess what? Allison Thompson had the nerve to tell me I was seeing things."

"Gaslighting. That's what happened to me," Viv sounded annoyed.

"I was surprised how angry I got. Walked out on her. After giving her a piece of my mind. We need to get to the bottom of this."

Rex stood and looked toward the door. "I hear the room steward. Time for breakfast."

. . .

Rex viewed the breakfast tray with two coffeepots and a covered dish and a basket. Lifting the metal lid, he inhaled deeply. "The eggs are still hot," he assured Viv.

Then he leaned closer to examine a basket of pastries. Filled with buttered toast, fresh croissants, and two over-sized cinnamon rolls, his stomach growled.

He reached for a slice of toast. "Have you been eating like this all week?" he mumbled. Then he made a point of staring under the table. "You don't look as if you've gained a pound."

"I've enjoyed more food than usual." Viv reached for a large spoon to scoop eggs onto her plate. "Something about the sea makes me ravenous." She lifted a full fork to her lips.

"Tired?" he asked.

"Not a bit," she assured him. "Completely rejuvenated."

"Everything was okay for you...last night?" He liked being complimented after lovemaking.

"Last night was delightful." She shoved a plate filled with eggs toward him. "Now it's time to tell me about that body going overboard."

Not the gushy type, my Viv.

He cleared his throat. "So here's what I saw..."

By the time Rex finished recounting what he'd seen the night before, they'd made it to the second pot of coffee. "More?" she asked.

"Yes, please." He lifted his cup for a refill. When he put his cup down he pulled out his cell phone. "I have a message," he scrolled with his thumb. "It seems my luggage has been delivered next door."

He felt himself relax. "Looks like we're back on track." He winked at her.

"Looks like we're more than that," Viv smirked. "Let's talk about our case."

"Our case..." he commented dryly.

"Neighbors in crime. That's us. So in a nutshell; one or two dead bodies have disappeared." She sounded matter of fact.

"One went into the sea, at least we know that," Rex said.

She took a bite of her cinnamon roll. "This is delicious." She licked the frosting off her lips.

"You're delicious." He tore off a bite for himself. "Do you think the guy tossed overboard was the same guy who fell off the elliptical?"

Viv paused. "There could be one body, or quite possibly two. I can barely remember what elliptical guy looked like. It all happened so fast, and then whoosh, the body's disappeared."

"The same with the body bag. Heave-ho and it disappeared. But it may be the same guy," Rex repeated.

She turned her head to gaze at him, a thoughtful expression on her face. "I think you're right. But we still don't know for sure. And we don't know why either. Who would be so dangerous they had to toss him in a body bag?"

"Who and why," Rex added. "Was his identity that important? It's a big risk getting rid of a person overboard. There might be someone waiting for him when the ship anchors."

"If it was family or a friend, they'd surely call the cops."

"My time in the infirmary. There was a body next to me on a respirator. Then I woke up and it was gone."

"Do you suppose they transferred the corpse to the morgue when you were going in and out of consciousness?" Viv asked.

"Possibly. And what if," Rex insisted, "that was the guy

at the gym. I think we've circled back to the same conclusion. Overboard guy is elliptical guy."

Viv looked toward the horizon again, taking a minute to think. "We only have a few hours before we reach Honolulu."

"And don't forget that memorial for Daddy," Rex added. "I'd like to go." He remembered the chapel and how he'd stood up to Allison. Once he disregarded the rules, he found his way to Viv's door.

"Did you meet Sandi Hughes?" Viv asked.

"Remember? I met her that first night at my show. She seemed a bit off to me."

"Carrying Daddy's ashes everywhere," Viv said dryly. "I saw more of Daddy than I saw of you for most of the week."

Rex sighed. "I don't know how you can forgive me."

She reached to pat his hand. "You do contrite so well."

"Really? I wasn't aware." He shot her a quick little-boy smile, the one that he knew was irresistible.

"But now we have a murder and a coverup to solve. And time's a-wasting." Viv pushed her plate away standing to her feet.

Rex stood up too. "Let's plan our first move. We need to get Allison or Redford cornered and have some of our questions answered."

Viv smiled. "I gave Redford quite a dressing down the last time the two of us spoke. I left in a huff from his office."

"Wish I could have been there." He glanced at her in admiration.

"I accused Redford of gaslighting me. Just a minute, I need to make a call." She walked to the room phone, picked up the receiver, and said, "You can come remove our breakfast tray now."

"You're adapting quite well to this life of leisure." He tossed his napkin on the tray.

"Maybe it's time to get dressed." She smirked.

"How about a shower first?" he invited. "Then we can take your phone to the IT desk and make a big scene. It will be fun. I can't wait."

"I prefer a bath," she said. "That shower isn't big enough for one, let alone two."

"It will have to be quick, considering we have work to do."

"Not a problem," she assured him with a smile. "I can do quick."

Rex and Viv stood at the IT desk looking alert and freshly bathed. He with his hair slicked back and Viv with a bright smile.

"Mr. Redondo. Ms. Rose," Redford addressed them.

Viv turned to Rex. "You go first, sweetie."

"We need to talk privately," Rex said with authority. "So call someone else to help the people behind us."

"And this is regarding..." Redford's fingers tapped the counter.

Viv glared. "Don't play dumb with Redondo and Rose. We're talking about the body," she said in a sharp voice. "Do I need to say that louder so everyone can hear?"

Robert's face drained of color. "Not at all," he forced a whisper. "Come this way."

43

VIVIENNE ROSE

Viv and Rex sat across the desk from Robert Redford. She watched with amusement as Redford squirmed under Rex's icy stare.

"Let me explain again," she said in her most ladylike voice. "Rex saw a body bag being dumped overboard last night. He reported the incident to Allison Thompson, who proceeded to tell him that he was seeing things."

Redford's left eye began to twitch. Viv continued, "Perhaps we need to take your inability to handle our concerns directly to Captain Barclay. He needs to know what's happening on his ship."

"Oh no," Redford insisted. "That will not be necessary." He rubbed vigorously at the twitching eye. "I'm sure this is all a misunderstanding. You're not familiar with cruise ship procedures.

"We have to keep a log of everything we drop overboard. Even the waste"—he blinked—"has to be recorded. For example, once the sewage leaves the toilet, it travels to our onboard treatment plant. Then it's filtered and heads to an aeration chamber. Once the waste is cleaned, it's sterilized using UV lights, and only then is it released into the ocean."

Rex, seemingly unfazed by Redford's attempt to deflect, glanced up at the ceiling. He lowered his eyes, amusement in his voice. "Talking about toilets and sanitation may fascinate you, old boy, but that's not what we're here to discuss."

"Were you head of the class of gaslighting 101?" Viv asked calmly. "We're talking about a body bag being hoisted over the side of the ship. A crime, if I'm not mistaken."

Redford's voice raised to a wail. "We also recycle plastic and cardboard. Once passengers disembark, we take the trash to offload."

"Interesting." Rex smiled. "But not the answer to my question."

Now Redford's voice became loud and even more desperate. "I guarantee you no one on this ship dumped a body bag. We'd see them on cameras for one thing. Every aspect of this ship is under surveillance."

"Surveillance." For the first time in their conversation, Viv felt a moment of doubt.

"But we can't get a look at the cameras, can we? So you're safe again," Rex commented dryly. "All of this conversation is a ploy to put us off until we hit the shore. And then wham. We'll be debarking, out of sight and out of mind."

Viv leaned closer to Rex. "What about Sutton? Can she alert the authorities in Honolulu? They could investigate once we dock." She watched Redford's face to see if he'd react.

To her delight, he jumped to his feet and his voice raised to a shout. "Oh no. You don't have to do that. We'll handle the complaint." He bent down to open a drawer. "Just fill out this form and I'll take it to the captain personally."

Viv took the paper. "I was sent this before but it never arrived." She sniffed with disdain. Glancing over the document, she realized, "So you had this form in paper format all along. Why didn't you give one to me that first day when I saw the man fall off the elliptical? Allison must have deliberately sent me a digital version that she knew I'd never receive. Interesting."

She nodded at Rex. "Time for us to go."

Rex followed her to the door, opening it for her to walk past.

Once they made their way to the corridor, she pulled him aside. "We weren't getting anywhere with No Relation Robert. I took the paper to end the conversation. It's time to go around him and speak to the captain."

"I didn't think you were satisfied with filling out a form."

"Not on your life!" she exploded. "What I do want to do is track down that Cricket person. I want to know why I got locked in the mortuary. Was she helping them to keep me out of the way? Speaking of which, we're running out of time."

"Cricket's probably cleaning up staff quarters this morning. We could try looking for her there." He pushed the elevator button to go down.

"I didn't realize you knew each other." Right then a familiar woman pushed her way into the elevator. Sandi sidled up next to Rex. Wearing a black dress with black flats, and a ridiculous-looking black straw hat over her light brown hair, she held the ubiquitous wooden box under her arm. "I'm hurrying to the chapel for Daddy's memorial. I hope you're both going to be there."

"We wouldn't miss it for the world," Rex murmured. A skeptical look came over Sandi's face.

"Don't you belong downstairs?" she asked. "I thought staff wasn't supposed to mingle with passengers."

"Viv's my neighbor back home," Rex began. "We've been friends for ages. Just ran into each other on the ship." He reached his arm around Viv's shoulders to pull her closer.

Sandi shifted the box to the other arm. "I see," she said in a voice full of doubt.

Before Rex could elaborate further, the elevator opened.

"See you at the memorial," Viv called to Sandi. She turned to face forward as the door slid closed.

After a few moments, Rex's warm breath touched her ear. "Maybe we'll run into the captain at the memorial. What do you think?"

Before she could answer, the elevator door slid open again.

"It's crowded this morning." Viv stepped out.

"Some people are intent on getting in the last bit of ship time," Rex mused. "We can use that hustle bustle to our advantage."

"Like how?"

"First let's chat up Tonya at the coffee counter. She may have something that will help our investigation. She's been a lifesaver for me."

"Has she now?" Viv dismissed the ping of envy.

"She rescued me right after I escaped from the infirmary," he explained. "What's that noise?" He pointed to her purse.

She slipped her cell out to look at the screen. "It's a stateroom charge from the other day. Now that message gets through just fine. But I didn't buy anything that I recall."

Rex glanced away, hiding his expression. When he looked back, she saw a tinge of red on his neck. "You might want to wait before looking at your bill. I may have used your room number when I was in a pinch."

She glared at him. Scrolling on her phone, she exclaimed, "Eight hundred dollars for a shirt, pants, and some flip-flops!"

"I really needed them. My you-know-what was hanging out, the hospital gown, and—"

"And you used my room number..."

"I thought if you saw the charge, you'd know I was alive. And maybe you'd be angry and come and find me. You know, to chew me out. I can always use a tongue-lashing. I missed you."

"Tongue-lashing my pajamas." She didn't really believe his excuse. But she did find it amusing.

"What pajamas? I didn't see any PJs." He leered at her. "Seriously, when I was sick, when we weren't texting or talk-ing, I felt awful. It started with brain fog and then a cough and it was hard for me to breathe. I had trouble prepping for my show in the usual ways, because my mental images froze up. I was just a mess.

"Then I felt dizzy and tired. Finally I woke up with an IV in my arm. Naturally I assumed I might not make it. Especially considering the guy next to me was on a ventilator."

Viv heard the tone of desperation in his voice. "But you were able to escape."

"It's hard to explain. I'm trying here. Aside from being physically ill, I felt as if I were being followed by a cloud of guilt. And then I kind of gave in to it, the feeling."

He looked away, rubbing his hand over his eyes.

"So I put the charge on your room. Maybe an act of desperation. I don't know. Seems kinda silly now." When he looked at her, she got the feeling that he wanted her to make sense of his unexplained behavior.

When she couldn't, Rex looked away, running his fingers down his arm, scratching at his sleeve.

"You're feeling it now," she said softly. "The guilt."

"I am," he admitted. "I keep busy. But there's something about this ship that's made it worse. And then being stupid and disappointing you. When I saw them dump that bag, I felt disappointment in myself. I can't shake the feeling. And I had...I had symptoms of... It's hard to talk about since my days in the Marines."

He gave her another puzzled glance.

"Have you ever spoken to anyone about this?" Viv asked gently.

"To Sutton. And a chaplain. In Afghanistan. A good guy. But I haven't seen him since I retired."

Viv took his arm. To her relief, the color had returned to his face.

He pulled her close. "I'm better now. Really, you have to believe me. You're like a tonic for me. When I put those clothes on your bill, it was my way of saying, 'Don't forget about me.'" He leaned to kiss her cheek. "I wanted to tell you that I was sorry. I made a mistake taking this job. I thought we'd be together during the day, right next door to each other sharing a veranda. When they moved me down with the staff, I knew right away I'd done the worst thing possible."

An idea popped into Viv's head. She knew what she needed to do. But for now, she only wanted to make him feel better. Viv held his arm as they walked toward the gym, giving it a slight squeeze.

44

VIVIENNE ROSE

They sat on the open stools at the end of the counter, waiting as Tonya brought drinks to another passenger. She took their room number and then made her way to Rex and Viv.

"What can I get for you two?" She looked right at Rex, ignoring Viv.

"Nothing for me," Viv answered, eyeing the woman up and down.

"Some answers and a latte for me," Rex said.

"Give me a minute." Tonya returned with a mug for Rex and a water for Viv. "I need to make it look like you're sitting here for a reason, so I brought water." She paused to add, "Would you like a wedge of lemon for that?" She pointed to Viv's glass.

"Oh no, I'm fine." Viv sensed that something was off with Tonya. *She's acting deliberately distant, at least with me. I wonder what went on with those two...*

Tonya watched as Rex took a sip of his latte. "I've been waiting for this," she said. "You asking me questions. I guess I always figured you'd realize that I was involved."

Viv glanced at Rex from the corner of her eye. *Involved in what exactly?*

"I am a mentalist," he replied. "I can read people's minds."

Viv did her best not to look startled. For their entire acquaintance, or friendship, he'd insisted he didn't read minds. Now he was telling Tonya that he did. *What's he up to?*

"That's why you knew." Tonya sighed.

Viv took a sip of water as Rex and Tonya stared at each other across the bar. *I'm no mind reader, but they don't seem closely connected to me.*

Viv cleared her throat. "Knew what exactly? Will someone tell me what's going on?" She made her voice sound just a bit helpless, as if playing the role of an innocent bystander. And then she nearly giggled, remembering another role. One she'd played years ago. Decades actually. A musical called *Guys and Dolls.* She was in high school.

Given the part of Miss Adelaide, the school paper called her performance wooden and inauthentic. It had hurt at the time, when her potential career as an actress tanked before she'd turned sixteen. But now Viv thought she was doing an admirable job playing the clueless girlfriend.

She hid her amusement by dabbing her lips with the paper napkin. *This isn't a role I'm playing now,* she reminded herself. *I really have no idea what these two are talking about.*

"Jon Jon and I were in a relationship," Tonya began. "Until he died."

Viv made every effort to suppress her surprise. She failed. "Who was Jon Jon?" She blurted. *Why two names? I assume he's an adult...*

"The previous mentalist," Tonya said quietly. "You knew, right?" She blinked at Rex.

"What do you mean, died?" He sounded genuinely shocked. "I was told he didn't show up for work and that's why they hired me in an emergency."

"He showed up for work," Tonya said. "But he lost his balance or something and hit his head on an elliptical. They took him away."

"I knew it!" Viv couldn't contain her excitement. She tugged Rex's sleeve. "That's the guy. Finally someone admits what I saw!"

Rex frowned. "But that makes no sense. Jon Jon was staff. He'd work out in the staff gym. He wouldn't be allowed to use the lido machinery." He looked behind him at the expanse of machines near the glass.

"Oh, he did a lot of odd things," Tonya said. "He liked to come up here just as the passengers came on board. The management didn't have the capacity to reprimand him because they were so busy.

"He liked to think he could get away with things. You know, it made him feel powerful. Not like the rest of us— underpaid and in fear of being fired.

"I warned him to stop, but he only laughed at me. Then I figured his in-your-face behavior was part of his mentalist persona. You're the second mentalist I've met, so it's not like I had experience." She looked imploringly into Rex's eyes as if for confirmation.

Viv watched the red creep up Rex's neck. *Interesting. Tonya may be on to something there.*

"I've been known to be—what can I say?—a bit pompous and opportunistic," he admitted.

And a ladies' man, Viv thought. Did Rex and Jon Jon also have that in common?

Rex glanced over Tonya's head toward the lineup of coffee mugs and tumblers behind the bar. "That's why you had the crystal ball. You said it was Jon Jon's, right?"

"I kept it," she sniffed. "He told me to hide it in plain sight during the day. It was part of his playfulness, letting me hold on to the ball. I'd sneak it to him right before each show and then he'd give it back. Usually when we met later."

Viv's eyes lit up. "I bet there's a recording device in the crystal ball. Is that why he wanted you to keep it? This is such a public location, you'd be able to overhear lots of conversations and help him out with his act."

Tonya frowned. "No, I never helped him. He knew everything himself."

Rex turned to Viv. "Jon Jon must have put a recording device in the hollow bottom of the globe so he could get people's information himself. How did I miss that? I looked the globe over but never unscrewed the bottom half."

Tonya interjected. "Do you mean he wasn't psychic? I thought all mentalists were..."

"He could have been psychic," Rex admitted. "But he most likely used other ways to assure himself he'd have the information necessary when he got on stage."

Similar to Rex, Viv thought.

"How long were you two, you know, together?" Rex turned the topic back around to Tonya.

"We'd get together on every cruise to Hawaii. Once we figured out we were, you know, a couple, we lined up our itineraries. It's encouraged by Aloha Cruise Lines. They like couples traveling together. And when we link up, it keeps employees from getting bored and almost guarantees they'll stay longer with the company."

"Not in the old days," Rex muttered. "They used to have stricter policies."

"Maybe things changed," Viv said in an agreeable tone.

By now Tonya warmed to her topic. "At first Jon Jon and I just ran into each other a couple times of year. But lately we've signed up on back-to-back tours. Until he had that accident." Tonya's eyes brimmed with tears.

Viv had heard enough. She had another agenda. *If we spend too much more time with her, we'll have no choice but to pack and get going. And then Robert Redford will get his way.*

"Was Jon Jon single?" Rex asked.

"Yes, as far as I know." Tonya dabbed at her eyes with a napkin.

"Any close family?" Viv continued.

"He made a big point of saying he was unattached." Tonya looked perplexed before turning to Viv. "I felt guilty not admitting to you what I knew, but I wasn't allowed to talk about it. No fraternization with passengers, you know."

"Yes, I remember." Viv turned to Rex. She figured by their line of questioning they were on the same page. "So there won't be a wife or sister or cousin to meet him on the dock when we get to Honolulu?"

Rex picked up on her point. "So no one would miss him if he were to be thrown..."

Viv sent Rex a sharp glare, hoping he'd get her drift and end the conversation; she did not want to finish Rex's sentence.

If Tonya figured out that Jon Jon may have been shoved overboard, she might burst into tears and then they'd need to comfort her. *Crunch.* The window of opportunity would close as the passengers debarked, sniffing their welcome leis, rushing to get in line for the hotel transports.

To her relief, another passenger arrived at the coffee bar. Tonya went to take his order. "Let's go," she told Rex.

He followed her across the room to a corner table, where they sat down.

"So the previous mentalist..." he began.

"Was named Jon Jon," Viv finished.

"And he must be the guy you saw fall off the elliptical," Rex concluded.

"If he was, then he may also be the guy you saw pushed off the promenade deck," Viv added.

"And without a wife and close family, no one would ask about his whereabouts." Rex frowned.

"So Aloha may have been betting that Jon Jon might not be missed right away, if ever," Viv said.

"They started their false narrative by telling me he just didn't show up." Rex sounded terse. "I don't like being lied to."

A loud voice could be heard coming from the coffee bar. "Hello, Miss Bertha," Tonya called.

Bertha Alcott rested her cane against the bar and leaned over the counter to speak.

"I'll get that right away," Tonya replied. When Bertha turned around, she locked eyes with Viv.

Viv smiled at the older woman and gestured to an empty chair. She spoke in a low voice to Rex. "I think the Old Lady of the Sea is coming our way. Would you grab that empty chair so she can sit down? And watch out for that cane. It gets in the way. I nearly took a fall just the other day."

Rex stood and pulled out a chair just as Bertha arrived at their table. "You two finally found each other," she said. "I just wanted to say hello, but I don't have time to stay for a chat. Have to get to the memorial on deck three." She hobbled back to the bar as Tonya handed her a to-go cup.

Bertha didn't take the cup. Instead she directed, "Would you have a steward deliver the drink to the chapel? I'll need fortification for the service. Memorials are always so sentimental." She leaned heavily on her cane, making her way toward the exit.

Viv needed no other reminder. "Let's wait for Bertha to go first. Then we'd better follow. I want to be there for that memorial."

Rex waited for Viv to be seated before he took the chair on the aisle. He'd explained to her in a whisper, "I want to be close to the food. Maybe Cricket will be there."

Viv estimated some sixty people were in attendance, seated in folding chairs arranged so an aisle was left in the middle. She wondered, *Why would people take their vacation time and attend a memorial?*

They most likely didn't know Sandi's father. She shook her head. *I bet it's because people are kinda bored before we disembark, and they dropped in to see the ashes tossed into the sea. Take a few selfies with the captain, and off they go.*

And then on cue, a man held up his camera to take a photo of his wife standing in front of the table where Daddy's wooden box had been placed. *#SayingGoodbye,* Viv thought.

She looked for Sandi and found her sitting in the front row. Separated from Daddy, she appeared forlorn. *How hard is that, not having other family to support you at a memorial for your father?* Viv felt a heaviness over her heart until the Old Lady of the Sea made her way down the aisle.

Heading to the front, she raised her hand in the air, offering a queenly wave to people already seated.

After turning in the aisle to bestow a smile on all of the mourners, Bertha sat down in the front row.

Sandi has company at least. And who better than Bertha Alcott.

Rex leaned closer to whisper, "I want to have a word with Cricket. She's setting up the table with the food. I intend to interrogate her about locking you in the morgue."

"I found that body bag stuffed with clothing in a morgue," Viv said. "I also find it kind of hard to believe that there would be a morgue on a cruise ship."

"Fernando confirmed it was the ship's morgue," Rex argued.

"And when did he tell you that?" Viv said.

"Right before I saw you. Last night. We had a long talk." His eyes narrowed.

Viv lifted her chin. "Get back to Fernando. What did you tell him?"

Rex shook his head. "Not now. We can talk later. But from what he said, I'm certain that the cold locker was behind that other door."

"So off you go. Have a chat with Cricket. See what her story is and then hurry back. I think the captain just arrived. It's time to bid Daddy a final farewell."

45

REX REDONDO

Rex watched Cricket rearrange a pile of napkins on the white tablecloth. Her eyes were focused downward as she nervously picked up the pile and moved it to the other side of the round meat platter.

"The food looks good," Rex said. "I wouldn't think the cruise line would be so accommodating for such a somber affair."

"The cruise line has all sorts of ways to make passengers feel welcome," Cricket spoke in a low voice.

"I guess so." Rex was not convinced.

"That's what I'm supposed to say if anyone questions this event," she responded. "The service is about to begin. May I help you with something?"

"Just wanted to thank you for bringing my luggage upstairs. I thought after our week of me avoiding you and then how you locked Viv in the morgue, you might not be that accommodating."

Unless one of us required a memorial. Then we'd get lots of food and a big farewell.

"What do you mean?" Cricket looked confused.

"You know what I mean. I saw the panties. What day of the week were you?"

"None of your business," she snapped, turning her face away.

"Oddly, I also discovered another pair in the safe, and now they are missing," he continued. "So what's the deal with the fancy underwear? Does it have a significance other than necessity?"

Cricket spoke in a low voice. "I was his Tuesday and Thursday girl." She cleared her throat. "And Tonya was the Monday and Wednesday choice. He kept his weekends free for more spontaneous hookups."

Rex felt his gut turn. Despite his reputation, the panty explanation made him slightly nauseous. He knew he was judgy when it came to more than one partner at a time. He didn't admit that to people because it was no one's business.

"The thing is," he told Cricket, "Tonya was wearing the Tuesday panties on a Wednesday. I found that very odd."

"You would." Irritation flared in her voice. "I think that's how men are, concrete thinkers when it comes to sex. Women don't care what day of the week is embroidered on panties. If they're clean, then wear them." Cricket walked away, not waiting for Rex's response.

I guess this conversation is over.

Once he sat down, Viv turned to him. "What did you learn?"

"That women don't care what day of the week is embroidered on their panties," he said.

Viv didn't hesitate to add her two cents. "Such a stupid idea, putting the day of the week on underwear. I pick the ones that are clean. Plus panties with days of the week are kind of childish. Something a mother would buy for her toddler who was learning to dress herself."

"I never thought of that," Rex said, "never having had children." He shrugged.

The sound of tapping on a microphone interrupted further discussion. "I'd like to welcome all of the people who gathered this afternoon as we help Sandi celebrate the life of her father."

On cue, Sandi began to sob. "I'll miss you, Daddy," she called, her voice shaking with emotion.

Bertha, sitting next to her, offered a cloth handkerchief. Sandi snatched it and covered her face. One loud blow of the nose later, the captain continued.

"We've put together some words, and then we'll remove the ashes from the box, adjourn to the promenade deck, and distribute them to the sea. Afterward, Sandi would like to invite you to stay for refreshments and conversation.

"We'll have an open bar and lots of nibbles. So be sure to stick around." He smiled at the mourners before adding, "Don't eat too much! You need to get swimsuit ready for those Honolulu beaches. And that being said..." He reached into his pocket. Adjusting his glasses, he read from a list. "Don't forget to pack your bags and have them outside your door for a quick departure. You don't want to miss check-in at that luxurious hotel you've already booked." He shoved the paper back in his pocket, giving a nod.

"Color-coded tags will be put on the bags so you can find them in the terminal as you debark. This can be quick and efficient, but only if you pack and follow instructions. Otherwise you might get left on the ship. No aloha for you!" He wagged his finger.

Because Rex worked other cruises, he knew the drill. The captain's speech reminded him of someone wrapping a stale cookie in a fancy box. Instead of warning people to pack and not delay, he'd tried to make it sound funny.

The captain took a pause and then began the service. "We are gathered here today to celebrate the life of..."

Sandi leapt to her feet. She swayed left then right, an animalistic wail hurtling past her lips. Rex's spine tingled.

"I can't do this. I can't let go, Daddy!" Sandi cried out. She ran to the table and shoved the captain aside. Grasping the wooden box, she clutched it to her chest. She sprinted down the aisle, making a beeline toward the exit.

A look of horror came over Bertha Alcott's face.

Before reaching the exit, Sandi stumbled. Tripping, she collapsed to the floor. The box of ashes flung ahead, escaping her grasp. Rex leaned over to get a better look.

"Looks like we have an unanticipated incident," he mumbled. "Check it out."

Viv leaned closer as Sandi sobbed, "Daddy," her face planted into the carpet.

Viv squinted. "Do you see ashes? I don't see any ashes."

"Nope. No ashes. Just rocks."

"What's this all about?" Viv asked.

"I have no idea," he mumbled. But in fact, he did have an idea. He'd suspected since that first show. *I knew she was holding something back, but I went along. I was losing my insights even then.*

Low murmuring from the assembled grew louder. When no one offered a hand, Sandi scrambled to her feet. She ran down the aisle and out the door, leaving the rocks and the wooden box behind.

Tap tap tap sounded from the microphone. The captain spoke. "It seems the bereaved has been overcome by circumstances."

When no one bothered to disagree, he nodded toward the food tables. "But that doesn't mean we can't take advantage of hospitality and have a cocktail." He walked away to be the first one at the bar.

"That's not right, him drinking on the job," Viv murmured to Rex.

"Can't say I blame him. She's a handful, that Sandi."

"Yep." Viv took his arm.

After availing themselves of one drink and a couple crackers with cheese, Rex and Viv left the fake memorial and made their way back to her stateroom. Rex made a quick trip to his room, where he went through his luggage to retrieve the fortune globe. Returning to Viv's room, he sat down on the edge of the bed to think. "Would you mind..." He looked at her.

"Mind what?" She dropped her purse and slipped off her shoes.

"I want to consult the fortune globe."

"You brought it here?" She looked surprised.

"It's in my suitcase." He reached for the handle to pull his bag closer.

"So the globe is for real, not just a mentalist's prop?"

"Give me a minute. I'll show you and explain." He unzipped his bag.

He lifted the globe, letting the white cloth drop away. "So do you remember when we first met, when I borrowed your house key and took it home?"

"You mean stole my house key and used it in a show," she tartly reminded.

He shrugged. "Okay, I see why you think that. But it turned out okay, right? I wanted to get to know you and—"

"Yes it did," she said primly. "For now."

"Anyway, the fortune globe is similar to the key. It holds

a vibrational imprint. When I cradle it in my hands and then hold it to my forehead, the heat from my palms transforms the contents. On stage the heat from the spotlights also helps.

"The audience can't see the image but I can, and I saw who used it previously."

"But I'm not an audience and this isn't your show. Do you mean to tell me you used the globe for personal reasons?" Her skeptical expression made him feel uneasy.

Will she accept this or think I'm a lunatic?

"Yes," he answered her. "Think of it this way. I'm Rex, and separately I'm also a mentalist. As Rex, I can use the fortune globe for personal reasons."

Her eyes narrowed, so he kept explaining. "And I'm risking being called a lunatic by the most important woman in my life, just so you know." He gave her a hard stare.

To his relief, her eyes softened. She came to sit next to him on the bed. "I'm listening..."

"After the first show, I began to have symptoms, like I told you. The most startling was that I could no longer access my inner images. Probably why I didn't suss out what Sandi was up to right away. And then I didn't have Sutton or you to feed me ideas. So I kinda winged it for the last two shows."

"I noticed those shows were a bit different," Viv admitted. "As if you needed to keep things going and get the audience's approval."

"Correct," he said. "Of course, I didn't fool you." He leaned closer to kiss her cheek. "But now I'm feeling better, and I think I can use the globe for personal reasons."

He enfolded the globe in both hands. His voice shifted to a singsong cadence.

"And then I'll hold it in my hands like so." He inhaled deeply, then exhaled slowly.

The liquid inside the crystal began to swirl clockwise, then it reversed. The water transforming into a white cloud which turned into a dark swirling mass.

"And now I'm holding it to my forehead," he said calmly.

He tuned out Viv, feeling the cool crystal against his skin. Once he held the globe in front of his eyes an image began to form. He recognized the first image instantly. The IT desk. There was no lineup of passengers or anyone standing to help answer questions. Just the desk. It vanished into the dark mass as another image appeared.

There were three people Rex did not recognize. They all wore red shirts with a logo over the pocket.

Then the third image began to form. Rex waited for it to stop so that he could see more clearly. He closed his eyes and inhaled. When he opened his eyes, he stared at Viv, who watched him with fascination.

"So I got two things," he said, reaching for the white cloth to cover the globe. "Three, actually. But I couldn't discern the third one."

"I see," she said, her voice cautious.

"According to the first image, the IT desk isn't up and running. I assume until further notice. They probably don't want passengers having any last-minute complaints."

"I get that," Viv agreed.

"And the second image, that's the interesting one. My interpretation is that Aloha Cruises is changing their branding. Red shirts replacing blue. I'm not sure why, but it felt urgent."

As he spoke Viv tugged at the towel elephant sitting near her pillow. She held it close to her body as if for comfort. "Will your images help us get answers to our questions before we debark?"

"I don't know," he said matter-of-factly. "But I want justice, whatever that would look like."

He made his way toward the closet. He stopped. "You have a safe in here, right? May I put this inside?"

She stood up. "Of course." She spun the dial on the safe and waited. By the time he left the globe and turned around, Viv was sitting on the edge of the bed. She'd slipped her shoes on, looking determined.

He opened the door and waited. "I want to bid a special goodbye to the Old Lady of the Sea. Are you coming..."

"That sounds like fun." Viv breezed past. "We can grab a cookie on the lido deck and snag a cookie on our way."

46

REX REDONDO

Bertha Alcott opened her stateroom door. "To what do I owe this pleasure?" she said in a not too pleased tone.

Rex hustled past her, dragging Viv by the hand. "We wanted to say goodbye before the day of confusion and debarking begins."

"I suppose I should feel honored," Bertha said in a dry voice, closing the door behind them. "I'll call Cricket to bring us some snacks."

She reached for her room phone as Viv looked around.

Bertha's voice cracked with authority. "Yes, dear. Champagne too. To celebrate our last time together."

"So this is your place. I always wondered what a permanent stateroom would look like. I noticed walking in that the entire section has been set aside from everyone else; feels like a ship within a ship.

Bertha explained. "There's even a separate bar and lounge and dining room for people like me who travel consistently from one cruise to the next. And for any celebrities who require more privacy."

"I'm surprised you ever come upstairs to hang out with the regular people," Viv mumbled.

Bertha gestured toward her chintz-covered sofa, giving Rex a chance to glance over Bertha's head at the wall behind the sofa. It had been painted in the dark blue signature color of the cruise line brand. Photographs lived an inch apart, surrounded by black frames.

"I can see from all of these photos that you've known more than your share of captains. Look at those stripes. How many skippers have you met over the years?"

"Seven," she replied snappily. "Captain Barclay is new but so far he's my favorite."

Viv piped up, "He handled the memorial quite well, considering Sandi's unexpected departure."

"He did, didn't he? Poor young woman. She seems, if you don't mind my saying so, a bit unstable. And then those rocks. No one suspected she was faking." But the tone of Bertha's voice made Rex think she suspected all along.

"She's not the first," Bertha continued." I've met a handful of fake mourners in my lifetime. Three on cruise ships, as a matter of fact. Sandi would make the fourth." Bertha's lips held a faint smile.

"The reality is that a cruise memorial is a public event. Since Aloha wants to accommodate its passengers, they provide food at no extra cost. And then there are the advantages. After the service the goodbyes are very clean. No one need know you were just pretending.

"I noticed immediately that Sandi glowed when she got attention. People stopped to chat with her as she toted that wooden box around."

Rex observed Bertha's face carefully, wondering if he'd underestimated the clever old woman. Before he could ask more questions, a knock came to the door.

Robert Redford walked inside. Allison Thompson followed right behind.

Then Rex blinked because Cricket came next, holding a tray with an ice bucket and five champagne glasses.

"We thought we'd join the party to raise a toast to a remarkable voyage," Robert said.

All three of them in the same room with Bertha. Something's up...

Cricket slid the tray on the table. She made her way to leave.

"Aren't you staying?" Rex called out.

"Stewards don't imbibe with passengers. See you later." But before leaving, she hurriedly told him under her breath, "I'm sorry. For everything."

She closed the door behind her with a thump.

"Why don't you pop the cork and do the pour," Allison instructed Rex. Then she continued to speak. "We can toast the unforeseen opportunity of finding you right on our passenger list that first day. If you need a recommendation..." She smiled to finish her thought. When Rex didn't move to pour, Redford did the honors. He raised his glass.

"But now it's time to say goodbye. I've posted your paycheck. It will arrive within twenty-four hours in your account. Lots of cash to spend in Honolulu. Take your lady to a luau and a sunset cruise on us.

"The return flight has been comped for you both. And we've upgraded you to first class." He sat down and leaned back with a look of satisfaction on his face, along with a forced smile.

He thinks he's done. With no acknowledgement that they were using extra perks as hush money. Neither he nor Viv reached for a glass.

"Hot nuts," Viv said.

"Excuse me?" Robert looked toward her with a confused expression.

"That's what I like best about first class. They heat the nuts."

Rex hid a smile. *Leave it to Viv. Hot nuts indeed.*

Allison picked up the conversation with a smooth tone. "As part of our hospitable service and by way of saying mahalo, we'll have your steward collect your bags and escort you off the ship right after the final lunch." She cleared her throat to add, "Before the others. That way you can catch the private limo to the Hilton Hawaiian Village and check in before the scrum."

She sat back against the overstuffed cushion, the liquid in her glass splashing onto her lap. "Oops," she giggled, taking a sip.

So that's their plan, Rex thought. *They've offered up all kinds of upgrades and special deals. But what I want to know is how they found out where we're staying.*

"How did you know our destination, the Hawaiian Village?" Rex asked.

"We have our ways. And you'll find an upgrade there as well. Arranged by Captain Barclay, again as a thank you for helping us out."

Rex narrowed his eyes. "So we're both getting all of those perks—the upgrades and the special limo etcetera—and what do we owe you in return?"

Redford's mouth hardened. "That has to be obvious, Redondo. Keep your mouths shut. Both of you. That's what you owe us. Take the extras and go about your business as usual.

"No one needs to know about the body. And how about I make it even more clear? If you or that one"—he pointed to

Viv—"say a word, I'll make sure the cops will hear about how you made a nuisance of yourselves during the cruise.

"How you were caught in the morgue snooping around. Maybe covering your tracks. How you ran nearly naked in the corridors. Not exactly a recommendation for sanity, now is it? Even if there's no real evidence, the police will keep you for questioning and ruin the rest of your holiday. We'll be long gone by then. Inconveniently floating in the international waters of no-man's land."

Viv spoke up. "The police aren't dumb. Being a nuisance isn't cause for arrest. Otherwise half the passengers would be hauled away. You're going to have to come up with something more threatening than that."

Rex spoke quietly, with a surprising change of subject. "I wonder how you'll all look in those new red uniforms."

"What do you mean?" Redford thumped his glass on the table. He rubbed at his eyes.

Allison gave Redford a quick glance. "We have no idea what you're talking about."

"Yes, you do!" Bertha spoke up. "I don't know how he found out, but he did." She glowered. "Aloha has sold their shares of the company. The new cruise line will be taking over right after this voyage. All the employees have been fired. And I, an old lady, will be forced to vacate my stateroom."

She held her hands tightly in her lap.

In a flash, Rex understood, right as Viv's fingers dug into his forearm. "So that's what all of this is about," he stated calmly. "You dumped Jon Jon Mulroy to keep the cruise ship authorities in the dark about yet another death.

"The late-night parties and the cavorting finally cost you. Maybe upstairs was working well, until Jon Jon crossed the staff-passenger line. But the basic infrastructure was falling apart bit by bit."

"Just a change of business practices," Robert mumbled. "You don't know how hard it was after the pandemic. No one was booking cruises and it was nearly impossible to hire any help. We loosened up on our staff guidelines to attract and keep employees. It worked for a while..."

Allison corrected him. "It helped keep employees, but passengers were still complaining."

"What kind of complaints?" Rex asked.

"Well the last-minute cancellation of the mentalist unsettled people. Once word got out that the guy we've been advertising for months didn't show, we had to do something. That's why we were so eager to sign you on. Hoping no one would complain.

"And then some of the staff started to ask for extra tips. Our employees had their hands out despite the gratuity policy. Word got back about that. We deflected the first complaints but passengers went over our heads."

"I'm beginning to understand why you were so defensive with me," Viv mumbled.

"And then there were actually four deaths," Bertha said in a tart voice.

"Four!" Rex exclaimed.

"Not that it's any of your business." Redford glared.

Allison earnestly explained. "Before this cruise," she began in an earnest voice, "there were three other deaths in the past three months. Adding another was out of the question. They hired another captain with the hope things would get better. But we were informed in no uncertain terms that one more body on our watch and we'd be fired."

"None of it was our fault," Redford insisted. "The first

three were picked up by the shore police. Coroners determined one death was from alcohol poisoning. And then the next two... That was a bitter divorce situation. The custody battle brought them to blows one night. Both died of head injuries as people watched. The passengers wouldn't stop talking."

"Keeping a job is important, but so is justice," Rex remarked.

"You don't understand. So by the time Jon Jon lost his balance on the elliptical and hit his head in the gym, Robert and I knew. We had to clean that up by ourselves. Otherwise everyone's jobs would be at risk."

"So the only way out was to get rid of Jon Jon," Rex muttered.

"We shoved all of his gear into the body bag and off he went. Overboard," Allison said very matter-of-factly.

"Since he had no next of kin it wasn't a bad plan—until that one." Redford glowered at Viv. "When she wouldn't give up her claim, we needed to make sure she'd give up.

"Told her she was imagining things. Insinuated that she might be having memory problems." His eye began to twitch. "Once we separated you, we figured we'd be safer. You can convince one woman that she's seeing things, but not when her boyfriend believes her."

"But then she got the idea you weren't feeling well. I knew she'd try to reconnect, so we came up with another plan," Allison said. "Keep her looking and guessing, and then escort her off the ship."

"That's why you had me locked in the morgue," Viv muttered.

"Your bodyguard found you soon enough," Allison scoffed. "And he kept you busy."

"I suspected that you deliberately disconnected my ship Wi-Fi." Viv's anger lurked beneath her words.

Redford spoke. "Once we did some research, we saw that you didn't have a cruise travel plan with your provider. That helped our situation a lot."

"I suppose you poisoned Rex." Viv glared. "Was that also part of your plan to keep him in his cabin away from me?"

"Hey, wait a minute," Rex interjected. "Did you poison my food or something?"

To his surprise, Robert and Allison looked genuinely confused.

Robert cleared his throat. "No, we didn't make you sick. I have no idea how that happened. The last thing we need on a cruise is someone claiming they have noro or some other virus. I noticed you were off your food and staying in your room. So we told Cricket to keep a closer eye."

"And that's how I ended up in the infirmary..." Rex rubbed his hand over his arm. *The itch is still driving me nuts! But it wasn't them.*

"I woke up next to another guy in a bed," he protested. "Then he disappeared. Was that by any chance—"

"Jon Jon was brain dead. But we decided to keep him on a respirator until we figured out the details of dropping him overboard," Robert explained. "Once that was settled we pulled his plug and removed him to cold storage."

Rex felt confused. His mind fell back into guilt. *I abandoned Viv to fend for herself with these dangerous scammers. I'll never forgive myself.*

He grew quiet, digging his nails into his shirt.

Something about abandoning Viv triggered a memory...

"What I want to know..." Viv held her hand over his. "Stop scratching," she whispered in his ear. Then she continued.

"When did you realize Aloha had already been bought by another cruise line? And that all of your machinations and treachery were for nothing?"

"Had no idea until yesterday," Redford said. "We thought we were home free after the last dump of the body bag."

Dumping. Like a human life is no more than trash. Rex rubbed his nose with the back of his hand. The acrid scent of smoke and metal filled his nostrils. He coughed into his elbow. *Just like Afghanistan...*

Rex swallowed back a lump in his throat as Redford kept on talking.

Viv looked perplexed. "What I still don't understand is why Jon Jon was using the passenger gym in the first place. That was off limits, right?"

"Jon Jon was always pushing boundaries. He didn't need the job for money, so he'd show up on the passenger side whenever he felt like it. That's why we had so many rules in place. Basically to keep him in line."

"You could have just fired him," Rex said.

"This was his last cruise under his contract. So he knew he had one more opportunity to make us pay," Allison said bluntly.

"Disposing of a dead body, illegally dumping it into the sea—those are crimes," Viv reminded everyone. "But that's not the worst. Your big cover-up plan got in the way of figuring out how Jon Jon actually died. Did he lose his balance and topple over, or did someone give him a shove?"

She's got this, he thought. *She didn't need me or Fernando to protect her.* Glancing away, his eyes settled on the Old Lady of the Sea.

Bertha Alcott tapped her cane impatiently. She looked worried.

"What do you think, Bertha?" Rex's eyes narrowed. "About Jon Jon's fall?"

With one more thump of her cane, Bertha spoke. "Oh all right. I did it. I gave that scoundrel Jon Jon a shove with the tip of my cane. I was taking a stroll as the passengers were coming aboard. And then I saw him breaking the rules. No one else was there, so I casually walked over and gave him a good thump in the leg.He deserved it.

"I watched as he fell over, and I walked away. Imagine having sex every night with whomever he pleased. Cricket and Tonya are like family to me. And all that nonsense with the panties at his insistence. And then I found out..." She lifted her cane to jab Allison's leg.

"You were the Friday, Saturday, and Sunday girl. I bet those panties are still in your possession. Three women on board, having coitus with the same man, and no one to call Jon Jon out for his unconscionable behavior. And Jon Jon? What kind of a name is that! He's not a child. One Jon should be enough for any man."

Allison's face grew bright red. "Stupid old woman," she snarled.

Bertha sat back against the cushions with a huff, her cane resting over her knees.

Images began to spin in Rex's head. He turned to Robert. "How did the other people die again?"

"The first man had been drinking all day in the bar. That night he lost his balance on the lido deck and sustained a head injury. He bled out before the doc arrived.

"Then the quarreling couple got into a physical fight," Robert explained. "Passengers crowded around them as they screamed at each other. Then he toppled over in a rage. He fell into her. She lost her balance as a result. Her head hit a glass table. A shard of glass got lodged in her neck. She bled out before we could help.

"When the husband tried to stand up lost his balance and fell back down. His head bounced off the deck like a ping-pong ball. He never regained consciousness. Something about a brain aneurism. Very sad."

Rex felt a tingling up his spine. "So three people, including Jon Jon, lost their balance and fell over."

He shot a cold stare at the Old Lady of the Sea.

"All of those people flagrantly abused the tenth commandment." Bertha gripped both hands around her cane. "All that coveting. Everywhere I turned, one of them was making eyes at someone else's wife. And then trying to compete in the casino, playing craps, drinking to excess. Disgusting. All of those people required a reset—comeuppance for their behavior. I didn't kill them. I only meant to make life difficult," Bertha argued.

"She reminds me of my grandma," Robert sighed. "Quoting the commandments by heart."

Rex was speechless. *That innocent old woman.* He glared at Redford. "Surely you're not saying that your grandma was a cold-blooded killer, using scripture to back up her misguided interpretations."

Viv butted in. "You must have known Bertha was part of the problem," she stated firmly. "I think you gave her special license because of her age."

"Bertha didn't mean it," Allison insisted. "She was at the wrong place at the wrong time. She couldn't help that people trip over her cane."

"Oh, I intended it." Bertha thumped her cane against the floor. "Someone has to care about the morals of the ship. This is my home, don't forget."

Rex looked at the cane in her hand. *So that's the*

weapon, he concluded. *She tripped people, which didn't kill them, but it certainly put things into motion that led to the deaths of four human beings.*

Before he could warn Bertha about her right to an attorney, Viv asked, "Did you trip Sandi with her cane? Is that why the box went flying at the memorial?"

"Of course I did. Silly child. She pretended her father passed for attention. I noticed right away how she preened and giggled every time someone stopped to chat with her. Disgusting. Pride goes before the fall." Bertha smirked.

Rex held up his hands. "I recommend that you don't say anything more until your lawyer is present." Bertha's face grew pale. She began to object when Rex's phone rang. He reached into his pocket.

"Hey, boss," came Sutton's voice. She sounded uncharacteristically subdued.

"We got a confession," he told her, loud enough for everyone to hear. "It was Bertha Alcott. And Robert Redford and Allison Thompson as accessories. You can make that call now."

"I alerted the precinct. Just needed to fill in the blanks," came Sutton's response. "And tell Viv I'm on the other thing. Take care of yourself," she added in a soft voice before disconnecting.

Discomfort rose in Rex. *Sutton's acting oddly. Where's her usual banter? Has she gone soft on me?* He turned to Viv. "Sutton said to tell you she's on the other thing. What did she mean? And what is this about her seeing me soon?"

"That's for Sutton and me to know and for you to find out. But right now I want to get out of here. I don't suppose these three are going anywhere, unless they want to swim to shore." Viv stood.

Once they got to the door, Rex turned around. "Give me a second."

He lifted the cane from Bertha's hands. "I'm confiscating this as evidence. Now that you confessed your involvement, the CCTV footage will supply enough detail to put you away. The truth will set you free," he told her. "That's also in the Bible. Somewhere in John 8, if I remember correctly."

Viv took his elbow as they left the room.

47

VIVIENNE ROSE

Viv zipped her suitcase closed. She looked over at Rex, who waited by the door. "All done," she assured him, realizing that he'd been more quiet than usual.

Outside in the corridor, Rex propped her bag next to his against the wall. "They'll come for them in a few minutes. I got a text."

"Do we disembark now?"

"We have about an hour. Would you like to have one last look at the pool? Maybe we can chat and let everyone else do the hustle."

They stepped onto the lido deck and sat at the first available table. "This is where I sat when Jon Jon Mulroy fell off the elliptical," she reminded him.

Rex rubbed his hand over his arm.

"Don't scratch," she said. "Makes the itching worse. We'll get some prescription cream first thing."

He dropped his hands to the table, but then started playing with his fingers one at a time, rubbing his thumb over the nails methodically.

"Do you think we could have done more to get justice for Jon Jon?" Viv asked.

He looked up. "I always think I can do more. It's kind of my thing, you know. I keep trying. But mostly what I do isn't enough."

Viv nodded. "I would have loved to see people arrested. That might have made a difference. But now everything is up to the police. Will Honolulu take this seriously, you think?"

"Sutton assured me that someone would be meeting the ship as soon as it docked..." His voice trailed off, sounding unconvinced.

"You've seemed kind of down," Viv commented softly. "Anything you care to talk about?"

He forced a half smile. "I thought for sure they were slipping me something in the water to make me sick. So maybe I have an allergy to some specific chemical on board the ship. Even that spa scent seemed pervasive, like a cover-up for smells that are less welcome. People living in close quarters are smelly. I even wondered if the fish was dodgy, you know, a bit past its expiration date."

He began to trace his nails with his thumb again.

Viv knew that she had to handle this conversation with great care. After talking with Sutton, she suspected this time would come, but not so soon and not when they were alone. She'd hoped that Sutton would also be there for support.

Viv bit her bottom lip and took the plunge.

"Have you ever been to an intervention?" she asked quietly.

His head bobbed up, his eyes surprised. "You mean the kind they do for alcoholics and drug addicts? I don't think so. I thought they were dumb, if you must know the truth.

People need to stay in their own lane and mind their own business." He sounded quite sure of himself on that point.

Viv gulped, searching for her words. "I agree, mostly. For what it's worth, I've never been to an intervention either. But I need to bring up a hard topic."

His body stiffened. "Are we breaking up?"

"No. At least I hope not." She reached to take his hand. "Sutton told me some stories about your time in the military," she began cautiously, watching his face for clues to continue.

"Don't you girls have something better to discuss?" He looked relieved but wary.

"She's noticed for years that you get anxious in certain circumstances. That you have triggers that make you feel ill. So she did some research while you were away. Like most men you don't want to share your feelings." She smiled at him.

"She found out that certain smells, sounds, and feelings trigger the brain. The result can be different in different people. For you it seems to start with upper respiratory symptoms. Then digestive issues. Feeling woozy and lethargic. Your brain is sluggish and you might have a headache that lasts for days. Just what you described, your experience on this cruise."

"That's true." He looked almost relieved.

When he didn't bother to disagree, she felt her confidence return.

Rex admitted, "Now that I think about it, I felt so guilty as soon as I took the job. For leaving you behind, especially after you saw the elliptical incident. I literally abandoned you and walked away, and the reason was selfish."

His voice raised. "I've had bouts of this before. I never thought about a trigger. I'd take some cold meds and it would go away in a week or so. But this time it didn't go away."

When his mouth tightened, Viv spoke. "Sutton and I think that certain triggers bring up memories of your work in Afghanistan."

"How's that? I was just an intel officer. Not in combat." Rex looked away.

"According to Sutton you were within one hundred yards of the burn pits," Viv said. "And the toxic fumes that filled the air. You inhaled that air. You were close to the residue on the uniforms of others, which contaminated the entire camp. Marines who stood in the food lines. The chow hall. The shower trailers. And the work spaces and barracks. Even though you weren't one of the ones dumping evidence into the pit, you may be experiencing the memories."

"That was normal procedure," Rex insisted. "Open-air burning is a way to dispose of waste. The process is contained and approved by the military. It wasn't my decision."

"Like burning plastic and electronic materials," Viv said. "Sutton told me."

"I'm getting tired of hearing her name." Rex shrugged. "But I suppose you're not going to stop with this line of inquiry. Now that the two of you are in this together."

He glared at Viv. She appreciated that his old resistance was returning.

"Lots of veterans sued the government," she explained. "Most had breathing and lung diseases because they'd been exposed to the pollution caused by the pits." She kept her voice calm, hoping her words would sink in.

"I know about all of that," Rex said testily. "I even told Sutton years ago that we were lucky."

"But there's something more," Viv said. "What often goes unexplored. The emotions. The Marines who served in relation to the burn pits. And for you it had a unique quality. You were a witness, watching as Marines followed orders, knowing somewhere in the back of your mind that they may suffer later—"

"Just stop!" Rex jumped to his feet.

When one foot got caught under his chair, he reached to steady himself.

Viv waited for him to catch his balance. She nodded to his empty chair.

"I admit that I still feel guilty, ever since my desert tour. And now that I'm thinking about it, leaving you on the ship to do a couple of shows also activated my guilt. But those are apples and oranges. How is one a trigger for the other? Makes no sense...

"I never got close to the burn pits," he kept explaining. "Not like the rest. I was sitting back in my cushy intel tent, minding my own business. There's no way I can compare myself to the real troops who risked their lives. I suspected about the hazards of the pollution, but I never spoke up."

Perspiration broke out over Rex's forehead. Viv reached for his hand. He didn't respond but stared blankly ahead.

She continued to speak in a quiet voice. "So Sutton knows a guy. A retired chaplain who works with the Navy as a contractor. His specialty is identifying the emotional and spiritual malaise of veterans who served in Iraq and Afghanistan."

"I don't need to talk to anyone," Rex said firmly.

"She'd like you to talk to him while you're here. Maybe have dinner."

"I didn't come here to talk to an old Navy buddy," he groaned.

"It's just a dinner," Viv said. "I can hang out with Sutton."

"I keep forgetting about her. Sutton's a big nuisance," he commented dryly. "And I've heard enough about her for one day."

At that moment, an announcement came over the loudspeaker. "It's time for deck five to debark. Form a line in the elevator lobby. I'd like to thank you for sailing with Aloha Cruises, and don't forget you can sign up for your next sea worthy adventure at the first kiosk on the pier. It's still offered at a discounted price."

"The endless upsell," Viv commented dryly.

As they rolled their bags down the ramp, it was Rex who brought up their previous conversation. "You're forgiven. For bringing up all that nonsense about the burn pits and my past. I know Sutton pulled you into this. It's been a difficult week and I'm going to make it up to you at the Hawaiian Village. I promise. And our alone time is long overdue." He added with a mischievous grin, "At least I'm still good at that."

"Yes, you are," Viv agreed.

A group of people stood at the edge of the pier. They waved at passengers walking down the ramp. Viv pointed to a familiar face.

He turned to her with a look of disbelief. "What have you done?"

"Just taking care of the man I love," Viv said. She waved at Sutton and the man standing next to her.

His eyes widened. "Did you say—"

"Do you think I'd go to all of this trouble for my next-door neighbor, no matter how cute his dog is?"

A tentative smile replaced his scowl. "I don't suppose I thought of it that way. You really must like me."

"I didn't say like," she corrected. "Is hard of hearing another one of your symptoms?" As he registered his pleasure, she looked away, remembering their night together.

When he'd come to her room that night, she'd finally allowed herself to feel. It was the way he didn't bother to make excuses that opened her heart.

And then when Rex didn't run away as she probed him about his past, she knew for certain. *I've always been that kind of person. I watch what people do more than hear what they say.*

"Come on. Time for us to go." Rex interrupted her thoughts by taking her bag. He called over his shoulder sounding more like his usual self. "I need to introduce you to someone. He's a great guy. Starbuck Little. A chaplain and quite a character."

Rex's last words were nearly drowned out by the blast of the ship's horn. A commotion erupted at the end of the ramp. The crowd parted when two uniformed police officers rushed out of their cruiser.

Standing side by side, the two looked imposing, their sunglasses covering their eyes staring in the direction of passengers disembarking.

Sandi walked past, holding the box labeled Daddy under her arm. She looked forlorn, wearing teddy bear pajama pants and a sweatshirt, her hair piled in disarray on top of her head.

The female cop stepped forward to take her arm, directing her to a man standing in the crowd. He was quite tall and held the air of impatience. "I can't believe you did this again." He took Sandi's arm.

At the foot of the pier, Bertha Alcott walked slowly

toward the shore. Without her customary cane, she gripped Cricket's elbow for assistance. The male officer stepped forward to take Bertha's other elbow, nodding at Cricket to let go.

With Bertha firmly in hand, the officer walked away. His partner continued to scan the crowd. Rex took the handle of the suitcase and hurried forward with Viv following.

She was the first to ask. "Hello, Officer. Who are you looking for?"

"The ship's captain, for one. And then two of his crew," she said curtly.

"Let me guess. That would be Captain Barclay, Allison Thompson, and Robert Redford, no relation," she added to clarify.

The officer nodded.

Viv kept talking. "My friend and I were responsible for reporting Jon Jon Mulroy's accident and the disposal of his body at sea. You got the phone call from Sutton Drew, our private investigator, I presume?"

Rex took a quick look at Viv, his mouth hanging open.

"The captain just gave an announcement over the loud-speaker," Viv continued to explain. "So he hasn't debarked."

"Thanks." With long strides, the officer made her way toward the ship while stragglers pulled aside to let her pass.

Rex grinned. "I guess the cops will arrest them too, including the captain. Not because he was necessarily guilty, but because he's responsible for all employees on the ship."

He sighed. "I have to admit this part is very satisfying." He sent a puzzled look in her direction. "I think I felt guilty, but I also forgot you are the most competent woman I've ever met. A class act, Vivienne Rose."

"I used my time wisely this week," she admitted. "Let's just say that. I can't wait to do an internet search once we're unpacked, get all the gory arrest details."

"That works." Rex glanced toward the dispersing crowd on the shore. He sighed again.

"Go ahead. You know you want to," Viv encouraged.

He lifted his arm and waved in Sutton's direction. Not like she was hard to miss, wearing a red top and tight red shorts with cowboy boots. Even the black baseball cap couldn't hide her flaming red hair.

"She's gone red again," Rex commented to Viv.

"I can see that," Viv said dryly.

The man standing next to Sutton waved both hands in the air.

"It's good to see Chaps." Rex waved back. "I can't wait to introduce you." He urged her forward as they merged into the crowd.

Two days later, Viv and Sutton sat on the beach. They'd ordered margaritas, which sat on the low table between their chairs underneath the umbrella.

"This is nice." Sutton picked up her glass. "Sorry I'm not Rex."

Viv looked toward the shimmering blue ocean. Waves lapped at the sand as the sound of children's delighted screams filled the air. "No worries. The cruise was one surprise after another. Plus he's in good hands."

A man hoisted a toddler on his shoulders, walking into the sea. The little girl's high-pitched squeal met Viv's ear. She smiled and turned to Sutton.

"So who's taking care of Kevin and Miss Kitty?"

"Fernando," Sutton said. "He flew back on the first flight.

I think Palm Desert Police relieved him of his special assignment once he told them how you solved a murder case with your sheer persistence. Apparently he gave them plenty of info, because they no longer think you require a bodyguard."

Viv thought of Fernando, his warm brown eyes and quiet confidence. "He and Miss Kitty will get along fine." She leaned back into her chaise lounge, taking a deep cleansing breath.

"The tropical breezes are intoxicating. Makes me feel so relaxed. I could take a nap right now," she said.

"I echo that." Sutton pulled down the brim of her hat.

Viv watched as the waves eased up onto the beach and then drifted back toward the ocean. In and out. *So peaceful.* Viv sighed.

Sutton's phone rang, making Viv look up.

"Speak of the devil, it's the pet sitter," She held up her phone and answered the FaceTime call.

"Hey, girls," Fernando greeted them. "Are you using lots of sunscreen?"

"Put Miss Kitty on." Sutton handed the phone to Viv.

She held the phone as Fernando directed the camera toward her cat. Miss Kitty, her tail waving, sauntered across the room. She jumped onto the first shelf of her cat castle. And then, one paw in front of the other, she climbed to the top plateau, turning to face the camera. Her green eyes glared.

"Hello, Miss Kitty," Viv called in her coaxing voice.

Miss Kitty picked up a paw and began to lick, turning her head away.

Viv laughed. "Miss Kitty, I miss you!"

The cat's tail swished over her head.

Fernando's face filled the screen. "All is well here. Tell Rex that Kevin escaped and ran around the golf course again. I got him back. The fine will be in the mail by the time you get home. I guess they doubled it because it's a repeat offense."

Once she'd said goodbye, Viv handed the cell to Sutton. She closed her eyes, deeply contented.

A slight breeze brushed against her skin, scented with plumeria and the briny smell of the sea. In the distance, she heard someone singing from the outdoor patio bar.

"Somewhere Over the Rainbow" to the thrum of a ukulele. Another thought drifted past her consciousness. *I wonder what Rex has in store for our next adventure.*

She smiled softly before drifting off to sleep.

AUTHOR'S NOTE

I'm often surprised by my own characters; Rex Redondo's journey to his past was no exception. And then the loving way Viv and Sutton led him forward touched me deeply.

Years ago, I had the privilege of accompanying my husband to a Wounded Warrior event in Colorado Springs, CO. Each veteran had their own recovery story, filled with individual detail. I tucked away how I felt at the time, and to my surprise, Rex brought back my memory.

Each service member had a different approach to their healing. Many of those competing in the Warrior Games had experienced a limb amputation or orthopedic impairment. Many had visual impairments and severe neurological issues stemming from injury, stroke, or multiple sclerosis. I will never forget those with spinal injuries in wheelchairs, spinning around the basketball courts scoring points, bumping and scraping their way to victory.

I think those with severe traumatic brain injury inspired me the most. The injury is less obvious than a missing limb. Recovery requires a different approach entirely. With the help of recent studies about trauma and the brain, we've learned that reliving the traumatic incident isn't as helpful as once thought, and that recognizing triggers may be a better way forward.

We don't have to be soldiers, Marines, or sailors to know trauma. How many of us have dismissed our suffering as inconsequential, storing up layer upon layer of protection due to something that happened long ago. And then we're triggered, only to be told, "You're overreacting."

A trigger can come from anywhere. A scent. A sound. A memory. A feeling. And then we're thrown back to the original event, feeling trapped and victimized with no way out.

I'd like to thank my family and friends for supporting me while writing this book. I hope my cookie baking has made up for any hurt feelings that my, "Not now," words may have caused.

I'd like to thank my team, who help me get my books in front of the public. Ebook Launch for their creative covers, which do not involve AI, along with Christie Stratos and her team at Proof Positive.

Let's end with a quote from Bessel van der Kolk, from his book *The Body Keeps the Score: Brain, Mind, and Body in the Healing of Trauma.*

"Imagination is absolutely critical to the quality of our lives. Our imagination enables us to leave our routine everyday existence by fantasizing about travel, food, sex, falling in love, or having the last word—all the things that make life interesting.

"Imagination gives us the opportunity to envision new possibilities—it is an essential launchpad for making our hopes come true. It fires our creativity, relieves our boredom, alleviates our pain, enhances our pleasure, and enriches our most intimate relationships."

And because I'm able to share my imagination in writing, I dedicate this book to you, dear readers. And don't forget: the best is yet to come.

Bonnie Hardy

March 2024

ABOUT THE AUTHOR

Bonnie Hardy, a retired professional turned author, is celebrated for her two enthralling cozy mystery series. The first, set in the picturesque mountain town of Lily Rock, features amateur sleuth Olivia Greer, known for her uncanny ability to draw out confessions from the most unlikely people.

The second series, set in Palm Desert, features the mid-life duo mentalist Rex Redondo and his down to earth next door neighbor doula Vivienne Rose.

Inspired by Agatha Christie, Bonnie's captivating tales

of mystery and community masterfully blend fast-paced whodunits with clever sleuthing.

f   facebook.com/bonniehardywrites.com

instagram.com/bonniehardywrites

BB bookbub.com/authors/bonnie-hardy

g goodreads.com/bonniehardy

Between the Sheets

Redondo and Rose Neighbors in Crime Book Two

Chapter One
Vivienne Rose

"Take a look at him." Rex Redondo pointed. "He's just a toddler and really good on that tricycle." A young boy pedaled down the middle of the street, his chubby legs pumping.

Rex's hand gripped her shoulder. "Oh oh!" The small boy's bike leaned to the left as he narrowly missed running down the orange cone. Several had been placed in the street, serving as an obstacle course.

An older man stood nearby on the grass. "Keep going, Josh. Look out for the next one!" He waved at Rex and Viv, a look of pride in his wide smile. "Isn't he great? Just like Ross Chastain," the man shouted.

"Who's that?" Viv called out.

"You know," the man explained, "like the NASCAR driver. My grandson. He's something else."

The sound of a blaring horn made the hair stand on Viv's neck. A sleek gray Porsche slid around the corner. Driving past the residential speed limit, the car headed straight toward the little boy.

Viv gasped as brakes squealed.

Rex shouted in alarm, "Look out!"

The grandfather froze, his eyes wide with horror.

The trike hit a cone and fell in front of the bike. The boy tipped off the seat collapsing onto the pavement. The sound of an electric car engine whirred away as the child's piercing wail met Viv's ears.

She darted into the street toward the child. Bending closer, her eyes traveled over his body. "It's okay, sweetie. You'll be fine," she assured him. The little boy sat up, tears streaming down his face.

Smoothing back the hair on his forehead, Viv's trained fingers gently probed his small arm. *Nothing broken.* A cut on his chin oozed blood. She reached into her pocket, pulling out a wad of tissues. Dabbing at the wound, she smiled into his eyes. Her mind continuing to assess. *The wound can be cleaned, might need a stitch.* The next glance affirmed her opinion. Dirt from the road covered both of his knees. *A little skinned up.*

"Is he okay?" The grandfather bent over Viv, his hand reaching for the child.

The child thrust his arms over his head. "Grandpa," he cried. The grandfather reached down and scooped the boy into his arms. Viv watched the child cling to the chest of the older man.

The man spoke over the boy's shoulder. "My wife is going to be furious. She's always telling me not to let him play in the street." He bent his head to whisper assurances. "It's okay, buddy. I've got you. You're going to be right as rain." The child buried his face further into his grandfather's shirt. But the tears had stopped.

Viv stood. "I'd take him to the ER to have him checked out. Just in case."

Perspiration beaded down the side of the older man's face. "Good idea," he said with a nod. "I'm going to take him right now. And thank you." His voice choked with emotion.

Once the man left, Rex turned to Viv. "Are you okay?"

"What, about that?" She pointed to the trike lying in the street. The handlebars tilted backward, an orange cone trapped underneath the front wheel.

When Rex raised an eyebrow she answered his question. "I was really scared." She brushed her hands against her slacks. "I'm going to pick this up," she pointed to the trike again, "and then drag those cones out of the road."

"Why don't you let me help at least." Rex lifted the trike in one hand. Viv grabbed a cone and made her way to the sidewalk. In a matter of minutes Rex had stacked the others, leaving them on the grass.

"The car didn't even stop." Rex looked toward the community exit.

Viv's eyes narrowed. "Isn't that just what we wanted to talk to the board about? Kids playing in the streets, how dangerous that is. And now there's been an actual accident.

"I think he's going to be fine, only scrapes and bruises. Mostly, he was just frightened," Viv added, more to reassure herself and to calm down

"Did you see who was driving the Porsche?" Rex asked.

"A guy with a shaved head. Probably mid forties. He gunned that engine and didn't even stop to see if the child was okay." Viv shook her head in disappointment. "I only have first aid training. I do hope the boy is alright," she said again, feeling as if she should have insisted more strongly about having the child checked out by a doctor.

"So we'll bring that up at our first meeting," Rex assured her. "At the homeowner's meeting. We're still going, right?"

"I want to go more than ever," she stated firmly. "A fifty-five-plus neighborhood is not supposed to have children playing in the middle of the main road. Why do people think it's okay to treat the street like their backyard?"

He placed his hand on her elbow. "So we're a bit late. But let's take that indignation and put it to good use. Our first HOA meeting."

His voice sounded reassuring, but Viv still felt mad. Though she did agree with Rex, that the best course would be to take this up with the board. The list of community rules was long, but that didn't matter since there was no one to make sure they were enforced.

End of Excerpt
Go to bonniehardywrites.com
Where you will find links and bargains for you own copy of
Between the Sheets Redondo and Rose Neighbors in Crime
Book Two

Sign up on my newsletter
to receive all the latest news about my
Redondo and Rose Neighbors in Crime Series.

You'll receive a free short story download
as my thank you.
Happy Reading,
Bonnie

ALSO BY BONNIE HARDY

For a full list including summaries and Audible go to

bonniehardywrites.com/Books

<u>Welcome to Lily Rock Holiday Mystery Novellas</u>

'Tis the Season

All Aboard for Murder

Wrap it Up!

<u>Lily Rock Mystery Series</u>

Getaway Death

Influenced to Death

Deadly Admission

A Thymely Death

Deadbeat Dad

A Very Tidy Death

<u>Redondo and Rose Neighbors in Crime</u>

A Doula to Die For

Between the Sheets

Sight Unseen